# Ley Lines and Rabbit Holes

## A Rogue Destiny Novel
### Book 2

**Paul Tallman**

Cover art by Damonza

Published by Oliver-Heber Books

0 9 8 7 6 5 4 3 2 1

*To the Seven,*
*Your support is the only reason this book exists.*

# Chapter 1
# A Winter's Tale

Natascha Devi fought back a painful yawn. She stared out the front window of the slipstream, *Nevermore,* into the blackness of the Great Void. Hunting Ren B'gatti had taken her and Medesto weeks with little rest, and she was reeling from the exhaustion. The few stolen hours of sleep were all she had been able to get while her mechanized co-pilot, Gustav 7, flew them to the origin of a desperate distress call. It was nowhere near enough, but it would have to do for now.

Natascha glanced at the clock on the dashboard. It had been several hours since she and Medesto had found Ren hiding inside the medieval urban fantasy novel, *The Crimson Masque.* Ren had been a flight risk since his early days with the Raconteurs. Claymore Ives was the only one able to control his impulsive nature, but Claymore was no longer a part of their world. The thought made her miss him even more.

But finding the trickster was only the first step in the Raconteurs' mad scheme of having him shape-shift his way inside a dangerous company of escaped prisoners rampaging across the Mythic Cosmos. And even if Ren succeeded in infiltrating the band of outlaws, it did not guarantee they could stop the heavily armed marauders from locating whatever their leader, Mordecai Davos, was searching for.

Gustav 7 steered the ship through a black sea of glowing worlds toward a small, bluish-green ball in the distance. He clicked through several maps on the wide dashboard screen with one of his utility arms.

"The distress signal from *Fool's Errand* is coming from that world directly ahead," Gustav replied in a synthesized voice. Natascha yawned again and sat up in her seat.

"What do we know about this place?"

"It's a novel called *Cossacks: A Winter's Tale*, an alternate Earth history. It's a relatively new world, recently formed only a couple of years ago, so we have no established field houses. Montagu and Keating may have been the first from Rogue Destiny to step foot inside."

Nevermore's co-pilot continued. "The narrative says it takes place in the cold Russian steppes during Earth's First World War. Invaders from the planet Mars seek to enslave humanity. The Story centers on a small outlaw band of fiery Cossacks led by the world's *Logos Personae*, *Mykhaylo Rodchenko*. He and his army of horsemen are the last line of defense against an over-whelming, superior alien technology. It looks like there may be some supernatural elements as well, but nothing magical that I can see."

"Sounds interesting," Natascha said. "Too bad we're here for work and won't have time to look around. Once we're through the Word Canopy, try to patch through to *Fool's Errand*. Hopefully, we'll get a response."

"Roger that," Gustav replied. The automatron pushed a button with a metal appendage and pulled down a small lever on the console with another. A tiny flash of light shot from the front grille of the Slipstream. The small ball of energy struck the giant globe. Tendrils of electrical charge spread over its outer surface and an opening appeared. *Nevermore* shot through the keyhole.

The turbulence outside the ship died down as they descended into a new world. The distress signal indicated they needed to head west through a thick blanket of clouds. Natascha grabbed the radio receiver.

"*Fool's Errand*, do you copy?" she said. "This is *Nevermore*. We are in-world. Do you copy?"

Static crackled over the line, and then a voice answered. "*Nevermore*, this is *Midnight Run*. Good to hear a friendly voice. We picked up the same distress call and have a location on *Fool's Errand*, but no word from Montagu or Keating. Sending you our coordinates now."

The WayFinder screen flashed to life and a series of numbers and symbols scrolled across the bottom of the screen. Natascha scanned them. "Thanks, Danique. We have a fix on you. Be there in twenty."

"Watch your step, *Nevermore*. We've got hostiles north and east of our location. They appear to be part of the greater narrative and not interested in us, but they could still be dangerous."

"Roger that *Midnight Run*," Gustav replied. "*Nevermore*, out." The ship began a slow descent from a dead gray sky to a world blanketed in white. Large snowflakes swept across the windshield. Gustave adjusted course and brought the Slipstream in low over the tree line.

They followed the glyph on the screen until the tail of *Midnight Run* came into view. The fifty-foot-long Slipstream Runabout looked like a giant insect crouching in the snow. *Nevermore's* route thrusters slowed their descent through the snowy sky and brought them around to land. Natascha scanned the white landscape below as Gustav searched for a place to set down. He chose an open area hemmed in by trees twenty yards from the other ship and landed *Nevermore* in the deep snow.

Natascha opened the suitcase that held the vestments of her alter ego, Doctor Enigma. Stepping out of the confined space of the cockpit, she threw the trench coat around her, sliding her arms into the sleeves. She donned her gas mask and pulled up her hood. Two Tesla Peacemakers sat on the charging stations under the dashboard. She shoved them into the holsters strapped to each leg.

Gustav opened the skylight above them, letting snow drift into the cabin. The co-pilot's metallic base glowed blue from the anti-gravitational burner. He retracted his utility arms and flew up into the frigid winter day. The opening slid closed after him. With a push of a button, the side hatch opened and Natascha followed Gustav out into the cold. Snow and wind swirled around her as she sank to her knees in the snow. She pulled the keybox from her pocket to lock down *Nevermore*. The ramp rose and clicked shut.

Natascha could feel the icy chill even through her insulated clothing. The readings in her mask registered the windchill at 12 degrees below zero. She adjusted the thermal heating elements in her coat to stave off the biting cold. She pushed through the snow around the deeper drifts toward *Midnight Run*.

As she approached, the hatch on the side of the Slipstream opened and Gossamer 99 slid his eight-foot metal frame free from the confines of the cabin. The ship tilted as his weight shifted toward the door. He planted a large metal foot deep in the snowbank and stepped out. The Slipstream rocked back into place when he cleared the opening and stood in the silent falling snowflakes.

"Hello, Gossamer," Natascha said. The cyborg mech turned to her.

"Hello, Doctor Enigma." His voice was deep with an artificial tinge to the words. "We still have had no contact from Keating and Montagu."

Natascha leaned into the open hatch. "So what do we have, Danique?"

"The Story's Narrative is playing out about five hundred kilometers to our east," Danique replied. "So we're pretty far from the *Logos Personae*. The ships should be safe here."

Danique, Gossamer 99's older sister, sat in the pilot's seat and removed the headset from her dreadlocks. She put on a leather bomber jacket, a thick wool cap, and wrapped a scarf around her neck. After buckling a holstered Peacemaker on, Danique dropped out of the ship to the snow.

"You still have a bead on Montagu and Keating's signal, Gossamer?" Natascha asked.

"*Fool's Errand* is about 1500 meters west of here," Gossamer 99 said. "Over that rise and through those trees, very close to the edge of the Story."

"They must have found Mordecai," Natascha said. "That has to be why they're here."

Danique shrugged. "Don't know, but if we do run into the outlaws, Father will be relieved you're with us."

Sebastian Poe, the Raconteurs' chief mechanic, was protective of his children. His youngest daughter, B'Tori was 14 and worked with him in his shop, always within sight. Danique and Gossamer 99 were older, 19 and 17, and insisted on working in the field with the other Raconteurs. Sebastian had agreed to that only if the two teenagers took every precaution. They had to stay in constant contact with the WayFinder and were never to engage the enemy without experienced backup.

Even then, they were given only menial tasks, such as transporting dignitaries or picking up machine parts for their father. Both agreed to those terms, because the alternative would have been to die a slow death, cooped up in his shop, dismantling and rebuilding Slipstreams all day long. But every so often, they found themselves in an emergency situation, such as searching for missing Raconteurs in cold winter worlds full of alien invaders. Natascha could see the excitement on Danique's face.

Gossamer 99 led the way, forging a pathway through the snowdrifts for the others to follow. Harsh winds swept down from the surrounding hills and forests as they trudged through the cold. Danique complained immediately.

"I'm freezing, brother. Can't you go any faster?" She wrapped the wool scarf tighter around her neck.

Gossamer shook his massive wedge-shaped head and looked down at her. "The snow's deep. I'm doing the best I can." His metallic-tinged voice was full of sarcasm. "It's winter in a Russian novel about winter. It doesn't get any colder than this."

"Shut up," Danique shot back with a smirk. "Just because you're not bothered by the cold doesn't mean I'm going to stop griping about it." She shivered and patted her gloved hands together. Large snowflakes continued to fall. "Since you have internal thermal heaters to keep what's left of your innards warm, you could at least fake a little sympathy for your sister's plight and offer me a ride."

"I am sorry you are cold, and I am not, my sister," Gossamer replied. "You have my sympathy. Is that better?"

Natascha smiled behind her mask. She wasn't about to mention the heating elements in the lining of her long coat kept her quite comfortable in the sub-zero climate.

Gossamer 99 knelt in the snow and Danique climbed up onto his shoulders. She sat on the smooth flat area behind his massive head and wrapped a hand around the leather hand-holds for stability. Her younger brother continued pushing his way through the deep snowdrifts toward the direction of the signal. Natascha followed in the wide track left by the cyborg. Gustav floated at her shoulder.

"Are you getting any closer to locating Ren?" Danique asked.

"Medesto and I found him in a grimdark fantasy novel. He's on his way back to Rogue Destiny as we speak."

After a short hike, they came to a break in the trees. Natascha could tell from the frozen rocks crunching underfoot that there was a road buried somewhere beneath the snow that had not seen daylight for many months. The signal from their missing compatriots' transponder was getting stronger. They crested a forested hill, and in the distance, an ancient monastery of stone and mortar came into view.

The building was two stories high, set on a wide span of open ground. Next to the building, covered in snow, sat the slipstream *Fool's Errand*. The area around the single stone structure was flat and empty of trees. A thin stream of smoke rose from the chimney.

Gossamer 99 pointed to the monastery. "That's where their signal is coming from," he rumbled.

He stayed under the shadow of the trees. Danique dropped from her brother's shoulder to the snow. She pulled out her binoculars and scanned the front of the building. "No movement that I can see. What's the play?" Her voice was only a whisper, but it echoed in the still air.

"Danique goes with me," Natascha said. "We have to assume Montagu and Keating are in trouble, or we would have heard from them by now. We neutralize any sentries we come upon—don't kill them unless you have no other choice. Then we deal with anyone inside."

There was a sound in the woods behind them. Natascha grabbed Danique by the arm and pulled her down as the whine of a large hydraulic machine broke the crisp, cold air. Natascha saw movement in the trees to their left. She crouched in the snow next to Danique. Gustav hovered above the ground next to her. Gossamer stepped behind a thick tree trunk. Overhead, a massive saucer mounted atop a tripod of long spindly legs moved through the trees in fluid, elongated steps. The Martian invader's machine came within fifty yards before passing past them.

Gustav nudged Natascha's shoulder. "I am intercepting a radio transmission. Thirty yards to the east, there are three humanoid-sized hostiles moving this way. Lots of metal on the outside, but they appear to be organic underneath. They are communicating with each other, but I am unable to translate their alien dialect."

Natascha motioned for Danique to stay down, then raised three fingers and pointed east. Danique nodded and crouched lower until she was hidden in the snow. Natascha peered over the snowdrift.

Forty feet away stood three alien figures. They were seven feet tall with large, bulging heads encased in clear glass helmets. Their faces were small and squat, with prominent foreheads and exposed brains.

The trio of alien foot soldiers seemed to be having an argument amongst themselves. The tallest one's brain pulsated in rhythm with the wild gesturing of his mechanical arms. Natascha drew her Peacemaker and waited. After a back-and-forth conversation went on for several minutes before the three armed soldiers continued on their way, lumbering through the trees on long mechanical legs. Once they were out of sight, she signaled the others to come out.

"Gossamer and Gustav," she said, "stay here and monitor the area. Let us know if they come back. Danique and I will investigate the building and see if we can find our missing agents."

The two metallic Raconteurs remained in the woods as Natascha and Danique crept across the snowy field toward *Fool's Errand*. They reached the Slipstream and crouched by its rear engines. "I still don't see anyone," she said. "You?"

Danique lifted her binoculars and scanned the snowy fields

around them. "Nothing," she said. "No, wait. Thirty-five yards out, near the tree line. There's a lone figure heading toward us. Looks like another alien foot soldier."

Natascha motioned Danique to follow her to the monastery. They moved to the corner of the stone structure as the alien approached the Slipstream from the field. It appeared to be armed with a heavy gun that hung from a strap over one shoulder. It stopped at the base of the landing gear in front of *Fool's Errand*. There was a hum, and a flat grid of light emanated from the soldier's chest and scanned the metal hull of the ship. The alien walked to the rear engines, continuing to scan the underbelly, and began talking in an unknown language to unseen comrades.

Danique drew her Peacemaker from its holster. Natascha motioned her to stay where she was, but the command was ignored. The younger Raconteur made her way from the corner of the building to *Fool's Errand* and hid behind a claw of the landing gear. The alien ended its transmission and went back to scanning the right engine. Then it stopped, suddenly aware of another presence, and turned toward Danique, bringing its weapon up.

Natascha stepped into the open. "Over here!" she shouted.

The foot soldier hesitated at the sound of Natascha's voice. Both Raconteurs fired their own ray-guns at the bulbous-headed alien from different sides. The tall foot soldier lit up as the blue-red electrical charges from both weapons shook its body. The whine of gears fought the electricity coursing over it. After a few seconds, the creature gave a high-pitched squeal that sounded like pain and fell forward into the powdery snow.

Natascha went over to the fallen alien and picked up its dropped weapon. It appeared to be a laser gun of some sort, short, hefty, with a series of coils encased in thick glass. The barrel tapered to a large porcelain insulator wrapped around a silver electrode rod that protruded off the end, not dissimilar in makeup to her own Peacemaker, but no doubt more powerful. She lifted the alien's weapon with a grunt, but it was too heavy to use effectively, so she dropped it back into the snow.

The side ramp on the Slipstream stood open. Snowy footprints led up to the ship, then back to the building. Danique climbed the ramp to investigate the inside. She appeared moments later, shaking her head. "It's empty, and the keybox is gone," she said. Natascha nodded and pointed to the monastery.

They followed several sets of footprints in the deep snow to the front entrance of the building, still unchallenged by any guards. Danique put her nose to the window and shaded her eyes from the reflection. "There's embers burning in the hearth," she said. "But I don't see any movement."

Natascha tried the doorknob of the wooden door. It turned in her hand, and the door swung in with a push. The foyer area was small and narrow. The doorway lead into an open sanctuary with rows of wooden benches and statues of saints and angels along each wall. At the back of the room, a set of wide steps led up to a second story. A baptism fountain burbled in the far corner. The room was empty.

Both entered silently and looked over the wide room. Natascha searched the areas adjacent to the foyer but found no evidence of anyone having been there. She walked down a short hallway to the backroom Danique was inspecting. It was the only place that had any hint of warmth. The smell of ash and smoke came from a fireplace on the far wall.

Danique took off her gloves, added kindling to the glowing embers, and stirred the coals with a poker. A small flame licked up over the wood. She rubbed her hands together. "Looks like we missed the party," she said.

"Yes, it does," Natascha answered. "But someone was here." Something caught her attention. On the back of a chair facing the hearth was a long silk scarf. She picked it up. There was an intricate flower design surrounded by swirling Chinese dragons. Natascha recognized it right away. A birthday gift from a shy seven-year-old girl to her mother. Was it left behind by accident? Or as a warning?

"One problem at a time," she muttered.

# Chapter 2
# Things Left Behind

Ren B'gatti knew he was asleep. He tried to wake himself up but couldn't.

In his dream, he found himself walking alongside Claymore on a narrow path up the side of a steep hill. Between them, their prisoner stumbled along with his hands bound behind him. Ren grabbed Serralto Cardus by the arm to steady him as they crested the hidden path on the precipice of a high cliff.

Ahead of them, the dirt pathway lead to a giant tree, twisted and ravaged by time. At the base of its massive trunk, the greenish glow of a rabbit-hole illuminated the cool night air.

The silence weighed him down. He and Claymore had just won a great victory over the *Society of the Black Rose*. They had rescued the man who would prove their innocence in the assassination of Minstrel Cotty, the *Logos Personae* of *The Angels of Avalon*. All should have been right with the world, but it wasn't. Something was off.

Normally, Ren appreciated the quiet. In his opinion, people talked too much without actually saying anything of value. But Claymore's sanity grew more unstable by the moment and Ren was at a loss at what to do about it.

"So, what's the first thing you're going to do when you're a free man?" Ren asked his partner. "How about we have dinner at *The Djinn's Lamp*? Tell Babek and Asha the good news. They'll want to know."

Claymore continued to mumble softly to himself, his words too low for Ren to hear.

As they approached the rabbit-hole that would take them back to Rogue Destiny, Serralto ripped his arm free of Ren's grip. The man tried to run, but Claymore kicked his feet out from under him. Serralto crashed to the ground.

Claymore stepped over him and drew his pistol. He cocked the hammer back and pointed the barrel in Serralto's face.

"Don't!" Ren yelled. "We've won! All we have to do is get Serralto back the Raconteurs, then we're both free. The nightmare will be over!"

His partner turned toward him, his eyes empty of emotion. He mumbled something Ren couldn't understand.

"What?" Ren asked, cocking his head to hear over the wind.

"You're wrong," Claymore replied. "I'm never going to be free. Not from this madness. It'll only get worse until I'm completely mad and don't recognize my own life. I can't go on like this." He lifted his revolver.

"No!" Ren yelled. He thought Claymore was going to turn the gun on himself. "You don't want to do this!"

"Sorry, but I have to," Claymore said. He fired.

Ren felt like he was struck in the chest with a blacksmith's hammer. A piercing, burning sensation radiated through his upper body. He looked down to see blood running from a hole above his heart. His partner had just shot him.

Claymore fired a second time, then a third and a fourth. Ren staggered backwards as each bullet struck him. He fought to stay on his feet, but was forced further and further away from Claymore. This was a dream, he told himself, but the bullets striking him hurt none-the-same. He found himself teetering on the edge of a cliff. The rocks gave way under his feet, and he fell.

---

Ren woke to bright sunlight on his face. He shaded his eyes and tried to figure how long he'd been asleep, and why there was a blanket on him.

"Rough night?" a quiet voice asked.

Ren scratched the back of his head and rolled over to see Medesto sitting next to him on the stoop, reading the newspaper, *The Daily Inquisitor*.

Ren yawned. "Yeah, I was out late."

"You wanna talk about it?"

"No, I do not," Ren replied. A grin crept over the shapeshifter's face despite his soreness. He sat up and stretched his arms. Joints cracked as he twisted and flexed his muscles. A piercing twinge of pain reminded him the injury on his bare left shoulder had still not healed. Even a little.

"You said you wouldn't leave," Medesto said.

"No, I said I would be here when you woke up," Ren replied. "Not the same thing."

Medesto stood up and folded the newspaper. "Where'd you go?"

"For a walk," Ren answered. "Couldn't sleep. Thought I'd get reacquainted with the City after being gone for a year. That's always more fun at night."

"Did you get it out of your system?"

Ren shrugged. "For now."

Medesto pulled the alpaca blanket off Ren and threw it over his own shoulder.

"You're injured," the gnome noted.

An intense pain radiated down Ren's shoulder. The laceration had yet to close, let alone begin to heal. That was not normal for him.

"It's nothing," he said.

"Can you shape-shift?"

Ren didn't need to shift to know he couldn't. "No, I can't," he said.

"Then it doesn't sound like *nothing* to me," the gnome said. "I thought you healed fast."

"I got cut by some sort of magically enhanced blade," Ren replied. "It'll be fine. It's just taking a bit longer to heal than normal."

A disgusted look came over the gnome's face. "It looks infected," he said. "You'll need to have that looked at before Natascha calls in or you're not going to be of any use to us."

Ren did not need to be lectured about his duty and responsibility to the Raconteurs, not after the night he had just experienced. He climbed to his feet. A bundle of letters fell from his waistband to the stoop.

Medesto picked them up. "And what are these?"

"Correspondence between Mordecai Davos and his minions here in the City. I thought Gideon might find them interesting. Took them off Piqwic York after I ran into him last night."

Medesto thumbed through the short stack of envelopes. "And what were you doing running into Piqwic York?"

Ren didn't want to talk about the events from the night before. How he let Claymore leave Rogue Destiny without him. His partner had convinced him he was better off alone to deal with the slow burning madness that he would never come back from. What was Ren thinking? Claymore made him promise to help the Raconteurs chase down Mordecai and his gang of escaped ruffians. He should have said no.

The urge to leave welled up in him, but he pushed the thought away. He would stop Mordecai, then he would go after

Claymore. He sighed and changed the subject before Medesto could continue questioning about his nighttime activities.

"So you haven't heard from Natascha?" he asked.

"Nothing so far," the gnome replied. "I hope she's okay."

"Me too," Ren replied.

Medesto climbed to his feet and unlocked the door to the apartment building with his keys. Once inside, they climbed aboard an old-fashioned caged elevator.

"I need to make a stop on the third floor," Medesto said. He pushed the button. Ren stepped in behind him and closed the elevator's metal scissor gate. The antiquated elevator rumbled up three flights before it stopped.

Ren followed Medesto past several doors until the gnome stopped in front of room 315 and pounded on the door.

"I know you're in there, Pitzer," he growled. "I can smell those cheap cigars. I want the rent by tomorrow or I'm coming back and kicking this door in. This is your final warning!"

They walked back to the elevator. Ren chuckled to himself. The gnome pushed the button to the top floor and stood quietly as they ascended the seven stories to his apartment.

"So, are you a slumlord now?" Ren asked.

"Hey, I run a respectable establishment," Medesto quipped. "No need to get nasty. I just have a couple of freeloaders that need to be nudged a bit. Never should have listened to Gideon. He said, *Don't just sit on your money. Invest in real estate.* But I'm telling ya, it's been nothing but trouble."

"I'm sure," Ren replied. "It forces you to be around other people."

"What's that hanging around your neck?" the gnome asked.

"A souvenir I lifted off Piqwic York," Ren said with a grin. He held the talisman up by its chain. The blue gem at the center sparkled in the dim light. "I've been told it protects you from death. Didn't work too well for the last guy who wore it, though."

"So, you found him?" Medesto asked, not bothering to look over at Ren.

"Who?"

"Don't play dumb," Medesto growled. "You said *we*. There's only one person that could mean."

"Yeah, I found him," Ren admitted. "Claymore was tracking those responsible for killing Minstrel Cotty and we chased them down to a villa in Adezhda."

"The city of assassins," Medesto said. "Impressive. Who'd it turn out to be?"

"Common Council member, Serralto Cardus. He didn't kill Cotty himself, but hired someone to do the deed. Unfortunately, he didn't survive the night."

Medesto raised a bushy eyebrow in surprise. "You killed a council member?"

"No," Ren replied. "Claymore did. When we had him in custody, Serralta attacked us with an enchanted wand. Claymore just reacted. It's been a long night."

"How's he doing?" the gnome asked hesitantly, as if he didn't want to hear the answer.

Ren scratched his head. "Not good. He's left Rogue Destiny. Wouldn't tell me where he was going. I tried to convince him to come back with me, but after he killed Serralta, he insisted he was too dangerous to be around the Raconteurs."

"You could have called us to help," Medesto said.

"I mentioned that to Claymore, but he insisted we didn't need help. I think he wanted to do this himself, to erase the stain of his greatest failure."

Ren stretched the sore muscles in his arms and legs. He could feel the many bruises that covered his body were on the mend. They would be completely gone in a few more hours, but the throbbing pain down his shoulder refused to heal. The elevator rattled to a stop. They walked down the hall to Medesto's apartment.

Ren closed the door behind them and turned to Medesto. "Now tell me what you know about the *Paradigm Madness*."

The gnome went to a bookshelf filled with his eclectic collectables and memorabilia. One shelf was nothing but ancient books of various sizes and thickness. He pulled one hefty tome down with a small padlock. He grabbed a small hidden key under a nearby vase, unfastened the lock and handed Ren a book titled *The Origins and Curiosities of the Mythic Cosmos.*

"Page 234," Medesto said. "Chapter 17." He walked into his small kitchen and turned on the teakettle, before taking down two teacups from the cupboard and setting them on the small, round kitchen table. "It happens most commonly when someone leaves their homeworld for the first time," he said, not looking over at Ren. He dug through a second cupboard for a box of tea bags and set it on the table between the cups. "The mind is unable to comprehend the extreme shift in realities. They simply cannot accept the fact that we are all, at our essence, nothing more than inky words on a page. Characters inside a book."

Ren thumbed through the pages to chapter 17. The heading that read:

*The Paradigm Madness and Its Effect on Mortal Beings*
*Accounts of the Paradigm Madness date back as far as the foundation*
*of Rogue Destiny itself. No one has been able to pin down the exact*
*cause or why it will take some and not others. The most common*
*occurrence appears to be when someone wanders from their world of*
*origin and is forced to face the greater truths of our existence. The*
*mind is unable to accept the shift in reality. There is a slow hollowing*

*out of the soul until the individual is nothing but a husk of their former self.*

"He told me this had happened before," Ren said, "to another Raconteur."

Medesto nodded. "Shalal Barrick," he said. "Early recruit. She joined the Raconteurs right after I did. The madness had taken her already when she left her world, but she hid it well. No one realized it was an issue until several agents died in an ambush. We took her home and shortly after that, she disappeared."

"Just tell me how I save Claymore?"

"You can't," Medesto said, shaking his head. "No one can."

Ren closed the book and set it down. "I don't believe that."

"Whether you believe it or not," Medesto said, "it won't change his fate. Claymore's situation is unique. He was in the presence of Minstrel Cotty when the assassin killed him. The *Crucible Event* that destroyed *The Angels of Avalon* formed at the precise moment Cotty died and the mystical bond between the *Logos Persona* and their Story was severed. It ripped *The Angels of Avalon* apart at its foundation. His exposure to that broke his iron will. It's more than any mortal mind can take."

Building frustration and rage filled Ren's thoughts. He attempted to shift into something big so he could punch a hole in the wall. Nothing happened. The pain in his shoulder intensified. He sat down on the couch instead.

"It's not fair," Ren said, ran his hands through his wild hair. "If I had only been there to stop this from happening."

"Life's never fair when you need it to be," Medesto growled into his beard. "Don't blame yourself. You got Claymore out of there, along with five other condemned souls. They'd all be dead if you hadn't."

The kettle on the stove whistled.

"And if you were there when Cotty died, you'd be in the same place Claymore is," Medesto said. "Tea?" He poured steaming water into both cups.

"That doesn't make sense," Ren replied. "The assassin who killed Cotty was still in the room when I found Claymore. She was unaffected by any madness. The only difference between them was Claymore's head injury. It had to be what prevented him from protecting himself against the effects of the *Crucible Event*."

"You don't know that," Medesto said. "*The Angels of Avalon* burned up over a year ago. The assassin could be out there wandering around right now, suffering the same fate as Claymore."

Ren pulled himself to his feet. "She seemed sane enough when I killed her last night."

If the reply surprised Medesto, he showed no sign of it. "You have been busy. Gideon will want a full report on everything that happened in Adezhda."

"Gideon's going to have to wait."

"You're right. First, we need to get that shoulder looked at by a professional."

Ren fought the urge to go look for Claymore. He should have never let him out of his sight. But he remembered his promise to his partner. *Take care of my Raconteurs.* It was Claymore's last request. One Ren couldn't ignore.

"Then what are we doing here?" Ren said. The hammer above the fireplace caught his attention. He made him wonder what part it played in the gnome's past and if Medesto was hiding from something like the rest of them. His eyes dropped to a bent and soiled white piece of paper, the size of a playing card. He took it down from the mantle. It was a business card that belonged to a friend. He slipped it into his pocket.

# Chapter 3
# When the Walls Come Tumbling Down

"In here!" Danique called from the next room.

Natascha stuffed the scarf into a pocket of her long coat and hurried to see what Danique might have found. The young woman stared out a large window to the back of the monastery.

"What is that?" Danique asked.

Behind the building stood dozens of snow-covered headstones surrounded by a wrought-iron fence. Beyond the graveyard was a huge, round hole carved out of the ground, twenty feet wide and angled down into the dirt.

"I don't know," Natascha said. She went out the back doors onto a wide terrace. Danique followed her and together they walked to the edge of the massive opening. It sloped into the earth at an angle wide enough for her to walk down. The rim of the hole was blackened from heat. The smell of vegetation and burnt paper rose to meet them. The ground around the opening was partially thawed from the warm air rising out of it. Footprints from the building showed the tracks from a score of people.

"This is where Mordecai and company left this world," Natascha said, not hiding her disappointment. She pulled a scanning device from her pocket and checked the area around the gaping hole. After a few seconds, she looked at the read-out. "There's a ley-line running underneath this spot. This is how Mordecai's been jumping worlds. Gideon thinks it's with the use of a machine that rides the energy of the ley-lines and redirects them to new destination points. That's how he was able to spirit an entire cell block out of Lazaranth Prison undetected."

"That's not possible," Danique said. "Who could build something that could harness that kind of power?"

"I have my suspicions," Natascha said, fingering the scarf in her coat pocket. She was hoping she was wrong, but knew someone who had once hypothesized about such a machine. She led Danique back inside out of the cold. "Let's see if we can get *Fool's Errand* running. There may be something in the onboard memory that will help us find Montagu and Keating." They were halfway across the sanctuary when voices reached them from the hallway.

The sound of footsteps echoed from behind a partially opened door, mixed with the murmuring of human conversation. Natascha and Danique hurried to hide as the cellar door opened and three individuals appeared, each carrying a wooden crate. They set the boxes down on the front pew, next to several others.

"Hurry it up," the woman ordered. By her tone, she was in charge. "We need to load what we can and get out of here."

The trio started back downstairs. The woman stopped and held up her hand. "Hold up," she said, pointing to footprints of melting snow on the floor in between the pews. "Those weren't there before."

Natascha watched from her vantage point behind the stairs. The woman scanned the room with deliberate intent. Her eyes fell on the rekindled fire. She looked about the darkened interior, her hand fingering the butt of her pistol. She drew the weapon and motioned her companions to spread out.

"Hallo?" she called out. "We know you're here. Come out and let's have a look at you."

Natascha caught Danique's eyes and nodded. The young girl shook her head in response. She drew her Peacemaker and remained hidden behind the stairs. Natascha took a breath and stepped out from under the staircase landing, Peacemaker in one hand, the other hand inside her coat pocket.

The leader was a lean, thin-faced, pale woman. She wore a red regency coat with gold buttons and a high collar. Gold trim outlined the front of the jacket and glinted in the dim light.

"Put your weapons down," Natascha ordered. "You're all under arrest." She could feel the woman weighing her options, glancing about the room as if wondering whether Natascha was alone. Without a word, she knelt and placed her pistol on the floor. The two men followed suit.

"I'm looking for the owners of that ship outside," Natascha said. "And you're not them."

"No, I'm afraid we're not," the woman replied.

"Mind telling me where they are?" Natascha asked.

"We should be the ones asking questions," the larger of the two men said. He shifted the empty gun belt on his waist. "Spying on us like that. It's plain rude."

"I know you," Natascha said to the woman. "Tessa Baryessa. Someone who should be currently serving a double life sentence for crimes against the dying-earth novel, *All Tomorrow's Yesterdays*. The big gentleman to your right goes by Poor Boy Johnson. Not sure what his story is, but he's supposed to be in Lazaranth too. My apologies, but I'm afraid I don't recognize your other companion."

"Ephraim Campo," the third one said. He was a small man with close-set eyes and a nervous disposition.

"And you escaped from Lazaranth as well?" Natascha asked.

Ephraim Campo shrugged.

"Where is Mordecai Davos?"

"Who?" Poor Boy asked.

"The man who broke you out of Lazaranth Prison?" Natascha said.

"Oh, Mordecai Davos," Tessa said with a thin-lipped smile. "He left some time ago. We're supposed to keep an eye out for anyone who might be following behind us. I think he meant you."

Natascha lifted her Peacemaker. "Well, you're all escaped criminals, so I'm taking you back to Lazaranth—after you tell me where Montagu and Keating are."

"We're only criminals under the laws of Rogue Destiny," Poor Boy retorted. He stood well over six-feet with violent eyes and a cruel smile. His brown skin was darker than Natascha's own. "Out here, we're beyond her borders, free from the laws set down by others. Just down-on-our-luck travelers, salvaging what we can to make our way in an indifferent universe."

"I'm only going to ask this one more time," Natascha said, bracing herself for the response she knew was coming. She hoped Danique was ready, but could not see her behind the stairs. "Where are the two men that ship belongs to?"

"What if I told you they left and said we could have it?" Tessa said. She pulled a small black box the size of a deck of cards from her coat. It was a keybox, the same kind Natascha had for *Nevermore*.

Natascha's grip tightened on her Peacemaker. "I'd have to say you were a liar," she hissed through her gas mask.

"No, no, no. You got it all wrong," Tessa replied. "I swear, they gave us the ship with their blessings. Said we could fly it around a bit, get a feel for how she handles before we settled on a price."

"I'm still inclined to believe you stole it," Natascha said. Her heart pounded in her chest, fearing the answer. "Where are they?"

Tessa gave her a cruel grin. "Down in the basement," she said.

"Ossuary," Poor Boy corrected.

"Excuse me?" Tessa raised an eyebrow at her companion.

"I believe they call it an *ossuary*," Poor Boy said in a matter-of-fact tone. "This is a place of religion, where they keep the bones of the dead."

Tessa nodded in response and turned back to Natascha with a smile. "My apologies. They are down in the *ossuary*, but not up to accepting visitors at the moment. The price we settled on was their ship in exchange for their lives. In the end, we decided we wanted both."

Natascha's breathing tightened and gritted her teeth. She was too late. All that was left to her now was vengeance.

"So you abandoned Mordecai Davos and his grand quest?" Natascha asked, keeping her voice calm, even though she felt like screaming and laying waste to the three in front of her. Tessa moved forward a step. Natascha brought the Peacemaker up.

"Alas, we decided to part company with Mr. Davos," Tessa said. "He was a gracious host, but kept us to a pretty tight schedule, and we felt we were missing the more interesting details of the worlds we passed through. Our goals in life were just too different. We felt it was time to strike out on our own and see what's out there for ourselves."

"Where was Mordecai headed?" Natascha asked. She fingered the small device in her pocket.

Ephraim Campos spoke up. "We traveled quickly, never knowing where we were or where we were going next. Not even sure where we are now."

"How many are traveling with Mordecai?" Natascha asked.

"Too many for you to handle, Missy," Poor Boy laughed. "But I wish we had a chance to get our hands on Mordecai's marvelous machine. It was quite impressive. You should see it if you get a chance. Imagine a contraption that can actually punch a hole through time and space, creating a doorway into a new world. Quite amazing, if you ask me, but we'll have to settle for the flying machine outside."

"No one touches the ship," Natascha growled.

"We know how your little rocket ship works," Tessa said. "And we're flying out of here with or without your blessing. You see, we know who you are too. The infamous Doctor Enigma. The Raconteurs' ghost, who likes to pretend she's the *Dark Avenger* from some pulp novel, able to walk through walls and disappear in a wink. You work for that little self-righteous fool, Gideon Dumas."

Poor Boy gestured to the crates they had hauled up from the basement. "Our time with Mordecai has not been a total loss. We have plenty of old writings and antique journals to take back to Rogue Destiny and sell. Then we can start living the life we always felt we deserved."

Natascha could tell by the man's tone that the conversation was winding down. The tension in the air was palatable. She ventured another question. "What is Mordecai Davos looking for?"

"Couldn't tell ya," Tessa answered. "Wasn't that close to the man. Treated us like pack animals, hauling his piles of old papers all over creation. But enough with the small talk."

Tessa Baryessa pulled a gun hidden under her coat and fired. Natascha ducked behind the staircase as Poor Boy and Ephraim picked up their guns. Bullets ripped into the railing and balusters next to her head. Natascha pulled an incendiary device from her pocket and tossed it into the larger room. It exploded a moment later. Statures shattered and crashed to the floor.

Danique threw herself down at the base of the stairwell opposite Natascha. The young woman fired her Peacemaker, striking Poor Boy squarely in the chest with the electrical arc of energy. The big man staggered back, the jolt of electricity flowing over him. He lifted his gun and fired before he succumbed to the effects of the Peacemaker's electrical shock. The bullet struck the stone wall behind Danique.

Poor Boy fell to his knees and collapsed onto the floor. Danique shifted her attention to Ephraim Campo. Her next shot struck the sculpture of a saint, where the criminal took cover.

Natascha moved under the staircase to the other side and stood over Danique, trying to get a better angle on Tessa. The woman slipped behind the enormous base of a statue, firing back. Natascha spoke into the comm in her gas mask. "Gustav? We're taking fire and I need you and Gossamer in here!"

No reply.

Outside the front windows of the monastery, an explosion interrupted her train of thought. Natascha fired her Peacemaker again and dared a glance out the front windows. *Fool's Errand* lay on its side in the snow. Black smoke and flames rose into the sky from its fuselage.

A vague silhouette appeared in the thick fog over the forest. A fifty-foot-high Martian tripod waded through the trees like water toward the monastery. A beam of red light shot from the saucer's head. It struck *Fool's Errand* again, splitting the Slipstream Runabout in half and leaving a smoking trench of molten rubble in its wake.

The single red eye at the center of the alien tower went dark. The tripod cleared the trees, marching toward the monastery on stilted legs. Natascha yelled into the comm again. "Gustav, talk to me! What's going on out there?"

A static reply answered. "Gossamer and I were under attack by the patrol we encountered earlier. The invaders used a jamming signal to confuse our communications. I could hear you, but couldn't answer."

"Are you okay?"

"Gossamer put down all three. Appears the invaders don't breathe well in this atmosphere with their glass helmets smashed in. They did have some interesting tech. Might be something we'll want to salvage before we leave..."

"Focus, Gustav," Natascha said. She fired again as Tessa moved between statues, but the fugitive was too fast to get a clear shot. "Are there any other tripods headed our way?"

"No others are showing up on my radar. I am on my way to you."

Natascha watched the tripod close in on the monastery. Its center eye began glowing, dim at first, then brighter and brighter. A piercing sound split the air and a deep red light filled the room from outside before a laser shot out.

"Danique, run!" Natascha yelled. The laser sliced through the front wall of the building like it was paper. The red beam continued forward, sparing nothing in its path. It cut through the wall, past the staircase to the back rooms. The force of the explosion knocked her to the floor behind the stairwell.

The destructive ray dissipated with the sounds of a turbine winding down. Natascha peeked over the edge of the landing. The red glow of the eye went dark, its charge spent.

"Gustav, I don't know how long we have before the tower's laser recharges. One of the foot soldiers dropped a weapon in the snow behind *Fool's Errand*. It was too heavy for me to use, but you might be able to bring that thing down with it. Another laser hit will bring the whole building down on top of us, so hurry!"

"Roger that."

Tessa remained behind a statue. She leaned out and fired randomly in Natascha's direction. Ephraim Campos had hidden behind a statue in the laser's path. There was nothing left of the statue or the man behind it but a three-foot trench of molten stone that ran the length of the building. Danique was nowhere among the rubble. Panic gripped Natascha.

"Danique!" Natascha yelled, fear of the unthinkable welling up inside her. There was only silence. Her thoughts went to bad places.

"How about we call this a draw?" Tessa yelled from her hiding place. "You go your way and I'll go mine. No hard feelings."

"Not going to happen!" Natascha answered from behind the staircase. She could ghost herself through the wall to safety, but she would never leave Danique.

She saw her co-pilot emerge from the edge of the forest, flying across the open field toward the burning Slipstream. The hovering automatron slowed near the back of the ship, scanning the ground for the weapon. Out beyond the burning ship, the tripod marched on in the monastery's direction. Its giant red eye began to glow again.

"Gustav?!"

"I see it," her co-pilot replied, pulling the laser weapon from the snow. He seemed to take a moment to figure out how to fire it. He held the soldier's weapon with three of the four appendages hanging from his undercarriage. The tripod's red eye grew bright as it reached its full charge.

Without appearing to aim, Gustav fired with uncanny accuracy and hit the mid-joint of one of the tripod's long spindly leg. He took a second shot, hitting another of the tower's three legs. The Martian War Machine stumbled, fighting to remain upright.

"Gossamer's on his way," Gustav told Natascha.

There was a deep thudding on the ground that grew louder as it got closer. Gossamer 99 came running out of the trees across the snowy field behind the towering machine and threw his full weight against the damaged leg. The machine buckled under the strike and the Tripod toppled over onto the top of the monastery.

Natascha looked up as the ceiling above collapsed under the weight of the war machine—and tons of stone and timbers crashed down on top of her.

# Chapter 4
# Worlds within Worlds

"How's your shoulder holding up?" Medesto asked. He stared out the small window of the cab.

"It's sore, but nothing I can't handle," Ren replied. In truth, the pain had gotten worse. Much worse. The gash across the back of his left shoulder had intensified to such an extent that his left arm and hand had gone numb. He'd received the injury the night before when he rescued his partner Claymore from the hands of *The Society of the Black Rose*. But he wasn't about to let anyone know the anguish he was in at the moment.

The horse drawn Hansom Cab stopped in front of an ancient building of stone, brick and mortar that stood hidden behind a high rock wall. Two owl statues sat on each side of an iron gate. The sign on the gate read:

The Order of the Memento Ex-Libris
For the Remembrance of All That Is and All That Has Come
Before.
~ Omnium-Gatherum ~

.    .    .

*The Order of the Memento Ex-Libris'* obsession with documenting every scrap of information throughout the Mythic Cosmos bordered on madness. Like the Raconteurs, they had agents everywhere, mapping, charting, and recording everything. Unlike the Raconteurs, who were intent on protecting the integrity of the cosmos, *The Order of the Memento Ex-Libris* was consumed with recording it.

Ren knew little of the mysterious organization, but had visited the facilities once, long ago, with Claymore. They were in pursuit of a rogue agent who had betrayed the Raconteurs and was working with a group of thieves trying to reach the most tightly guarded secret in Rogue Destiny. The location of the Great Library.

The Great Library was rumored to be hidden somewhere within the vast archaic depths of the building. It held a copy of every book. and therefore every Narrative to every Story, within the Mythic Cosmos. If the knowledge contained in those volumes ever fell into the wrong hands, it would undermine the safety of the worlds the Raconteurs sought to protect. The thieves failed to locate the library, thanks to the Raconteurs. It strengthened the bounds between the two organizations.

"*The Order of the Memento Ex-Libris*, huh?" Ren said. "That's quite a name."

Medesto chuckled. "The Order tends to be a bit self-aggrandizing. Their field agents call themselves the *Bedlam Chasers Society*. It an inside joke. Chasing *chaos* and all that." He pushed the call button inside the box at the gate. A voice answered a moment later.

"Welcome to the Omnium-Gatherum," the cheerful female voice said. "How may I help you today?"

"This is Medesto Bodenhammer with the Raconteurs. I don't

have an appointment, but I need to speak to Pasquali Eco if he's available. Tell him it's an emergency."

"One moment please."

Medesto glanced over at Ren's obvious discomfort. "Hang on, bud," he said. "We'll be inside in a minute."

Ren tried not to move any more than he had to, but if the pain radiating down his shoulder increased any more he knew he was going to pass out. The box crackled as the voice on the other end came back on.

"He'll meet you in the main lobby. Please come through." The iron-barred door next to the main gate buzzed and Medesto pushed it open. A domed roof sat atop the massive building. Towering spires, one on each corner, stretched skyward, giving the byzantine architecture the illusion they supported the very skies above the city.

Ren followed the gnome up the front steps into the entrance way to a coatroom. The arched doorway led to a lobby with a counter of polished wood. Two clerks looked up as they entered. A large, rotund man in bright clothes and a red skullcap filled a doorway beyond the counter as they approached.

Pasquali Eco gave them a broad smile. "Medesto!" he beamed. "And Ren B'gatti! Good to see you both. What brings you in today?"

"Hello, Pasquali," the gnome said. "Sorry to bother you, but we have an injury caused by some sort of magical weapon. It's refused to heal, and I hoped you could help us."

"Well, come on back to my office." He motioned them to follow and disappeared into a backroom. Ren lead the way around the end of the front desk and through the decorative archway. They followed Pasquali to a low-ceilinged backroom. The walls were covered in maps and charts showing the farthest reaches of the Mythic Cosmos. Tables cluttered with books and scrolls filled the room.

"Sit down." Pasquali pointed to an empty stool. "Let's have a look."

Ren gingerly slipped his shirt off and sat down. His wound burned with a blistering hot pain across his back. He leaned forward with his elbows on his knees.

The alchemist slipped on a pair of magnifying glasses that made his eyes look comically large and leaned in to inspect the wound. Ren could feel warm breath on his back as Pasquali examined the infected skin around the incision.

"This is a nasty cut. How long ago did this happen?"

"Six, seven hours," Ren replied. "Normally, a clean incision like that should've healed by now." He winced as Pasquali carefully probed the injured area with his fingers.

Pasquali picked up a device from his desk. It was the length of the alchemist's hand and resembled any number of instruments that Charley or any other technician that worked for the Raconteurs would use. With the a press of a button, the device hummed to life, and two small antennae rose on each side. A light pulsed in slow rhythmic succession as he passed it over the infected area and then checked each of Ren's pupils. He read the apparatus' reading with a perplexed look on his face.

"This does not look good." The alchemist raised an eyebrow. "Can you raise your left arm?"

"A little," Ren said. He tried, but his arm was heavy and numb. It rose a couple of inches before he winced and lowered it back down.

"There is nothing more I can do here," Pasquali concluded. "Your wound is infected and if we don't act quickly, it may be beyond what I can do. This requires a solution that lies beyond the borders of Rogue Destiny. We need to get you off-world immediately."

"How long is that going to take?" Medesto asked. "Maybe I should wait here. We're waiting on a call that we need to respond to immediately."

"Not to worry, I know a place that isn't far at all," Pasquali replied. "Only a rabbit-hole hop away. Time moves differently there. Who knows, we may be back even before we have left. It should slow the advance of the infection and allow me to reverse the effects of any contamination. I'll get you back as quickly as possible, so you can get on with your business."

Medesto scratched his salt and pepper hair. "Have you seen anything like this before?" he asked. "Because I sure haven't."

"It does not appear to be poison, but it is spreading quickly," Pasquali replied. "I'll know more when we get to my research laboratory. In this case, magic can only be healed by magic."

Pasquali lead them to a wide assembly hall, lined with the desks of robed scholars and bespectacled researchers, their heads down, lost in their work. People carrying armloads of books and folded maps swept by them. More statuettes of owls filled the nooks of the bookshelves in the walls.

They passed through the hall to an adjoining corridor down a set of stairs to a metal-reinforced wooden door. Pasquali unlocked it with a key attached to his belt by a silver chain. The door opened to a private office. The room was small with only a desk, bookcase and a large plush chair in front of an unlit fire. The alchemist lifted a rug and grabbed the steel ring of a trap-door beneath it. He pulled it up. The familiar hazy light of a rabbit-hole illuminated a staircase that wound downward into the darkness.

"This building dates back to the early years of the City," Pasquali said. "It's taken me decades to construct this passageway to my liking. It leads to my private research laboratory." He descended the iron steps, twisting his bulky frame sideways to navigate the narrow staircase. Ren followed with Medesto bringing up the rear.

As he descended the stairs, Ren was struck with the disorienting vertigo of leaving one world and entering another. Medesto grabbed his arm to steady him. For a few moments, he couldn't tell if he was upside down or not and closed his eyes. His hand gripped the railing tightly as he continued down the metal steps until the sensation passed.

After a couple minutes, the poor lighting gave way to bright daylight. The twisting staircase ended at a stone pathway. In front of them, Ren saw a great garden of trees and fountains interspersed with fragrant flowers of all shapes and colors. The path lead to a wooden bridge that crossed a babbling brook. On the far side, a quaint cottage waited for them, like something from a fairy tale. Songbirds flittered about the trees as Pasquali unlocked the front door to the cozy little house.

"What is this place?" Medesto asked. The interior of the cottage looked like some mad scientist's laboratory.

"My private retreat, where I can relax and work undisturbed," Pasquali replied. He lifted a hand and snapped his fingers. The dozen candles set around the front room flared to life, casting everything in a reddish-orange glow. "It's close enough I can tap into the magic of the nearby world, *A Blood Curse for an Eternal Prince*. The proximity allows me access to some of my lost sorcery, but we're still far enough away so nothing I do will interfere with the mechanical workings of the narrative."

"So, we're in a *pocket-world*," Medesto quipped.

"More or less," Pasquali said. "Also known as a *pocket-dimension*, although the differences are minor. This is a world within a world, a nebulous place, not quite here, not quite there. It's quiet, and I enjoy the solitude."

"Where's the sunlight coming from?" Ren asked. Even

breathing was painful for him now, but this place fascinated him too much to keep his questions to himself.

"Who can say?" Pasquali replied with a laugh. "It's all part of the mystery of a place that shouldn't exist. A pocket-dimension needs a light source and here it is for us."

Ren and Medesto followed Pasquali to a back room full of alchemist equipment. Tables and shelves held all of the sorcerer's equipment, flasks, gas burners, and glass vials of various sizes, each labeled and corked. A small cot sat in the far corner.

Pasquali tapped on the empty table top at the center of the room. "Climb up and lie down on your stomach while I prepare something to dull your pain."

Ren did as he was asked. Pasquali switched on a small burner under a large beaker of cloudy liquid. He took a white cloth from a drawer and dipped it in a bottle of brown paste.

"Hold still while I apply this salve," he said as he gingerly dabbed the infected area around his wound. "It should numb your discomfort considerably. So, tell me how you obtained this injury."

Ren intended to keep the details of the previous night as vague as possible. What happened with Claymore was no one else's business. Even Medesto did not know all that happened.

"There were two attackers," he replied. "One had white robes with a hood and black mask. The other was opposite. Black robes and white mask. Their feet were clawed, bird-like. They phased in and out as we fought from one room to another."

Pasquali removed his spectacles. "I'm guessing this did not occur within the boundaries of Rogue Destiny or her surrounding islands."

"How'd you know?" Medesto asked. The stoic gnome fidgeted in place. He stood back from the examination, but Ren could tell he was anxious to help in some way.

"There's a nasty discoloration of the muscle and skin around the wound," Pasquali said. "It looks like unclean magic at work here, something that could never happen within the borders of the City."

Ren winced at the touch of the cloth. "We were in Adezhda chasing down a fugitive."

"Ah, the infamous City of Assassins," Pasquali murmured. "Interesting. May I inquire as to who you were with?"

"I was alone," Ren asked.

"But you just said *we*," Pasquali replied with a sly smile.

Ren swore under his breath. The injured shoulder pulsated in agony down his shoulder and had grown to the point of making him delirious. The medicine Pasquali applied did little to lessen the jarring pain. He glanced over at Medesto.

"You're among friends here," the gnome said. "You can speak freely in front of Pasquali."

Ren laid his head back down on his crossed arms. "Okay," he quietly said. "Claymore and I chased a suspect to Adezhda when we had a bit of a run in with *The Society of the Black Rose*."

"Ah, Claymore Ives," Pasquali replied. "That's even more interesting. I have not heard that name in some time. Given the recent prison escape and your sudden return to Rogue Destiny, I figured the two may be connected. So you say the hooded attackers wore masks? What did they look like?"

He dropped a handful of reddish seeds into a stone bowl and ground them to dust with a pestle, before dumping the contents into the roiling white liquid.

"Very birdlike. If fact, their whole appearance struck me as birdlike. One nicked me with the tip of its polearm before I could get out of the way."

Pasquali chuckled. "This was more than just a nick. Sounds like the work of *The Scions of Arubus*. A cultish group who work for various organizations, legal and otherwise. I've been hearing rumors of their activities inside the City recently. Their disciples hire themselves out for bodyguard work to various criminal organizations to fund their leader's exorbitant lifestyle."

"I've heard of them," Medesto said. "Gideon is convinced they're pursuing a more sinister agenda than just bodyguard work for the likes of Mordecai Davos and his ilk."

"If they were your attackers, you're lucky to be alive, Mr. B'gatti," Pasquali quipped. "Going up against both the *Scions of Arubus* and the *Black Rose*, I'm impressed you came away with only this. I can assume since Claymore is not here, that he did not return with you to the City?"

"No, he did not."

Ren took a deep breath, trying to focus past the agony radiating through him. "I created a diversion," he said. "So Claymore could slip away with our suspect. I ran into two the enforcers before I could get myself out."

Pasquali opened the doors to an apothecary cabinet and searched through several small drawers before taking a large vial out and holding the dull blue liquid up to the light. The label read: Thaumaturgy 19C7. He pulled the stopper off and poured the bottle's contents into the liquid bubbling over the burner.

"Dangerous business," Pasquali murmured, not looking up from the concoction he was mixing. He poured several colored liquids into a large clear bowl. The various pigments mixed together but never quite lost their separate brilliance. Then the bubbling liquid was mixed in. The contents of the bowl grew thicker as he stirred it. He strapped a respirator over his face and donned a thick apron. Pulling on elbow-length rubber gloves, he consulted a thick book of crinkled, yellowed pages that sat on a pedestal next to his worktable.

"Brace yourself, this is going to hurt," Pasquali warned. "It's designed to force a chemical reaction, pulling the contaminates from the wound." He set the steaming bowl down on the table before he dabbed the thick liquid onto the wound. Ren winced as the ointment oozed down into the open gash. It was neither cold nor hot. He felt it course through his veins until his whole body tingled.

Ren blew the air from his lungs to steady himself against the sudden searing pain. His injured shoulder throbbed with a torment he'd never experienced before. In the past, he had been stabbed, shot and beaten dozens of times. This was on a whole different level. He felt the dark magic welling up inside him until his body was completely numb.

"Corrupted magic is very dangerous," Pasquali said as he worked. "Leaving Adezhda severed the magic from its source and slowed the spread of the putrid rot. If you had stayed there much longer, you'd most likely be dead now."

Ren tried to answer, but realized he'd lost any control over his voice. Words came from his lips, but it was not him speaking. It was not his voice. Someone else spoke through him.

"How are we doing, Mr. B'gatti?" Pasquali asked. His voice echoed from a distance.

"Better, thank you," a disembodied voice answered. Ren shouted, hoping someone would hear him, but no sound came out. He tried to calm himself against his rising fear. He was aware of a presence he often felt, mostly in the quiet moments when he was alone.

Only the night before, while he lay half drowned on a sandy beach outside Adezhda, the same voice had spoken to him. He called himself *Rhune*."

Ren had always been aware of a presence that followed him everywhere. It felt familiar to him, even if at times he doubted it was real. The voice only manifested when he was at some vulnerable point physically. He'd never worried about it before because it had never interfered in his life. Until that moment, the voice had only been an annoying echo in the back of his mind.

No one knew about the shadow that often whispered in his ear. Not Natascha or Medesto. Even Claymore was left in the dark. Now he wished he had told someone, anyone, as an unseen force pushed him further into the recesses of his own mind.

"Do not fear." The voice echoed inside his head. "I am here to break you free of this prison."

Ren felt the sensation of falling. He screamed a warning to Medesto and Pasquali, but no sound came out. Then everything went dark.

# Chapter 5
# Ley-lines and Rabbit-holes

Natascha pressed a button in her glove as the giant saucer-shaped head of the alien war machine crashed through the roof of the monastery on top of her. A green mist rose up around her, mixing with her chemically treated clothing and gas mask. Everything went black as tons of stone and timbers rained down on her.

The Raconteur stomped through the tons of debris piled high over her. She emerged from the darkness, like a ghost rising from the grave, to see Gossamer digging through the rubble.

"Danique?!" the cyborg bellowed. His simulated voice sounded strained. "I don't see her." He tossed aside large chunks of wood and stone as panic set in.

"Over there," Natascha said, pointing to the doorway leading down to the ossuary. "She may have made it to the cellar."

Gossamer waded through the debris, pushing aside an enormous chunk of stone blocking the way and threw the door open. He thrust his metallic head into the narrow opening.

"Danique?" he yelled. "Sister, are you down there?"

A faint voice answered. "I found Keating and Montagu."

"Do they need medical attention?" Natascha yelled.

"No," Danique replied. Her voice broke and was almost inaudible.

Natascha walked to where she had last seen Tessa. The statue she had been hiding behind was now buried under the rubble. At the edge of a stone slab, the tip of a boot was visible. Natascha didn't need to see any more and turned away in disgust. Poor Boy was nowhere to be seen. She decided he had suffered the same fate as his companions, and she was not about to go looking further. They had more important things to tend to at the moment.

Danique appeared at the top of the basement staircase. She was shaking and pale. "They're both…," she said, fighting back tears. "They were beaten and cut, then finally shot." The young girl leaned back and slid against the wall to the floor.

Natascha sat down next to her. She pulled off her gas mask and gloves, letting the snowflakes falling through the open ceiling land on her face. The air was still and strangely peaceful, despite the death and destruction all around them.

"What do we do now?" Danique asked. "Mordecai was here, so we go after him, right?"

"No," Natascha answered bluntly. "I need you and Gossamer to take Montagu and Keating home. There's nothing more we can do for them now except make sure they get a decent burial."

Danique stood up. "You may be a few years older than me, but I've seen more death than any Raconteur," she said, her voice getting louder as she talked. "Dying is nothing new to me or my brother. Mordecai may not have kill Montagu and Keating himself, but he *is* responsible for what his people did here. You can't leave us out of this!"

Natascha ignored the outburst and climbed to her feet. "We need to get moving before any more tripods or foot soldiers happen by." She spoke into the comm hidden in her collar. "Gustav? Go get *Nevermore* and bring her around."

The flying automatron appeared at a hole in the front wall of the building. "Roger that," he said. "Give me twenty minutes." He disappeared across the snow at a furious speed.

Gossamer stood guard as the two women completed the grisly task of bringing the remains of two of the oldest active Raconteurs up from the ossuary.

"Not enough left of the escapees to take back for identification," Natascha said. "But both of you should still get the bounty on them. Remember their names—Tessa Baryessa, Poor Boy Johnson, and Ephraim Campo. You'll have to identify them from the records at Lazaranth. I'll vouch that they're dead."

The young girl looked up at her, not even trying to hide the pain in her eyes. Natascha knew Gossamer felt the same under his steel shell. Montagu and Keating had been like surrogate uncles to both of them.

"I'm going after Mordecai alone," Natascha said. "That smoking hole out back is how he jumped to the next world. I need to follow him, find out where he landed, so we can slip the shape-shifter in with his followers."

"Renny's going after Mordecai by himself?" Danique asked. "Isn't that dangerous, even for him?"

"Not if he behaves himself," Natascha replied. "He's only supposed to gather information and find out what Mordecai is looking for. Then he'll contact us, so we can end this. And I'll make sure Mordecai sees justice for what was done here."

Danique and Gossamer were too young and inexperienced to face what waited beyond the yawning entrance of the rabbit-hole. Sending them back to Rogue Destiny with the bodies of the deceased Raconteurs would keep them safe, and Sebastian would be relieved his children were out of harm's way. Both were too polite to argue with her.

"And make sure their families are contacted," Natascha added.

After their grim cargo was loaded into *Nevermore*, Natascha watched the ship disappear into the snowy sky. Gustav would drop Danique and Gossamer off at *Midnight Run*, then both Slipstreams would head home. She pulled out the scarf she had found and smelled the perfume on it. The silk scarf was a one-of-a-kind custom-made 1936 Malcolm K. Richards limited edition. There was only one person she knew who had such expensive tastes. It belonged to her mother.

*One problem at a time*, Natascha thought.

Gray ash covered the snowy ground around the scorched edges of the rabbit-hole as Natascha approached. The air surrounding the opening still smelled of burnt paper. She traipsed down the sloping pathway into a fifteen-foot-wide circular tunnel. The ground was loose dirt, but there were no tread marks or evidence of the portal machine, only the footprints left by Mordecai and his people.

Something was not right. The ley-line should have condensed the distance between this world and the next into a single doorway. She stood in a dark passageway.

She clicked the side of her gas mask to bring up her night vision and stared forward. The artificial rabbit-hole narrowed in places. The floor and walls of the tunnel were uneven and rough, with large, malformed globules of discolored growth. Many of them seeped dark liquid that filled the passageway with a noxious smell.

The dirt ground beneath her boots cracked like thin ice as she moved along the tunnel. At one point, her boot broke through the floor up to her knee. She cursed under her breath and awkwardly pulled it free.

Natascha examined the hole her misstep had created. Under a thin layer of dirt, the floor of the tunnel was brittle, withered like a dried-out husk of a dying plant. She grabbed a handful of debris from the floor. It crumbled to dust in her hand. The tunnel was hollow underneath her, and all that separated her from the utter blackness of the Great Void was a layer of dead vegetation. She scrambled to her feet.

A true ley-line was a living organism pulsating with life. The cosmic fiber that connected all worlds together throughout the cosmos. Veins of vibrant energy snaked through the walls, giving off a greenish glow. The organic ley-line grew out from the roots of the giant Wayward Trees that speckled every literary world.

But this tunnel was not natural, only a poor imitation of a real ley-line. It was unstable and dying. Bits of debris fell off the walls and ceiling around her. She quickened her pace, unsure how long she had before the ley-line collapsed out from underneath her.

Natascha continued along the uneven ground as it wound and twisted for far longer than she would have liked. She climbed a decaying rise. In the distance, the light of a new world shone through the end of the tunnel. Natascha breathed a sigh of relief.

She continued forward, then stopped. Tessa Baryessa had said she and her companions remained behind on Mordecai's orders to prevent anyone from following. They also claimed to have deserted Mordecai's party to strike out on their own. The problem when dealing with desperate fugitives is that they were never truthful about their intentions. She wondered if there might be others waiting at the end of the rabbit-hole. The thought caused Natascha to rethink her reckless rush through the tunnel. She drew her Peacemaker. The answer came a moment later.

Gunfire erupted out of nowhere. Two figures stood momentarily silhouetted against the opening and fired at Natascha before disappearing into the shadows of the tunnel. More of

Mordecai's minions left behind to discourage anyone from following.

Natascha dropped to the ground and fired her Peacemaker. Her shot went wide and hit the decaying wall beyond her target. The multicolored beam from her pistol lit up the area of darkness around her opponents.

One shooter crouched behind a large mound at the edge of the light. She was female. The other was male and remained in the shadows on the opposite side. Natascha reached inside her coat for a small explosive device but remembered where she was and switched it out for a smaller silver orb. She tossed it to where the man crouched, and a burst of light went off in a blinding flash of brilliant white. Her night vision automatically compensated for the change in lighting, protecting her eyes as she dashed forward and shot the disoriented female with a blast of voltage from her Peacemaker. The female's body spasmed from the electrical shock before she fell to the floor of the tunnel.

The male shooter shielded his eyes from the piercing light. He pulled something off his belt and threw it blindly toward Natascha. The canister bounced past the Raconteur. A moment later, it exploded. The concussive force knocked Natascha forward to the floor and the whole tunnel shook. The surrounding walls began to split and crack.

Natascha did not wait to see what would happen next. She took off at a sprint over the uneven ground. Large horizontal cracks appeared in the walls, splitting wider as she ran past them. The wind picked up as the mouth of the tunnel tore free from its connection to the world in front of her. The distant light seemed miles away. Natascha ran faster.

The floor crumbled under her boots, causing her to stumble more than once. There was no time to grab either of Mordecai's lackeys, so she reluctantly left them to their fate and sprinted toward the beams of sunlight filtering through the dust at the tunnel's end. There was a great rumbling groan as the final moorings tore free from the world to which it was attached. She leapt through the doorway, catching the ragged edge of the opening to the new world with both hands as the tunnel fell away beneath her.

Natascha clung by her fingertips, dangling over the yawning blackness of the Great Void, fighting to gain a foothold in the loose dirt. The mouth of the rabbit-hole became a wind tunnel. Dirt and debris blew over her as it was sucked through the opening. Her foot caught a dried root from the edges of the dead ley-line. She reached up far enough to grab a handful of scrub brush. The grass came free from the ground before she could pull herself out. She slid back.

Hands grabbed her arms. Winds whipped around her, and she looked up in the faces of two men who pulled her through the opening onto firm ground. She rolled onto her back, breathing hard. The ley-line gave one last ominous groan in its final death throes, then disappeared into the darkness behind her.

One of the men picked up her Peacemaker from the ground where it fell. He stood examining the weapon's polished chrome casing, and the parabolic dish and diode at the end of the barrel.

Natascha's first instinct was to thinks these were more of Mordecai's people. She rolled to her feet toward the one holding the Peacemaker and knocked the weapon from his hand with a sweeping kick. She followed that by landing a boot into the man's midsection. The second man held a sharp scythe in both hands.

Another foot sweep put the man on his back. He landed with a hard exhale of air. The crescent blade flew from his hands and stuck in the ground next to his head. Natascha picked up the fallen Peacemaker and stood over both of them.

The men stared up at her, fear in their wide eyes. One glanced at the gaping hole in the hillside and then back at Natascha. It took her a moment, but judging from their clothing and calloused hands, these were locals, probably field hands curious about the smoking hole left in their world. A horse and cart full of straw waited on the nearby road confirmed her suspicions.

Through the yawning opening in the hillside behind her, Natascha regarded the dark Void beyond this world. The escaping air pulled at her coat.

She turned to the two men lying on the ground. "My apologies," she said with a slight bow. "I mistook you for someone else." She pulled her hood back and removed the gas mask, facing the warm sun before taking a long breath of fresh air. She returned her Peacemaker to its holster. "Where am I, and have you seen anyone else emerge from that hole?"

"No, we were just passing by when we saw the hole in the hillside," said one.

"You're in England," said the other. He pointed up the dusty road. "Old London is three leagues that way."

"Forgive me for the way I reacted." Natascha dug into an inner pocket of her long coat. "For your troubles." She tossed a Rogue Destiny Gold Sovereign to each of the laborers. The origin of the coins meant nothing to the two men, but gold translated across all languages and worlds.

Old London. So she was in England, or one of them anyway. Natascha had traveled many Englands through many different realities. In her own homeworld, she had received four years of education at Cambridge before inheriting the mantle of Doctor Enigma from her father. Each London she passed through was its own unique variation on the ancient city, but the layout of the streets was surprisingly similar. That would help her navigate the city, but it still didn't tell her what Book she was in.

"How much will it cost to catch a ride to Old London as quickly as possible?" Natascha asked. She could tell the two men were still processing the incredible events of the last few minutes. "Your cart?" Her voice was urgent, but she checked her anger. "I need transportation to the city."

She handed each of them another gold sovereign. Both men stared at the coins with avarice in their eyes. One of them snapped out of his daze. "Yes. We would gladly give you a ride to the city," he said.

"Good," she said. "But I have to send a quick message before we go."

Natascha pulled a narrow device from the protective sheath strapped to her leg and switched it on. The Echo Transponder took a moment to warm up before the map of this new world appeared on the screen.

The number of ley-lines and rabbit-holes in a literary world was in direct proportion to the number of fantastical elements the Narrative had. A Story steeped in magic could have dozens of doorways to and from the world, while a novel of dystopian survival may only have a single rabbit-hole. Whatever world Natascha now stood in, there were four ley-lines running throughout it.

The Raconteur stood in front of the opening as the gaping hole diminished in size. It was a relief to see that the artificial ley-line would leave no permanent scar on the world. Soon it would be as if it had never happened. The broken ley-line might even grow back over time.

But before it disappeared completely, Natascha needed to get a message to Rogue Destiny. She fiddled with the controls of the Echo Transponder until a signal flashed on her screen and the light shone with the same glow of the ley-line's organic green hue. She typed a quick message on the screen:

McGuffin has been located.
Tracking but no idea how long target will remain.
Coordinates to follow.
Hurry.
Enigma out.

With the push of a button, the message was sent on its way through the unseen ley-line beneath her feet, far across the Mythic Cosmos. It would take hours to reach the Raconteur's Wayfinder in Rogue Destiny, but it would give her location to the Raconteurs.

In the distance, a dirigible floated slowly among the clouds, which gave Natascha some idea of the level of technology she would find here. It looked like she was in a steampunk world of leather and gears. She had been to many of them before and was familiar with the genre.

Now she needed to find out what threats this world might have beyond the outlaws she chased. There should be a field house in Old London. She would start there.

"OK, I'm good, let's go," Natascha said to the laborers. She climbed into the back of the hay cart and plopped down on the soft straw. Her muscles ached, and she relished the moment of quiet. She lay back in the straw as the cart bounced down the road. The warm summer's day washed away the memories of the frozen Russian world, the loss of her friends, and the musty memories of the dying ley-line.

"Now to find Mordecai Davos before backup arrives," she muttered.

# Chapter 6
# The Unexpected Visitor

Medesto watched Ren's body convulse before he slumped unconscious onto the table. The streaks of pigment that moved across the trickster's skin slowly disappeared, leaving him the color of bleached bones. A dark ochre bubbled up from Ren's wound.

"What's happening?" the gnome asked.

"Extracting the poison takes a toll on the body," Pasquali replied.

A rancid odor filled the room as the oily liquid spewed over Ren's back. Black drops splattered on Pasquali's face, respirator and apron. Medesto gagged at the noxious stench.

When the black liquid contacted the surrounding air, it began to solidify. Pliable strands of the hardened magic snaked to the edges of the table like creeping vines or the tentacles of a great monster. Medesto started toward Ren, wanting to help, but not knowing how.

"Stay back!!" Pasquali ordered. "Do not come in contact with the corruption! This solvent will contain the spread of the ethereal magic by altering it to solid matter, like freezing water to ice."

Medesto backed away. "Blood and thunder, what a stink," he muttered under his breath.

Pasquali pried the curling strands of magic off the tabletop with his gloved fingers. The inky substance clung to his hands like spider webbing. He wrapped the dark tendrils around his fingers and submerged them in the bowl of milky solution. A soft hiss broke the stillness of the room and the corrupted magic dissolved in the swirling liquid. Pasquali waved the vapors rising from the bowl away with his hand.

He grabbed the ointment soaked rag and wiped his gloves clean.

"Hang on, Mr. B'gatti," Pasquali said. "Just a bit longer."

The entire process took several more minutes. Pasquali scrubbed the last remnants of the cursed magic from the table and floor with a thick cloth. Thin wisps of smoke rose off the trickster's skin, only to dissipate in the cool air.

Medesto glanced at Ren's gash. The injury finally began to heal. Pasquali covered the wound with a damp cloth.

"Thank you, Pasquali," Medesto said with a smile. He helped gather the dishes used in cleaning out the wound and took them to a small sink across the room.

"Always glad to help out the Raconteurs," Pasquali replied. "Our alliance with your agents has benefited us both throughout the years."

On the table behind them, Ren stirred. There was a heavy thud as something solid hit the floor. Medesto turned at the sound to see Ren had rolled off. He smiled and shook his head.

"Hopefully, Ren will be more careful in the future. You won't always be around to help us." He looked back at Pasquali to see if his attempt at a joke drew any response. The sorcerer stared past him at the empty table.

"Medesto?" Pasquali whispered.

"What?"

"Who is that?"

A dark, shadowy figure that did not resemble Ren B'gatti rose up on the far side of the table.

The light reflected off Ren's indigo skin. He grabbed the edge of the tabletop and stood to his full height, taller and larger than he had been the moment before.

"Is this some aftereffect of the corrupted magic?" Medesto whispered.

"I'm certain I destroyed all of it," Pasquali said. "No, this is something else. Have you witnessed him in this specific form before?"

"No," Medesto replied, shaking his head. "I assumed, after what he just went through, he'd need to rest before he could shapeshift again." He'd seen Ren change shapes hundreds of times, into a myriad of creatures and false faces, but none of them looked like the massive form standing before them.

"Did we just release something evil into my laboratory?"

Medesto took a hesitant step forward. "Ren?" he said. "Are you okay, buddy?'

The imposing figure turned toward the gnome. Almond-shaped eyes, now solid black, bore into him. The indigo skin shimmered like shadows under the candlelight. The wedge-shaped head rested on a thick, muscled neck and shoulders. Whoever inhabited the body in front of him, it was no longer Ren B'gatti.

When the trickster decided not to be stubborn, arrogant, argumentative or self-centered, he tended to carry a relaxed, laid back disposition. He was always ready for the next fight, but, ironically, rarely sought out conflict. His time with Claymore had that much of a positive influence on him. The figure standing there was commanding, aware of everything in his immediate vicinity and seething with the desire to prove he was the dominate force in the room. In other words, a predator.

Pasquali fidgeted in place. "May I inquire your name, good sir?"

"I am known throughout my lands as *Rhune*," the dark stranger rumbled. He looked about the laboratory. "Where am I?"

The sorcerer leaned in close to Medesto. "Any ideas on how we handle this?" he whispered.

"Nothing comes to mind," the gnome replied. "Give me a moment to think."

"I don't know if we have that much time," Pasquali replied.

Rhune grabbed the heavy worktable and threw it aside with one hand. It crashed against the wall, cracking the plaster and shattering a window. He stepped up to Pasquali.

"I said *Where am I*?" he hissed.

The rotund sorcerer took an involuntary step back, bumping into the apothecary cabinet. The bottles inside rattled as he caught himself. His eyes darted to Medesto, full of concern and fear. The gnome knew what the look meant. Whatever happened next, *this monster could not be allowed to leave this room.*

"You are in Rogue Destiny, sir," Pasquali said with a slight bow.

"Liar!" Rhune bellowed. "I am somewhere between worlds! I can feel it!" He backhanded Pasquali. The sorcerer flipped around into the alchemy equipment. Beakers shattered and chemicals sizzled on whatever surfaces they fell on. Pasquali pushed himself up. Blood dripped from his nose and mouth.

The misshapen head turned on the gnome. Rhune glared down at him. Subtle shifting hues of various colors swirled across his naked chest and over his bald scalp. His skin rippled in response. He was trying to shapeshift. Medesto could not let him do that.

He didn't want to hurt Ren, if that was even possible, but he needed to put this creature down before he wreaked any more havoc. Because of their height difference, it would be easier to let Rhune come at him.

The rippling effect continued over Rhune's upper body, and his muscles swelled for a moment, then stopped. Rhune stared at his hands. Medesto could not be sure, but it appeared Rhune was unable to shape-shift. He braced himself for the inevitable attack.

The punch came faster than Medesto could follow. Fortunately, decades of living dangerously had conditioned him to react instinctively. His hand came up without thought, and he stopped Rhune's massive fist before the blow landed. The sheer force behind the punch pushed him back a step.

Medesto gripped Rhune's fist tighter and pulled him close. He cocked his other arm back and delivered a thundering counterpunch to his assailant's face. Rhune flew back into the wall, the impact breaking through the wood paneling. He raised his head and struggled to get up.

The gnome rushed forward and hit Rhune in the face with all of his considerable strength. The shadowy figure collapsed to the hardwood floor. Medesto pressed a boot down on his naked chest.

"Stay down," he ordered, pointing a thick finger in his face.

Rhune did not stay down.

A taloned hand seized Medesto by the throat, cutting off his breath. Rhune rose gracefully to his feet, lifting the gnome from his feet. Medesto dangled in front of him. From the corner of his eye, he saw Pasquali pulling open doors to a cabinet on the wall. He prayed the sorcerer was searching for something that would bring a quick resolution to the fight.

To buy some time, Medesto struck Rhune in the face again. A thundering blow that should have taken his head off or at least loosened the grip on his throat. Rhune's head snapped to the side, but he otherwise remain unfazed. His fingers tightened around the gnome's throat. Medesto struggled to get air.

Pasquali came up behind them and smashed a large beaker of sparkling liquid against Rhune's face. The glass shattered, and tiny scintillating bursts of colors exploded in the air.

He threw his head back and gave a desperate cry of rage mingled with pain. He stumbled back drunkenly, releasing Medesto and grabbing at his face. Smoke rose through his fingers.

Medesto dropped to the floor. He picked up the overturned worktable in both hands and slammed it down onto the blinded creature. Rhune fell to his knees. A deep growl came from his throat as he labored to get up. Medesto brought the table down on top of him again, with all the strength he could muster. The cabin shook from the impact. The thick wooden tabletop snapped in two over Rhune's head.

The dark intruder crashed to the floor. He groaned once, then fell silent. Medesto took a step back. He held half the broken worktable at the ready, waiting for the shadowy figure to move. This time Rhune stayed down.

"What just happened?" Pasquali asked. His breath came hard as he tried to calm himself. "I've never seen anything like that."

"I'm not sure," Medesto replied, keeping a watchful eye on the figure crumpled in the corner of the room. "What did you throw at him? Acid?"

"Actually, it was common unicorn urine," Pasquali said. "As bodily waste goes, it's the purest of all urines."

"Well, it did the trick," Medesto quipped.

"Exactly," Pasquali said. He nudged him with an elbow. "I know a little shop in the merchants' district that can supply you with the urine you could ever need."

"Thanks, I'll keep that in mind," Medesto replied. "How'd you know it'd work?"

"I didn't," Pasquali replied. "It was just a lucky guess. Unicorns are among the purest beasts in the cosmos. I postulated, given the temperament of our guest, that he would not react well to it. He struck me as an impure, possibly evil being, and it's never good for creatures of such disposition to come in contact with the pureness of the unicorn."

"Or even their urine," Medesto said. He chuckled and shook his head.

"Exactly," Pasquali grinned.

The unconscious shape on the floor stirred. Medesto raised the table, ready to strike, but the dark figure spasmed, before slowly morphing back to the familiar form of Ren B'gatti.

"Help me get him to the bed," Pasquali said. Medesto tossed the broken table to the side and together they lifted the unconscious trickster gently to the small bed. Ren's labored breathing came in short, shallow pants.

Medesto watched Ren until his breathing returned to normal. The trickster lay unmoving on the cot, one arm hanging lifeless over the side.

So was this even the real Ren B'gatti? The thought had never occurred to him before. He suddenly realized how little he knew about the enigmatic trickster who had joined the Raconteurs at Claymore's insistence. Medesto knew the rumors of how Ren had fallen out of the sky into the Dreaming Sea, only to be rescued by a passing fishing boat. How he wandered the streets of Rogue Destiny, with a low level street gang, *The Gentlemen of the Open Road*, until word of a shape-shifter running around the city reached the notice of Claymore and the Raconteurs.

After what he had witnessed today, Medesto wondered if the Ren B'gatti lying on the bed had been a deception the whole time. What if Tempest was right? Maybe Ren was not who he said he was? Could they trust him at all now? The thought scared him. But what if Ren didn't even know the truth himself? That scared Medesto even more. If that was the case, then had they just met his alter-ego? He rubbed the bruises on his neck to remind himself that Rhune was very real and very dangerous.

Ren's eyes slowly opened. He blinked when he saw Medesto and Pasquali staring down at him.

"What?" he asked.

"Welcome back," Medesto said. "Is there something you need to tell us?"

"I was having weird dreams about unicorns." Ren sat up with no apparent pain and rotated the arm of his injured shoulder to loosen it up. "What would I have to tell?"

"Why you tried to kill us?"

"I haven't tried to kill anybody today," Ren replied. He glanced at the broken equipment strewn around the lab. "All I remember is blacking out from the sudden, stabbing pain."

"Well, somebody just a gave us rough time," Medesto said. "He called himself Rhune. Who is he?"

Ren shrugged. "I don't know."

"You're lying."

Ren couldn't help himself when it came to mischief. It was in his nature. But he had a certain *tell* when he was being untruthful. Something he was not even aware of. If he spoke the truth and was accused of lying, his anger would flare. If he was actually lying and got called out, he stayed calm and tried to over-explain the situation or try to change the subject. Medesto often goaded him with accusations to get him to reveal whether he really was telling the truth.

"I honestly don't know," Ren replied. His demeanor remained calm. "He claims to be me. But he can't be me because I'm me. I think we should be getting back."

Pasquali cleared his throat. "I may have a theory as to what is going on here. It's a phenomenon scholars call the mirror-effect. The impossible event of a person being in two places at once. Whoever you truly are, Mr. B'gatti, and wherever you are from, when you left your homeworld, this other entity was somehow left behind."

"I don't understand," Ren said.

"When someone leaves their world of origin," Pasquali said, "the laws of *transmitigation* take precedence. Many extraordinary powers or abilities are often lost. For instance, I was a great sorcerer in my homeworld. In Rogue Destiny, I am a magician without magic, and of no great consequence to speak of. These islands are a dead zone, like so many other worlds around us. *Transmitigation* encompasses many unique capabilities, but magic is the most common."

"But you lit the candles with a wave of your hand."

"You are quite right," Pasquali replied. "As I mentioned before, this little pocket-world is close enough to the nearby fantasy narrative that I can draw from its well of magic. It only allows me a few unimpressive parlor tricks, just enough to assist me in my experiments. It's a refreshing taste of who I once was."

"So Rhune is an echo of me," Ren said. "Like part of my subconscious?"

Pasquali shook his head. "This Rhune character appears to be trapped in your shared world. I'm only speculating here, but your alter-ego may be who you really are. If Rhune is the dominant personality, that makes you the echo."

Ren stared at the floor in wide-eyed disbelief. Medesto could tell he was processing what this all might mean.

"Have your researchers made any progress in finding where Ren is from?" Medesto asked.

"Unfortunately, no," Pasquali replied, stroking his goatee. He put a hand on Ren's shoulder. "I've had my people looking for your story of origin since Claymore requested it after you first showed up in the city. Nothing in our research has revealed a shape-shifting trickster that matches your exact criteria within any narrative."

"But what happened today should help, shouldn't it?" Medesto said. He raised an eyebrow at Pasquali. It took the scholar a moment to understand Medesto's intent, but then things fell into place for him.

"Oh, of course!" Pasquali said with a bit too much enthusiasm. "Not to worry, Mr. B'gatti. The events of today should aid us in our search. All this time, we've been searching for the wrong person. Now that we have a name and physical description to work with, I have no doubt we'll have answers before you know it." He looked over at Medesto, but the gnome could only roll his eyes.

The sorcerer looked around at the wreckage left by their uninvited visitor. He threw up his arms in frustration. "I'll come back later and clean this up. You said you had an appointment, so we should get back."

Pasquali strode out of the cottage. Ren and Medesto followed him down the path and over the bridge toward the spiral staircase. When they emerged back in his study, Pasquali pointed to an antique telephone that hung on the far wall.

"You can use my private phone," he said. "Just dial nine first."

"Thanks," Medesto said. He put the receiver to his ear and dialed the number to the Raconteurs' central office on the rotary phone. It rang twice before someone answered.

"Hello?" a feminine voice said. "This is Central."

"This is badge number 0013," he said. "I'm calling to see if *Nevermore* has checked in yet?"

"Hold on, while I check the registry dispatch," the voice on the other end of the line said. "Ah, yes, it looks like we had a call logged in just over an hour ago."

"Can you tell me what it says?"

"*The McGuffin has been located, but no idea how long target will remain. Coordinates to follow.* There's also a note attached to the file stating Gideon's been asking for you."

"Thank you," Medesto replied. "Let Gideon know we're on our way in." He hung up the phone. Ren stood in the corner, looking around the room with his hands in his pockets.

"They received a message from Natascha an hour ago," he said. "She has a location on Mordecai. They're prepping *Bad Mojo*, so we have to leave."

Ren held up a bent, smudged business card and smirked. "We need to make a stop before we head over to the Obtuse Turtle."

# Chapter 7
# Confessions

Ren climbed onto the back of the three-wheeled street taxi and sat in the rear seat. Neither he nor Medesto had spoken a word while they stood outside the gates of *The Order of the Memento Ex-Libris* waiting for the taxicab.

Medesto gave the address to the driver and climbed into the seat facing Ren. The gnome's brooding eyes bore into the trickster. The taxi pulled out into traffic.

Ren refused to look at him. "What now?" he growled.

"You want to talk about what happened back there?"

"No, I do not," Ren replied.

"Okay, then I'll do the talking," Medesto growled. "Rhune knew right away he was in between worlds. Pasquali said the pocket-world was neither here nor there. Maybe that's how he was able to take control of your physical body. That combined with your weakened state from the corrupt magic flowing through your veins. This has never happened before, right? Because you would have said something if it did."

"Not that I know of," Ren replied, although he often heard whisperings at the edge of his thoughts. Just the night before he had been sent flying out over a bay in Adezhda by a weather manipulating sorceress. He blacked out when he hit the water, and woke up safe on the beach, not knowing how he got there. Either way, he had never lost control of himself the way Medesto had said.

Medesto gave a sigh of relief. "Good, I'm convinced Rhune took over control of your body because of your weakened physical state. But fortunately, he's helpless in holding onto control of your shared body. That is a good thing, given how aggressive and dangerous he is."

Ren watched the pedestrians along the sidewalks. The open-air, three-wheeled taxi wound through the crowded streets, dodging delivery trucks.

"I'll have to take your word for that," he said. "Did he really attack you?"

"Yes, *you* attacked us," Medesto replied. "I saw him morph back into you after I put him down."

"So what are you saying?"

"That you'll need to tread carefully. There's no telling what may give Rhune permanent control over you. We're all in uncharted territory here."

The address on Mucluc's business card took Ren and Medesto to a destitute part of the city near the industrial district. It wasn't easy to decipher the name of the street on the smudged card. Their destination turned out to be down several back-streets where the pariahs of Rogue Destiny congregated.

Ren rotated his shoulder to loosen up the muscles. They felt weaker than they should have, but moved easily enough and he was free of pain. Pasquali's methods proved to be better than he imagined. His injury quickly became a passing inconvenience.

"We don't have time for this," Medesto grumbled.

"Then make the time if you want my continued cooperation," Ren said without looking at him. "Last night at the Pithy Fool, Odd Bod said Mordecai ordered the deaths of my old gang, the *Gentlemen of the Open Road*. Then he implied it may be time to hunt down Mucluc, like he did the others. I wasn't there to protect the others, but I can at least make sure Mucluc's safe before I leave. He may not be the brightest star in the sky, but you'll never find a more loyal friend."

Mucluc's room was on the basement level. Medesto pushed the elevator button going down, but after a few seconds realized it wasn't working and looked around for the stairs. Ren spied them across the way, and they took a creaking wooden stairwell to the building's lowest level.

The hallway was dimly lit by a single, bare light bulb. The air hung dank and humid as they found Mucluc's apartment number. Ren rapped the back of his knuckles on the weathered wooden door. There was no answer, but the door was unlocked.

"Hello?" Ren poked his head in, then pushed the door wider.

The apartment was a long single rectangle, not really meant to be living quarters. Ren assumed it had once been a storage room. Bare drywall covered the walls and standing water was everywhere. The stench of mildew and other unknown foul odors filled the room. A single bulb hanging in the middle of the ceiling provided the only light. A small window slit at street level looked into a narrow alleyway. It was decorated with short, flowered curtains that were partially drawn shut. Exposed pipes and electrical wiring wound their way along the walls.

A large floor sink for dumping mop water had been converted into a makeshift shower with a metal loop connected to the wall supporting a torn mildewed shower curtain. The floor's tiling was pulling up in spots and had deep stains from hundreds of spills and probably the constant drool from the corners of Mucluc's mouth. Empty boxes of breakfast cereal were strewn about on the floor, with more piled on a small table against the far wall. Candy wrappers and empty bags of chocolates and sweets crinkled underfoot as they walked in. The room was heavy with the smell of things that Ren did not want to identify.

"He's not here," Medesto commented. The trickster walked past him. His footsteps squished in the mildewed carpeting.

"I can see that," Ren grumbled. He paced the room, looking for anything that might help him learn the fate of his slow-witted friend. Maybe he was still walking home from last night. "We need to backtrack and see if we can find him."

"No, we need to get to the Obtuse Turtle," the gnome replied. "We have a ship waiting for us. I'm impressed with the concern you have for this guy, but there are more pressing matters to attend to. Mucluc will have to be on his own for now."

Ren turned on the gnome. "I'm not leaving until I know what happened to him. If Odd Bod found him, then I have a score to settle with him and the rest of *The Society of the Black Rose*."

"You're going to go after all of them?" Medesto asked.

"If I have to," Ren replied. "Claymore and I managed just fine last night."

"Claymore's not here, is he?" Medesto grumbled into his beard. "Ok, what if I talk to Gideon and we send people out to search for Mucluc while you're gone? Will that get you on *Bad Mojo*?"

Ren thought about that for a moment. "Alright."

"I'll see what I can do." Medesto replied with a sigh.

The cab ride to the Obtuse Turtle was silent. Ren stared out the window, holding the letters taken from Piqwic in his lap until the floating coach bobbed to a stop. Medesto grabbed his traveling bag and stepped out. Ren followed him to the front entrance of the public house.

"You go check in with Gideon," Medesto said. "I'm going to see if *Bad Mojo* is ready to leave and let them know we're here."

Ren watched Medesto amble away toward the landing pads.

He walked through the lobby to the back offices and knocked on Gideon's door.

"Come in," a voice responded. Gideon sat behind a wide desk, stacked with papers and books.

"Ah, Mr. B'gatti," he said. Ren tossed the bundle of letters on the desk in front of Gideon. He picked them up and untied the string.

"What are these?" he asked.

"Letters from Mordecai sent to his lackeys here in Rogue Destiny," Ren said, unable to contain a touch of smugness in his voice. "I went out and did some snooping last night. I asked around and ended up confronting Piqwic York. Took those off of him."

Gideon pulled one letter from its envelope. He put on his reading glasses and scanned it. He got up from his chair and went to a bookshelf crammed with large leather-bound books. He pulled one out called *The Short but Fruitful Life of Peter Magpie*. Hidden in the middle of the thick tome was a file of papers. Gideon took it out and placed the book back on the self. He laid the file out on his desk and flipped through the loose pages.

"Here." Gideon removed a yellowed piece of paper from the stack and handed it to him. It was the partial remains of an old handwritten letter. The date in the corner indicated it had been written over twenty years earlier. "This is the only known example of Mordecai's handwriting," Gideon said. He set the yellowed page down next to Piqwic's letter so Ren could compare the two. "The letter to Piqwic was not written in Mordecai's hand. Most likely a surrogate penned it."

Ren's eyes darted back and forth between the writing on both pages. "The handwriting's not from the same person," he muttered. "Why does that matter?"

"I find it curious," Gideon said, removing his spectacles.

"There are systems of magic where one's handwriting can create a link to that person and leave them open to magical influence, the same way blood magic links the targeted victim by their blood. Mordecai may fear that might happen to him."

"What do you know about the *Book of Days*?" Ren asked.

"Only the myths and legends everyone's familiar with," Gideon said. "Baltazaar Gedde protected the city he built with magic throughout his 500 year reign. Little is known about how this was accomplished, but it is believed he created a conduit between his homeworld and Rogue Destiny that allowed him access to his magic. The details of how the sorcerer-king accomplished this were recorded in a single tome called *The Book of Days*. It details the founding of the city and Baltazaar's life. But it was lost, stolen from his crypt centuries ago, and its whereabouts currently unknown. Claymore was looking into the Book of Days' whereabouts before the events of *The Angels of Avalon* occurred. I wonder if there is a connection."

"I'm beginning to believe there may be."

"So, you think *The Book of Days* has resurfaced?" Gideon asked. "And this is what Mordecai's searching for."

Ren nodded. "But why would Mordecai want to bring magic back to Rogue Destiny? He's no wizard."

"That is the question you must find the answer to," Gideon answered. "He has never exhibited any magical inclinations, so why would he search for an item that he would not be able to use? He would never allow another to wield such a weapon—it would be too great a threat to his own power. But there may be other secrets within the pages of *The Book of Days* he is after. Good deductive work, Mr. B'gatti. You may be on to something."

"We'll find out soon enough," Ren promised. An unaccustomed feeling of pride welled up inside his chest. Claymore would have been proud. For some reason that mattered to him.

"That is our hope," Gideon said. He got up from his desk. "I have arranged for the finest guide in all of Rogue Destiny to escort the team. He should be arriving shortly if you wish to wait out front with me."

"I've nowhere else to be," Ren said. He followed Gideon from the office, through the lobby full of the bustling mid-day crowd, to the main entrance of the public house. They stopped on the front steps, looking out over a vast, landscaped parking area.

The hotel grounds spread out before them. Peacocks strutted by on well-tended swathes of grass dotted with bright-colored flower beds. A wide driveway lead from the open gates to a parking lot filled with every mode of motorized transportation imaginable. To their left were the stables for horses and other mounts. On the right were the security gates leading to the slip-stream landing pads and Sebastian's garage.

The crisp click of hard-soled shoes broke the quiet as Gideon strode out to the end of the walk and waited. The sky overhead glowed with the illumination of a thousand worlds. A refreshing breeze blew in off the sea. Looking up, he took a deep breath and exhaled. Ren stood beside him.

"Thank you again for your help," Gideon said quietly. He looked down as if deciding what to say. "You and I have not had a chance to talk privately since your return. This has been a diffi-cult year without Claymore. After the breakout from Lazaranth Prison, I was certain he would contact me, but he never did. I just hope he's okay."

Ren sympathized with Gideon's concern, and debated if he should say anything about the night before. At some point, Medesto would tell Gideon he had been in contact with Clay-more, so Ren figured he might as well confess his sins now, if only to control the narrative.

"I ran into Claymore last night during my search for Morde-cai. We ended up in Adezhda, chasing down Minstrel Cotty's killer. That's when I found Piqwic's letters from Mordecai."

"You saw Claymore?" Gideon's eyes went wide. "How was he?"

"He's getting worse by the minute," Ren replied. His temper flared again. "The *Paradigm Madness* is eating away at his soul. I tried to convince him to come back with me, but he said he was too much of a threat to the Raconteurs. So he's left for good. I shouldn't be here! I never should have left Claymore alone. Not in his condition."

"Then why didn't you stay with him?"

"Because he told me to go," Ren replied. "I always did what he told me to. It's how we operated. He makes the decisions, so I don't have to..." He paused.

"Make any moral decisions for yourself?" Gideon interjected.

Ren didn't answer.

"Did you find Minstrel Cotty's killer?" Gideon asked.

"Yeah, it was a council member," Ren replied. "Serralto Cardus masterminded the assassination. But Claymore killed him before we could get him back to the Rogue Destiny to stand trial."

"That is unfortunate." Gideon shook his head. He suddenly looked exhausted, weighed down by the burden of keeping the Raconteurs operating after the loss of his friend and cofounder.

"There's something I need you to do while I'm gone," he said.

"And what is that?" Gideon replied.

"I need you to have your people find someone for me. Goes by the name Mucluc Ludlow. Odd Bod and the *Black Rose* will be looking for him to get revenge on me for the damage Claymore and I did last night."

"I suppose I can do that."

"It's not a request," Ren growled. "Otherwise, I'm not getting on *Bad Mojo*." He tired of people asking for things from him.

Now it was his turn to call in some favors. "Then I need you to keep him here at the Obtuse Turtle until I get back."

"I suppose we can find somewhere to keep him safe."

Gideon stared at Ren for a moment. "You are a dichotomy, Mr. B'gatti," he said, stretching a hand in front of him. "Much like this great City around us."

"What do you mean?" Ren asked.

"A place like Rogue Destiny should not exist. Every literary world out there comes from somewhere, a book or a series of stories. The words of those stories create the foundation the world was built on, but Rogue Destiny has no foundation of words. The City of a Thousand Moons has no reason to exist, but here we are. Rogue Destiny is neutral ground, void of any magic, paranormal or supernatural abilities of any kind. The gods themselves are no more than exalted mortals here—even the strongest would wield only a tiny fraction of their true power. And like this City, you are also of two minds. One understands the need to help others, and the other is self-absorbed, seeking only what seems interesting in that moment."

The click-clack of hooves on the cobblestones interrupted them. Ren looked up to see a tinker's wagon swaying back and forth as it made its way through the front gates toward the stables across the parking lot.

Gideon walked out to meet the wagon. Ren followed. "You are torn between two very different paths," Gideon continued. "One road leads to sacrifice and helping others, putting their needs before your own. The other road leads to self, doing only that which gives you pleasure, while ignoring the needs of others. One day, those two sides will collide, and you will need to choose one path or the other."

"We are among the fortunate, Mr. B'gatti," Gideon went on. "To know what we know and choose to use that knowledge for the betterment of everyone. The Raconteurs protect the literary worlds from outside interference and corruption, risking every-thing to ensure the safety of the multitudes. That is our great burden, and worthy of any sacrifice that we have to make. That is the most important work there is. Countless lives have been saved by our efforts. We are not the legendary heroes glorified in Literature. We are merely background players that allow those heroes to shine. They may save the day in the Narrative, but we are the ones standing in the shadows who ensure their Story always continues. No hero in any Story can claim to do what we do. We do this by choice, and that makes us more honorable than any character or *Logos Personae* could ever be."

"I would never consider myself honorable," Ren said. He looked up at the bright worlds floating weightless above them. "I've done terrible things." The revelations from that morning of who he might be echoed in his memory. What if Rhune was the dominant personality, like Pasquali suggested, and Ren was just the afterthought?

"We all have regrets, Mr. B'gatti," Gideon said. "The best Raconteurs over the years haven't always been the ones who followed the rules. That might make you one of the greatest Raconteurs of them all." Gideon chuckled at his joke. "Our success was never greater than the brief time you worked with us. I have complete faith in you and your abilities. That is why I chose you for this run. Nothing is more important than the protection of this City. If we allow Rogue Destiny to fall, then all of Literature itself is in peril."

The small wagon drew closer, and Ren could see it was laden with clinking pots and pans and bric-à-brac dangling off the sides. It was being pulled by a sizable razorback boar. On the driver's seat sat a small figure wearing a straw hat holding the reins of the cart.

"This is our guide?" Ren asked.

"Yes, it is," Gideon said with a smile. "Raffles Bonhomme.

He's a contemporary of Bijou Antilles and the best tracker there is. He knows more than anyone about the nature of ley-lines and how to navigate them. Although he's a bit eccentric in his methods, his expertise will be invaluable to you, *and* he owed me a favor."

Gideon smiled and stepped out beyond the sidewalk to greet the peddler's cart. The wagon pulled to a stop. The small driver hopped to the ground in front of Gideon and removed his straw hat to reveal two long ears and a furry face with a beaming smile.

Their guide was a talking jackrabbit.

# Chapter 8
# Bad Mojo

"Raffles, thank you for coming," Gideon said warmly.

"Ma pleasure, G'deon," Raffles said. His thick Cajun drawl chewed up the words. The two-and-half-foot tall jackrabbit's long ears poked out of holes in the straw hat as he waddled up to them.

The jackrabbit hooked both thumbs in his leather vest and clicked his teeth. Ren's gaze followed the scars and splotches of missing fur from Raffle's face to his exposed arms and chest. The mark of a true adventurer. It was what Medesto would have called *A life well lived.*

"Always 'appy ta help out da Rac'oteers," Raffled clucked. "We 'bout ready ta go?"

"Just waiting for you," Gideon replied. A young porter ran up to the cart but retreated when the large boar gave a sloppy snort in the boy's direction.

Raffles produced a carrot from his pack and handed it to the pig. "Bocephus, ya be good," the rabbit said. "You gonna be sleepin' here 'til I get back." He patted the round side of the beast and offered the reins of the rickety cart to the porter. "Sorry, 'bout dat, son. He get ornery when it past his bedtime."

The porter hesitated but stepped in to take the leads. Bocephus snorted on his shoes, but the boy slowly led the rotund swine and jingling cart toward the stables.

Raffles looked around and smacked his lips. "Let's load up and get dis wagon train rollin'," he said, rubbing his paws together. "Ya keep dem flying ships over dere, don'cha?" The jackrabbit ambled off in the direction of the landing bays. He adjusted the small rucksack on his back, where a pair of long fishing knives were sheathed on either side of the pack.

Ren followed Gideon and the rabbit along the stone walkway through the gates to the Byzantine landing bay. A half-dozen Slipstream Runabouts filled the vast courtyard, but they were only interested in the one with *Bad Mojo* painted in bold script under the cockpit. It was in its final stages of fueling, and several figures labored away, loading gear and supplies into the cargo hold.

*Bad Mojo* resembled an immense interplanetary hot rod. Her overall shape was greatly influenced by the posters of hot rods and muscle cars that Sebastian hung in around his workshop. The slipstream's squat form rested atop retractable landing gear. The hundred-foot-long vessel was the largest of the Raconteurs' fleet. It rose twenty feet above the landing pad. The cockpit windows were narrow and dark, with four port windows dotting each side.

Exhaust pipes sprouted from under the front hood down along the undercarriage. Painted flames accentuated the underside of the windows and splayed out along both sides. Two large Nomad IX Coldfire engines sat mounted off each rear quarter. It was one of Sebastian's finest creations and the envy of the Raconteur fleet. Ren stopped for a moment to admire the craftsmanship of the massive transport.

He saw Medesto leaning against the landing gear at the front of the ship, talking with Gideon and Raffles.

"Been in the city long, Raffles?" Medesto asked.

"Nah, I was just passin' through to collect some debts." The jackrabbit spit out bits of the cherub root he was chewing on. "Den Gideon called, and here I am, heading off on this little jaunt wit you."

Ren paced around in front of the slipstream, growing more restless by the minute. He still could not believe his mentor and closest friend was inflicted with the Paradigm Madness. It was inconceivable that anything could be powerful enough to break Claymore's iron will, let alone some sickness of the mind and spirit. Gideon continued to engage in small talk with the rabbit. When there seemed no end in sight to the conversation, the trickster wandered off to find *Bad Mojo's* pilot, Sinjin, and see if he could goad him into getting them out of there.

Ren found Sinjin standing next to Sebastian at the rear of the ship. They were in the middle of an argument about the safest route to take.

"There's too much of a chance of hitting electrical storms if you pass through sector seven," Sinjin said, pointing at a red area on the flat screen in his hand with a taloned finger. "It's too dangerous this time of the year."

"Not if you circumvent the storms and go through the Fairy Tale worlds here and here," Sebastian said. "Those worlds are far away from the radiation coming off the storms that mess with your navigation." The Raconteurs' chief mechanic had yet to find insulation strong enough to protect the delicate electrical systems of the Slipstream Runabouts from the violent storms and radiation that filled the Void. It frustrated him to no end.

Sinjin's head bobbed up and down in agreement, finally satisfied with their chosen route. His head tapered from a lengthy neck to a long snout with coal-black eyes and a toothy smile. He was large, round and reptilian with a potbelly, and walked bent over with a prominent hunched back that reached six feet from the ground. Two rows of spiny bone spurs ran down his spine and tail. He followed Sebastian to the front of the ship.

They noticed Ren for the first time. "Good luck to the both of you," Sebastian said. "Stay safe and don't do anything stupid." He turned back to his garage, dragging the tether attached to the portable respirator on his back behind him.

The pilot of *Bad Mojo* gave a wide grin when he saw Ren. "You're back. Long time gone, B'gatti. You sticking around after this time?"

"We'll see," Ren answered.

Sinjin was a member of the Salmagundi, a race who once resided on a lava-rich world in the science-fictional Novel *World at the Edge of Time*. He was an infant just out of the egg when his homeworld was destroyed in the same fashion as *The Angels of Avalon*. The sole survivor of his race, Sinjin had been brought back to Rogue Destiny, where he grew up under the rough-and-tumble ways of the Raconteurs. He was big, tough, and would die for anyone he thought to be in danger.

"You hear about Claymore?" Sinjin asked in his deep, gravelly voice.

"What about him?" Ren asked. He worried what Sinjin was about to say next.

"He was part of the Lazaranth escape. Disappeared that night and hasn't been seen since. Weird, huh?"

"Yeah, that is," Ren said, relieved Sinjin didn't seem to know about the madness inflicting his old partner. Behind Sinjin, across the courtyard, Ren spied a familiar-shaped blob standing in the shadows of the gate to the land bay. It was Mucluc.

"Never got to tell you how sorry I was for what the Council did to Claymore," Sinjin said. His gravelly voice cracked a bit. "Setting him up like that to take the fall for *The Angels of Avalon*."

"Thanks, I appreciate that," Ren said. "I've learned to roll with the punches in life. Excuse me, would you, Sinjin? There's one last loose end I need to tie up before we go. Can you give me a few minutes? This won't take long."

"I'll give you as much as I can," Sinjin grinned. "Listen for the horn."

Ren started across the landing bay to where Mucluc stood, looking around nervously, and rocking back and forth from one foot to the other.

"How'd he find us?" a voice behind Ren asked. He turned as Medesto ambled up.

Ren grinned. "I have no idea. I'm just glad to see he's okay." It was a relief to know his friend was safe. Mucluc came off as slow-witted and denser than stone, but under that appearance there was a unique intelligence at work. If Mucluc wanted something bad enough, he would make it happen.

"You need to send him home," the gnome growled. "I understand you have a soft spot for him, but tell him to go back to his apartment and stay put until you return. That's if you're even coming back after you get your slipstream and go search the cosmos for Claymore. Where will Mucluc be then once you leave for good?"

As they approached Mucluc, all seven eyes widened, and his frog-like face lit up. "Reen Boogatti! I found you," he croaked.

Medesto smiled and stuck out his hand. "My name's Medesto. Nice to meet you." A huge smile on the creature's wide face, and he stuck out one of several flippered tentacles. There was a squishy sound as their hands met, but he continued to shake the appendage out of politeness.

"I am named Mucluc Ludlow. Glad to know you too, Maydeesto," he said with a proud grin.

Medesto's hand came away dripping with a sticky greenish slime. He glared at Ren, but the shape-shifter only shrugged. He looked around for something to wipe his hand on while

Ren brought Mucluc over to where Gideon was talking to Raffles.

Gideon raised his eyebrows as the six feet of slimy mottled bulk and multiple eyes came toward him, but composed himself quickly. "And who do we have here?"

Ren put a hand on his friend's shoulder. "Gideon Dumas, this is Mucluc Ludlow. I need you to keep him safe and out of sight until I get back. You can take any expenses he incurs out of my fee."

"Mr. B'gatti," Gideon said. A rare flash of anger crossed the face of the diminutive leader of the Raconteurs. "We have more important things to focus on than your altruistic pursuits. While I can appreciate your concern for a friend who is down on his luck, we are not a flophouse for every destitute individual you come across."

Ren was unfazed by Gideon's words. "Then figure out some other way to stop Mordecai, cause I'm not leaving unless you find a place for Mucluc to stay until I get back."

Gideon gave a deep sigh. "This is not the time for such nonsense," he replied. His tone was even, but his face indicated he was not happy with the trickster's sudden demands.

Mucluc rubbed his sticky appendages together nervously. "I have had enough fun and friendship for one day. I am tired and hungry."

"I'm working on it, buddy," Ren said, turning back to Gideon. "I have reason to believe Odd Bod may come looking for him. He has no one else to turn to. If you want me on that ship, promise me you'll keep him safe while I'm gone. Find him something to do around here, make him feel useful. He has no qualms about how dirty the job is."

"Do you no like me, Mr. Gideon Dumas of the Raconteurs?" Mucluc croaked. "You will like how hard I work if you give me job."

"Yes, I'm sure I will, Mr. Mucluc," Gideon said with a forced smile.

"Ludlow," Mucluc corrected.

"Excuse me?" Gideon asked.

"My name is Mucluc *Ludlow*, sir," Mucluc said. "So I would like ta be addressed as *Mr. Ludlow*, like any respectable citizen of Rogue Destiny should be."

"I apologize, Mr. Ludlow," Gideon corrected himself.

"Kind of grows on you, doesn't he?" Medesto quipped.

Gideon sighed deeply and pinched the bridge of his nose like he was fighting a sudden headache. "Very well, there is a sizable suite being remodeled at the end of the hallway in the fourth floor attic. He can stay there until you return. That will allow him some privacy and keep him out of the way of the other guests. Take him around to the back elevator behind the kitchen. I'll have room service send up something for both of you. But this discussion is not over, Mr. B'gatti."

"Is it ever?" Ren responded. "But thank you. I appreciate you looking after him."

Gideon almost smiled at the apology. "And what does *Mr. Ludlow* prefer for dinner?"

Ren laughed. "He'll eat anything. Bone, gristle, marrow, and all, and it doesn't have to be fresh either. Also, any decadent desserts you have. That would cheer him up. He has quite the sweet tooth."

Mucluc started drooling at the corners of his mouth. "I very much enjoy the cereals for breakfast. Do you have any of those?"

"Take him up there and get him settled in.," Gideon said. "But hurry, they're finalizing preparations for your departure."

"Come on, Mucluc, I'll show you where you'll be staying," Ren said. The monster nodded and followed him. Mucluc stared up at the glowing worlds overhead as they crossed the landing pad to the delivery entrance by the kitchen. Ren cracked the screen door open enough to look in. No one was in sight, so he led Mucluc down a back hallway to the staff elevator, and they took it to the fourth floor.

Ren made sure the hallway was empty before walking Mucluc to the last room on the floor. The door was unlocked, and they ducked inside. The shape-shifter flipped on the light to reveal a room in complete disrepair. It felt good to help someone who had nothing to give in return except friendship. They came to a narrow door that Mucluc had to squeeze his wide frame sideways to get through.

The floor was stripped to the bare wood, and the walls were nothing but exposed beams and electrical wiring. Parts of the ceiling had been recently repaired with the extra fresh lumber stacked in a corner. Ren pulled a tarp off the bed. "This is where you'll sleep when you're not working. You need to stay out of sight from the other guests. Understand?"

Mucluc looked around the room and nodded his approval. "This very fancy. No water drips and a bed to sleep on."

"Yeah, these are good people," Ren said. "You'll be safe here while I'm away." The blare of a horn broke the air outside. *Bad Mojo* was announcing it was time to leave.

Mucluc clucked gleefully as he waddled over to a large, beaten leather recliner and plopped his sizable rump down, grinding his backside into it until he was comfortable. The worn out chair creaked in protest under his weight. "Please, please have a seat, and we talk the small talk," he said. His face split into a wide grin of satisfaction.

"How are you doing?" Ren asked.

Mucluc shook his bulbous head pitifully. "Since you lost my job for me, I spent all the night walking to the Obtoose Turtle. My feets hurt, but I cannot complain. I have good friend in Reen Boogatti, who got me new job."

Ren smiled. "Well, Gideon said you could stay up here, and he would find work for you," Ren said.

"You mean I cannot go home to my apartment?" he gurgled. There was panic in his choppy, throaty voice.

"It's not safe for you to go home right now."

"But I like my home," Mucluc replied. "When things go bad, I go dere and den things not so bad. It not much, but it is mine." He pushed himself to the edge of the recliner. "This is all getting too stressful. I don't think I want your job anymore."

"It's all right," Ren assured him. "The Obtuse Turtle will be your new home for now. I didn't want you to know this, but I found out what happened to the *Gentlemen of the Open Road,* and I think you're in danger."

"Why would I be in danger?" Mucluc croaked. "The *Gentlemen* just a stupid bunch of street punks who got demselves killed. Dat what I was told."

"By who?" Ren inquired.

"Oolong Bok told me dat a few days before he died. He said all da *Gentlemen* dead 'cept him and me."

"And then Oolong died?" Ren asked. "How?"

"Dey told me he was robbed and shot down by peoples unknown. At work, Rough Tony laughed, and said he fell on some bullets. Everyone laughed, but I not get joke. Who would leave bullets just lying around on da ground for child to find? Dat not safe at all!"

"Well, I believe they were killed on orders from Mordecai Davos."

Two of his seven eyes looked up at the ceiling in thought, like he was trying to unpuzzle something. "Why would Mordecai Davos, Dmitri the Confessor, Piqwic York, Three Finger Louie, or Odd Bod care enough about de *Gentleman of de Open Road* to kill dem? We try to pay our tribute to dem if we ever stealed anything. Were dey upset we never stealed anything?"

"No, it was because I refused to work for Mordecai," Ren said. "The *Gentlemen* paid the price for my decision."

"So Tote Rossiter, Sozo Vantage, Anon Bousso, Sojourn Swoboda and Oolong Bok are all gone because you wouldn't work for Mordecai Davos?"

"Yeah, I'm sorry. I don't want to scare you, but they could come after you next."

"You not need to be sorry. You not join the criminal Mordecai Davos. You always loyal to the *Gentlemen*. No one can do more den dat." Mucluc's mood went dark and somber. "I not afraid of dem. They get near me I crack 'em good." He pounded a flippered tentacle down onto the armrest of his chair. "I get dem," he whispered. *Bad Mojo's* horn went off again.

"I have to go, buddy," Ren said. "There are worlds to save."

"You such a good hero, Reen Boogatti," Mucluc muttered. "Anybody would be lucky to have you save them. You don't have to worry 'bout me. I be fine in my fancy new room. Thank you for watching out over me."

There was a knock on the door and a waiter rolled in a cart heaped with food. There was chicken and roast beef and fried fish and boxes of breakfast cereal. Ren popped open a couple of soft drinks and handed one to Mucluc. The shape-shifter lifted his in toast. "To the *Gentlemen of the Open Road*. Long may they be remembered."

Mucluc smiled a big phlegmy smile, and they clinked their bottles together. "To Tote and Sozo and Anon and Sojourn and Oolong. Dey my friends and I miss them."

"I know you do," Ren replied. "So do I. Those were good days." They tapped their bottles together again.

Ren stayed until the monster had eaten his fill. Mucluc laid back in his chair, rubbing his plump belly. A few moments later, he snored away, lost in slumber. The recliner creaked under his weight.

*Bad Mojo* blew its horn several more times, but Ren didn't care. They weren't going to leave without him. He watched as his pitiful friend slept. Mucluc was just trying to find his way in the City of a Thousand Moons like everyone else. He covered the beast as best he could with the blankets and smiled at his friend before leaving the room.

# Chapter 9
# Tales of Grandeur

Ren's mood turned sour as he took the stairs down to the main floor of the Obtuse Turtle. Now that Mucluc was safe, his thoughts went back to something that had been formulating in his head since his return to Rogue Destiny. His mind was flooded with everything going on around him. He needed to decide what would be his best course of action to end this quickly so he could go search for Claymore.

It was dangerous, but the best plans always were. Ren would simply kill Mordecai at the first opportunity and steal this portal machine out from underneath him. It would put an end to the needless loss of life the Raconteurs had suffered. Gideon would have his machine, then Ren could collect payment for his services and be on his way. He had not come back to Rogue Destiny to be a hero, but even he knew the universe would be better without Mordecai Davos. He headed down the stairs through Sebastian's workshop and emerged onto the Byzantine landing bay.

Gideon waited for him at the bottom of the steps leading up to *Bad Mojo's* main cabin. "In Medias Res, Mr. B'gatti," he said. "Happy hunting. And thank you again for the letters. I am sure they will prove invaluable once I have had the chance to study them in closer detail. They may answer some pressing questions about Mordecai's actions and help us prepare an appropriate defense against him."

"I'll get the job done," Ren said. He took one last look at the Obtuse Turtle, wondering if this was the last time he would see the public house. Somehow, he doubted it. Something always drew him back to Rogue Destiny, no matter how many times he tried to leave it behind.

Ren walked up the side ramp into the main cabin of *Bad Mojo*. Sinjin was at the controls of the ship, talking to Sebastian through a headset, and making his final checks before departing. His scaly bulk filled the cockpit. There was a co-pilot's chair, but it would have been a struggle to squeeze past the reptoid's mass to get to it.

The two aisles of ten seats faced the person across the aisle. Ren pushed past Tempest, then looked back, wondering what she was doing there. She smiled at him, grabbed her bag from the overhead compartment, and returned to her seat. Charley sat next to her, punching away on her scanner.

He could feel the crystal blue eyes of the Raconteur's Chief Security Officer studying him as he moved down the aisle, but he didn't give her the pleasure of knowing it was annoying him. Raffles laid back in his chair with his hat pulled down over face. Ren took a spot on the far side of Medesto, the furthest he could get from Tempest.

Medesto pulled a field bag out from under his seat. "Food and water for the trip," he said, setting it in the trickster's lap. Then he reached under the seat again with one hand and held out a pistol in a holster. "And you might need this at some point."

Ren grinned and took the weapon. He wrapped the leather belt around the holster, shoved it in his field bag, and stowed that under his seat. Then he laid back and tried to sleep before they arrived at their destination and the fun began. The soft leather cushions under him were comfortable, but his mind was not ready for sleep. He was already thinking past the killing of Mordecai to how he was going to find Claymore while convincing the Raconteurs to leave him alone.

Ren knew they would be watching him after he completed this job. He glanced at the cast of players that would accompany him on this mission and realized these were decent people, just trying to do an impossible job. The engines powered up, and the Slipstream Runabout vibrated. He closed his eyes and pretended to sleep so no one would talk to him. The ramp at the rear of the ship closed with a loud clank, and *Bad Mojo* slowly rose from the ground.

"So you think you're ready for this, B'gatti?" Tempest called from down the row.

"He's not so dangerous," Ren replied. "Mordecai Davos is nothing but a petty cutpurse. It'll be easy enough to find what he's up to and stop him. Especially when he won't see me coming."

"We'll see if Mordecai agrees with that," Tempest replied with a laugh. "We're not dealing with another common street thief. His criminal reach goes far beyond Rogue Destiny. I've heard stories he does business with scores of worlds across the literary universe. I only wish the Common Council would see this man as the threat that he is. There are many who still doubt his existence."

"And that's exactly what Mordecai wants," Medesto said. "For people to doubt he exists. To think he's nothing but a myth created by the criminal underworld to keep the weak and gullible in line. He wants to be seen as a ghost that's used to frighten small children into behaving, anything but a threat to the power structure of Rogue Destiny." He leaned back and closed his eyes. There was rustling on the other side of the gnome, and then a loud yawn. Raffles pulled up his straw hat.

"Ever been ta *The Enchanted Shillelagh of Finlay*?" the rabbit said. "Beautiful world, very green, but wit unspeakable horrors hidin' b'hind every rock. You 'aven't seen trouble 'til ya been chased 'cross a world by a buncha angry leprechauns throwin' their little bits of magic at ya. Dey caught me 'fore I could reach de rabbit-hole to get me off-world, so I 'ad to stand trial before da ancient Lepr'chaun Court of Sheerudimon. Nasty bunch of little buggers, ya couldn't reason with dem. I 'ventually escap'd, but not witout some reminders of da fun time we had togeth'r."

He pulled the vest off his shoulder to reveal where the fur had been burned away, leaving a nasty scar. "But dat was nuthin' compared to de time I got caught between dese two Scandinavian fire wyrms. Dey was fighting over da treasure of Gristovel. Norwegian legends are as dangerous as dey get. Den I found out too late someone already got ta da treasure. Barely got out o' dat alive wit nuthin' ta show fer it." He raised his arm and pointed at his elbow with a stubby clawed finger. "You see dis scar?"

Tempest laughed. "That's cute, little bunny. But try battling through hordes of radioactive zombies on a derelict space station, trying to reach the escape pods. Lost good people to those monsters. Isn't that right, Charley?"

The dirty-blonde technician looked up from the tangle of cables she was connecting to her scanner. On her face she wore a pair of optic-scope eyeglasses with wire rims and four different eye loupes of varying magnification. "You've told that story enough times. I figure it has to be true," she said. "I wasn't there, but radioactive zombies are definitely bad." She went back to examining the wire circuit board propped up on her knees.

"Enough with the war stories," Medesto growled, not bothering to open his eyes. "We have hours of being cooped up together, so keep it down. Some of us are trying to sleep."

Raffles rolled his eyes. "Why dey call you *Charley*?" he asked. "Dat ya given name?"

"No, it's Constance," Charley answered. "After my mother. She started calling me *Charley* after my father died. That was his name. She said I was the last part of him that she had to hold on to."

Raffles gave her a smile. "Dat hard when a child loses a parent."

The rabbit turned to Ren. "So, Gideon tell me you a skin-changer, huh? A doppelganger, a mimic, a Frei's Shadow? Wat dat like?"

"It's interesting," Ren said.

"I bet it is," the rabbit grinned. "Can ya change inta anyting?"

"Pretty much."

"Where ya from?"

"Don't know," Ren said with a shrug of his shoulders. "Just kind of fell out of the sky one day. Don't remember the details."

"Fell outta de sky, huh?" Raffles asked with an eager nod. "With no memory? Who does dat? Dere's gotta be a story in dere sumwhere, and I bet it's a good one. I tink ya could be Mythic, same as me and Bijou Antilles. Dat got the markings of a folk hero all over it."

Ren slid down in his seat and closed his eyes. "I've never been much of a hero. I'm here for the slipstream promised by Gideon. When the mission's over, I'm gone."

He could feel the rabbit staring at him. He looked over to see Raffles dig in his vest pocket and pull out a circular flat stone. He held it up to one eye and looked at Ren through the hole in the center. The green stone gave off a dim glow.

"What're you doing?" Ren asked, finding himself slightly annoyed by the rabbit's continued antics.

"Dis a seeing stone," the rabbit replied. "It tell me if you magical or not."

"And?"

"If you was, it'd be glowing like da mornin' star. So dat tell me you ain't."

"It's glowing a little," Ren said.

"True," Raffled replied. "Dat mean you prob'ly come from a place dat has magic, but you just ain't magical you'self."

"Anything else?"

"Well, you ain't celestial or demi-god." Raffles cocked his head and laughed as he kept studying the trickster through the stone's opening. "Or any sort of deity for dat matter. You too skinny. Ain't got da physique of da gods or da hum of constrained power like da fae." He stopped talking, his furry expression contorted into a mask of concern. "But dere's a shadow hanging off ya. A powerful one. Like dere's more to ya than we seeing."

Ren caught a glance from Medesto. After the events of that morning and the previous night, Ren still didn't know who or what Rhune was, but this was not the place to talk about it.

"What do you mean?" Ren asked, sitting up in his seat.

"Sumting ain't quite right with our changeling here," Raffles replied. "Your aura is off kilter. And I'm getting a second image, like dere two of ya. You know anyting about dat?"

"No, I don't," Ren said. He tried to act uninterested, but was starting to feel uncomfortable from all the attention.

"How is that supposed to help him?" Tempest asked.

"Didn' say it would," Raffles replied, throwing Tempest a dirty look. "But it more den he knew a minute ago."

"So, what does that make me?" Ren asked.

"It mean you prob'ly a cryptic," the rabbit replied, nodding his head. He slipped the stone into a vest pocket.

"Cryptic?" Ren responded.

"It mean you just not classified inta any of da other groupings. Dat you unique, a one-off."

"So that would narrow down what Book I'm from?"

"Not witout more details. Der are thousands of worlds out der with both magic and cryptics. Dey thick as molasses in some places."

"Thanks for the help."

"Sorry I couldn't tell ya mo'." And with that, Raffles pulled his hat down over his eyes and nestled back into his seat. "Everyone should know where dey from."

"Like you said," Ren said with a glance at Tempest, "it's more than I knew a minute ago."

The conversation ended as the slipstream left Rogue Destiny's airspace for the blackness of the Great Void. The hum of the engines filled the cabin with a gentle rhythm. Sinjin's voice came over the intercom. "Get comfortable. We got a while before we get to where we're going."

Raffles lay curled up in his seat, snoring softly, his foot twitching every few seconds. Medesto was reclined in the seat next to him, hands on his chest, with his eyes closed.

Tempest stretched her long legs out in front of her and pulled a wide-brimmed hat down over her face.

Ren realized he didn't know anyone on the ship other than Medesto and Sinjin. Field work was never easy, even under the best of circumstances, and everyone reacted differently to the pressures. Places that appeared quiet and peaceful often turned out to be the most dangerous. There were local authorities to deal with, and the military, always the military. Anything from a lone city guard to a vast conquering army could be a hazard. At any time, a random event could interfere in the Narrative without realizing it. Nothing was predictable, and even the most seasoned Raconteur always tread carefully. There were one of a thousand things a Raconteur had to watch for every time they were in the field.

His own safety was never a concern—he was a survivor. It

was that rush of facing the unknown he was always chasing. But experience told him that hunting a madman and his army of heavily armed fugitives meant not everyone with him was going to come out of this unscathed. Tempest's reputation spoke for itself, and Medesto was a tank in battle, the strongest individual Ren had ever known. He would do what he could to protect the others, but he might not be able to save everyone. He hoped this team was ready for what lay ahead.

Tired of thinking, he leaned back in his seat and watched the circular worlds of light flit by the windows. He closed his eyes. The vibration of the cabin was soothing to his sore body. After what seemed an eternity, exhaustion finally won out, and he drifted off to sleep.

# Chapter 10
# Old London

Natascha watched *Bad Mojo* descend from a moon-drenched sky onto a wide, empty field. She climbed out of the truck she had procured for them and walked over to meet the ship. The ramp lowered from the back of the slipstream. Several silhouetted figures stomped down the sloping metal incline to the moonlit grass.

Medesto led the group, followed by Tempest Vondersteen and Charley Lovejoy. A tiny figure with long ears that could only be Raffles ambled behind them. He and Natascha had met once a long time ago, and she wondered what role the Cajun Folk Hero played in this. Finally, the lean form of Ren B'gatti wandered down the ramp.

"Charley, where is the *Logos Persona* currently located?" Tempest asked. "Is there any chance we'll stumble across her path while we're here?"

The young tech checked her scanner. "The novel's called *The Gaslamp Adventures of Asher Grey*, so I'll let you all come to your own conclusions about who the *Logos Personae* is. She's an explorer who travels the world fighting giant monsters and mad scientists. She's only in Old London for the first four chapters and spends the rest of the book on the *Forbidden Island of Antediluvian* hunting some great beast."

"What chapter are we in?"

"It looks like chapter thirteen. The whole story cycle lasts for eight days."

"Good to see you again, Raffles," Natascha said. "I didn't know you'd be coming on this run."

"Raffles is here as a guide and consultant," Tempest said through tight lips. "We need his expertise on ley-lines and their relationship to the rabbit-holes."

"Las' minute decision on Gideon part," Raffles chuckled. "He ask'd me ta check on da condition of da lines after dat machine had its way with dem."

Natascha nodded. "Well, you have your work cut out for you," she said. "The hole Mordecai left in that hillside over there has mostly closed up. He's been jumping worlds by means of some kind of machine. I followed him and his crew through an artificial rabbit-hole that turned to dust and collapsed under my feet. It was like the ley-line dried up and died. Not sure how we're going to reverse that kind of damage."

"Do you have the location of Mordecai's current whereabouts?" Medesto asked.

"I tracked him to a bookseller's shop in Old London," Natascha replied. "He's been holed up there since I signaled you my location," Natascha said.

"Did ya get a look at Mord'cai?" Raffles asked. "What'd he look like?"

"It was too dark," Natascha answered. "I didn't see any faces."

"How could you be sure it was him?" Tempest asked.

"Because many of those with him were still in their Lazaranth prisoner uniforms," Natascha snapped back. She did not like this woman. She tried, but Tempest didn't let anyone get close to her. "And I saw the Grimm Jester leave for a few hours, and then came back. If the Jester's there, then Mordecai is not far away."

If Tempest kept up with the attitude, some adjustments on Natascha's part might be required to correct the problem. Natascha held her tongue and took the high ground. She glanced at Medesto. The gnome rolled his eyes and said something inaudible under his breath. Ignoring Tempest, she pointed to the truck she had commandeered from a dairy farm.

"I've secured us transportation to Old London. The shop is about an hour from there, so we need to get moving."

"Ren, let's load up," Medesto said, raising his voice enough to indicate it was time to focus on why they were there. "Tempest, let Sinjin know Natascha and I will be back as soon as we can."

Raffles held out a tiny paw to Ren. "It a pleasure ta talk ta ya, skin-changer," Raffles said.

Ren shook it with a smile. "You too, rabbit."

Tempest turned away without a word. "Charley, with me," she ordered. "There's gear to unload and not a lot of time to study the area where Mordecai entered this world. We have a lot to do in a short time."

"Good luck, Ren," Charley yelled over her shoulder as she ran after Tempest.

Natascha led Ren and Medesto to the delivery truck hidden under the trees. It had a cow and chicken painted on the side with the words *Randall's Farms, Where Quality is King.*

"If she keeps it up, Tempest and I are going to have words," Natascha fumed.

"She hates not being in control," Medesto said. "It's who she is. Gideon said she used to be a general in some Royal Space Corp back in her homeworld. At least she'll be staying here and out of our way."

"Well, if she keeps it up, she'll find out exactly who I am," Natascha replied.

"I'll drive," Ren said. He ran to the cab and jumped into the driver's seat. The key turned in the ignition, and the engine gave a violent electrical buzzing sound, but did not turn over.

"Move over." Natascha shoved him in the shoulder. He slid into the passenger seat and saw Medesto frowning at him through the window. The gnome grumbled under his breath. He opened the back door of the crew cab and climbed in.

Natascha pulled the headlights on. "The ground vehicles here are powered by steam. You have to warm up the engine's solenoid before she'll start." She pushed a silver button at the bottom of the dashboard and held it for a few seconds, then pumped the gas pedal and turned the ignition key. The engine coughed, then sputtered and roared to life. She threw the truck in gear, and they roared down the dirt road toward Old London.

An hour later, a large metropolis city came into view. Old London was enormous. The closer they got, the more impressive it became. *The Gaslamp Adventures of Asher Grey* took place in an industrial age of steam-powered marvels. High smokestacks belched soot into the air. Airships of every shape and size floated among the high spires, citadels, and steepled bell towers. In the distance, the tallest structures looked to be docking stations for the ships. Natascha followed the tracer left at the spot where she had been watching the bookseller's shop.

The drive through town took longer than she would have liked. Finally, Natascha stopped on an empty street in front of a closed floral boutique. She pointed to a corner shop of brick-and-mortar across the intersection. The sign out front said *Oldman's Rare and Antique Books.* The front windows were covered with decorative iron bars, and the display window was a simple arrangement of books and book-related merchandise. The three climbed out of the truck.

"They gained entry through a door around back," Natascha said. "The archive is in the basement under the bookstore. There's been a lot of people coming and going, mostly one or two at a time, leaving up the street that way." She gestured north. "Has to be some kind of shift rotation, giving everyone their turn to eat and rest. Mordecai was still in there when I left to meet you."

Medesto put a hand on Ren's shoulder. "You ready for this?" he asked.

"That's what I'm here for," Ren replied. He pulled off his shirt and handed it to Medesto, followed by his pants. The gnome stood butler-like next to him, holding Ren's clothes draped over his other arm. Natascha turned her face away from the naked trickster. Modesty was not one of Ren's strong suits.

"Now, just keep your head down," Medesto said. "You're not here to cause trouble. You are here to gather information. Do not engage the enemy. Find out what Mordecai is searching for and where it is. Then get to the nearest safe house and contact us. We'll take it from there."

Ren nodded, but said nothing. Natascha didn't like that response.

"And don't kill Mordecai!" Medesto admonished. "We want him alive to stand trial. We don't need another Serralto Cardus."

Natascha turned around and kept her eyes on Ren's face, not daring to look down. One of his eyes was icy blue and the other bright green. "If, for some reason, they see through your facade," she said, "I want you to get out of there and head back to *Bad Mojo*. We'll be nearby for the next few hours if you need us."

"I'll be a good boy," Ren said. He winked at her. "I'll contact you as soon as I find anything out." He dropped to all fours as his body shrunk. Fur sprouted from his head, along his back and down his limbs. A moment later, he was a skinny alley cat with a brindle-colored coat and a gouge in one ear. He stretched his front legs out to get comfortable with the change in size. His eyes were still icy blue and green. He looked up at her through the eyes of the cat, then padded across the street, disappearing into the fog.

# Chapter 11
# The Book Depository

Two armed men stood watch outside the basement entrance to the bookseller's shop. One at the bottom of the stairwell next to the closed door. The other leaned against the wall at the top of the steps. Ren padded toward them in the form of the ally cat. His natural eyesight was exceptional, even in the dark.

The two sentries were of no use to him. If there had been only one, he might have had time to switch identities with him, but two guards made that impossible without causing a ruckus. Ren needed to get inside, find a way to separate someone from the herd, and take their place. Then he could work his way in close to Mordecai..

He crept unnoticed to the edge of the stairwell, waiting for an opportunity to sneak past the guard standing at the door. A minute later, the basement door opened, and a heavyset man handed the sentries each a steaming mug. Changing his shape did not give Ren the inherent smell of a feline, but the strong aroma of coffee was unmistakable.

He slipped through the metal railing and dropped to the ground behind the inattentive guard. Medesto was right, this was the part he enjoyed most, sneaking into the belly of the beast. He felt the adrenaline rush build as he padded like a shadow through the open doorway.

Down a short hallway, he followed the din of noise to a crowded basement. Rows of mostly empty bookshelves lined the walls. People sorted the volumes into stacks on two long tables at the center of the room. There were piles of discarded books and journals everywhere. Ren slipped past a female soldier who stood guard at the door. She held a stocky rifle of the science fiction variety. It was a high-tech design, dull gray with a stub barrel and clear round magazine full of small multi-colored balls under the barrel. Two similarly armed soldiers waited nearby, hidden from immediate view by standing in the gaps between bookshelves. She stepped toward the cat, but the trickster quickened his speed and scurried through the forest of legs away from her.

Ren did not want to arouse suspicion, so he stopped briefly and rubbed himself up against the leg of a woman rummaging through the shelves. She stroked her fingers down his back. The soldier stopped, watching them intensely. The woman set her books down on the table and picked Ren up, scratching him behind the ear. "Calm down, it's just a stray cat," she told the soldier. Ren purred and licked her hand.

No one ever suspected the cat.

The soldier remained where she stood for a moment longer, her expression hidden behind the reflective face guard she wore. Either embarrassed with so many eyes on her, or satisfied the feline was no threat, the soldier spun around and walked back to her post. The woman continued to pet Ren's head, then dropped him to the floor and returned to her work.

A familiar dread rushed through Ren as he crossed the room. It was followed by an overwhelming sense of foreboding. He spotted the cause of his uneasiness. Floating in the far corner was the dark wraith he had encountered outside the Pithy Fool. Its bony jaw protruded from under the heavy cowl. The rest of the wraith's face was swallowed in the darkness of the hood. Anyone passing by the Grimm Jester gave the monster a wide berth. A shiver ran down Ren's spine, even though he couldn't tell if the creature was looking at him or not.

Ren shook off the feeling and wandered freely through the crowd. He weaved his way across the floor, dodging the shuffling feet of people moving about as he tried to get an idea of what was happening from his low vantage point.

At the center of the room stood a well-dressed gentleman that had to be Mordecai Davos. Oddly, the man he saw standing in front of him was not what he had imagined. Mordecai wore a gray coat that reached to his ankle. He was of average height with a slim build, sharp, gaunt features, and a neatly trimmed goatee with long, slicked back hair. His dark, piercing eyes took in everything around him as he gave orders to his underlings. There was nothing particularly threatening or imposing about him.

So, this was the man who would bring Rogue Destiny to its knees, and claim the fabled city as his own? The criminal mastermind whose very name struck fear throughout the gambling dens and back rooms of the City's underworld. The unseen shadow who held sway over the highest reaches of power. Ren was not impressed. Now he considered killing Mordecai just on principle for misrepresenting himself.

The man next to Mordecai had the look of the scholar. He was nicely dressed, although his gray suit was dusty from travel. Every few minutes, someone would bring another notebook or journal to him. He would quickly peruse it with his reading glasses perched on his nose, then decide whether to drop it into a wooden crate at his feet or toss it aside onto an ever-growing pile of discarded books and papers.

Behind the two stood a giant of a man in a black western duster and flat-brimmed cowboy hat. The brute remained silent as a statue. His broad face shrouded by the brim of his hat. On the other side of Mordecai was a soldier who was as much machine as man. The weight of his artificial legs shifted on three-clawed metal feet. His arm ended in a lethal-looking weapon where his left hand should have been. The cybernetics designs reminded Ren of Sebastian Poe, the Raconteurs' chief mechanic back in Rogue Destiny. Although the cyborg in front of him had more advanced, sleeker components than anything Sebastian had grafted onto his body.

Mordecai appeared to be in a heated conversation with a hard-looking man and a small group of people.

"I beg you to remain optimistic, Yturri," Mordecai said to the man, who seemed to be the leader of the group. "We are close to our goal."

"You said that two worlds ago," Yturri growled. His heavy brow furrowed, shadowing his eyes. His long oily hair reached the cuff of the leather coat he wore. Under the jacket was the worn striped uniform from Lazaranth Prison. His thumbs were hooked in his belt, where a two-foot knife hung along with a holstered pistol. Two women and a man stood behind him, similarly armed.

"It won't be much longer," Mordecai protested. "We cannot afford to have any more desertions."

"Ain't your choice," the man spat. "You promised when we agreed to join you, we could leave at any time. Was that a lie?"

"Of course not," Mordecai answered. "You are free to do as you wish. I just hoped you would reconsider."

"We're tired of hauling your crap around like pack mules," one of the women said, her face visibly angry. "We've been at this for weeks, tearing up a dozen worlds with nothing to show for it. You won't even tell us what we're searching for. Tessa and Poor Boy left, and they're doing fine."

The cowboy in the black hat stepped up to Yturri. He was a full head taller and twice as wide at the shoulders than the long-haired leader of the group. The tension in the room intensified. Mordecai raised his hand.

"Let them go, Dark Angus," he said. "We do not want anyone with us who is not completely dedicated to our cause." The cowboy stepped back as the prisoners hurriedly gathered their belongings and headed out the same way Ren had entered. Yturri waited for the others to get out the door before he turned and gave Mordecai a smug grin. The criminal mastermind watched him leave from across the room with no expression.

Mordecai sighed. "I have treated my underlings with respect and generosity, Tomas," he said to the scholarly man next to him. "I have promised them a share of the City once we take it. Yet they still abandon us."

Tomas set the journal down he was studying. "We need bodies to carry our research back to camp. Forty-seven escapees agreed to join us when we left Bones Martyr Island, but between the deaths and desertions, we are down to less than twenty. We cannot afford to lose any more. The soldiers on loan from Tiberius refuse to carry anything other than their own weapons. They are only as loyal as the gold we pay them, and our gold is running low."

Ren darted from under his hiding place to the feet of Tomas. He rubbed up against the scholar's pant leg and purred loudly. Tomas picked him up from the floor and cradled him in one arm. Ren's chest rumbled as he was scratched behind one ear.

"You must remember these are high-security criminals you broke out of prison," Tomas said. "Their loyalties are fleeting at best. They see your respect for them as a personal flaw, not a virtue."

"That is a shame," Mordecai said with an exhausted breath. "Then I will need to impress upon those who remain that it is in their best interests to stay with us."

"How will you do that?" Tomas asked.

Mordecai turned to the cowboy. "Dark Angus, please show everyone how we handle deserters. If you would?" The man in black nodded and strode out the door, his boots echoing off the wooden floor.

Mordecai raised his hands, a pleasant smile on his face, and addressed the room. "Could I have your attention, please?" The room grew quiet as all eyes turned to Mordecai.

"I know we are all tired, and I am grateful for those of you who have remained at my side during our hunt, but there has been a steady exodus in our ranks. Once we find our prize, we will return to Rogue Destiny, and those who imprisoned us will pay dearly for their transgressions. It's been said revenge is a dish best served cold, but I disagree. I say revenge is best served amid blood and fire."

As if on cue, four rapid gunshots rang out in the distance. The genial expression dropped from Mordecai's face, and his eyes grew hard. "I freed you from Lazaranth Prison under no obligation to do so. I did it simply because I could. You joined my quest under your own free will and swore allegiance to me. I will hold you to that oath. From now on, anyone who tries to leave will be dealt with in the harshest terms." He motioned to the cyborg standing behind him. "Silium-Cinque-Niner, if you would show them I am serious."

The metal soldier nodded and raised his weapon. In unison, all the soldiers in the room stepped out from the dark nooks and crannies, their weapons at the ready. All five wore body armor with their short rifles hanging off a strap around their shoulder. Many had cybernetic limbs like their commander, Silium-

Cinque-Niner. The top half of their faces were hidden behind helmeted facemasks.

Mordecai smiled and clapped his hands. "Now, everyone, back to work." All five soldiers returned to their posts as Dark Angus walked in, having fulfilled his grisly mission. He reeked of gunpowder and death.

Tomas set Ren down on the maps and ley-line charts stretched out before him. He picked up a notebook from one of the stacks. "This archive has certainly proven more fruitful than the last few," the scholar mused, placing a piece of tape on the cover. He wrote something with a pen on the tape and dropped it into the crate next to Ren. "It's been exhaustive trying to retrace Harper Bellweather's movements based on nothing more than handwritten notes and watercolor scribblings."

Digging through the satchel at his side, he pulled out another notebook covered in doodles and colored drawings of fantastical creatures and vivid rainbows. He flipped through the pages until he found what he was looking for and laid the note-book down open on the table. "But I am confident this is where we need to go next. She's mentioned it several times throughout her writings, and she made frequent stops there within the time period she would have been in possession of the *Book of Days*."

Mordecai pointed a long finger at the map. "Then that is where we head next. Does she give details about what we can expect to find there?"

Tomas nodded with a tired smile. "Bellweather was prolific in her writings, almost too much for the purposes of our search. From what I have put together from cross-referencing her other writings, I am sure the *Book of Days* is there.

"Thank you, Tomas," Mordecai said. "Your history with the Order of the Memento *Ex-Libris* and knowledge of their methods have brought us this far, and I am confident you will take us the rest of the way."

Ren peeked over the edge of the box to see what it contained. The crate was filled with journals and notebooks of various sizes and colors. All had a white strip of tape showing the time and place they were found. They were covered with doodles and drawings of unicorns and dragons and mythical monsters of every kind. One notebook lay open on the table. Inside were more sketches and water-colored pages of cities with words scrawled haphazardly in the margins.

Not quite the deep intellectual works of a well-traveled scholar Ren expected Mordecai to be chasing. But if the leader of the *Society of the Black Rose* was this desperate to collect her writings, they must be of great value. Maybe this Harper Bellweather was some kind of mad genius.

Mordecai brushed Ren away from the crate. "Will someone get this cat out of here?" he yelled.

A shadow fell across the trickster. Dark Angus loomed above him. For the first time, Ren noticed a broken loop of rope hanging around the cowboy's thick neck. It looked like a noose. He drew his long-barreled naval revolver and pointed it at Ren's head. The hammer slowly cocked back with a click.

"Angus, not inside," Mordecai ordered. "We don't need the mess." The cowboy lifted his gun from Ren. A heavyset man walked by them, carrying an armful of books. "Doggs Borland, please throw this stray beast outside?"

The man called Doggs dumped the books on the table next to Ren and picked the cat up by his midsection. "I got 'em," Doggs said. He held the animal out in front of him and started for the door. Ren gave a pleasant purring sound in his throat and rubbed his face against his hand. The man's annoyed mood softened, and he brought the cat in close to him, stroking his back as he made his way through the crowded room to the back entrance.

"Where you goin', Doggs?" one guard asked as the man and his cat came out the rear door.

"I was told to get rid of the cat," Doggs answered.

"We passed a fishmonger's shop up the street," the guard said, pointing down the cobblestone lane. "Take it down there and leave him." Doggs grunted a reply and ambled up the steps to the sidewalk.

Two blocks later, Doggs passed the door of a closed fish market and turned into a narrow-trash- strewn alley. Large wooden barrels lining one side of the alley. The stench of rotten fish filled the crisp night air. The man kicked over a garbage can filled with fish heads and entrails. He dropped Ren in front of the mess. "Bon appétit, kitty," he said and turned away. Ren shifted to his natural shape. He stood up and mimicked the cat's meow.

Doggs looked back. "What now, little kitty? I'm not going to hand feed you..." His eyes went wide when he saw the naked shape-shifter standing where the cat should have been. "Where the hell you come from?" Doggs sputtered. "Hiding in the shadows, scaring the unsuspecting. And why are you nekkid?"

Ren delivered a blow to the man's throat to stifle any cry for help. Doggs staggered back. He grabbed his neck, choking on his words as he tried to draw breath. A hand dropped to the revolver at his side. Ren swept the man's legs out from under him. Dogg was a large, awkward man. He fell hard and slammed his head against the floor of the alley. Ren followed up with a punch to the face that laid Doggs out cold.

A familiar scent caught Ren's attention. He turned to see a green mist appear at the end of the closed off alley. The dark form of Doctor Enigma emerged out of the brick wall. The trickster looked down at Doggs. His face was a bloody mess, but Mordecai's lackey was unconscious.

# Chapter 12
## An Unlikely Reunion

**R**en waited for Doctor Enigma to walk up the alley. The emerald mist surrounding her slowly dissipated. "Worried I was going to run off again?" he asked with a wry grin. He dragged the unconscious Doggs away from the fish entrails and started pulling off his boots.

Natascha removed her gas mask. "Don't say that," she replied. "I saw an alley cat being carried from the bookseller and figured it had to be you. We haven't had a moment to talk, just you and I. Medesto headed to the Raconteurs' safe house to let them know what's going on. Have you found out what Mordecai's after?"

"I heard them mention *The Book of Days*," Ren said. He removed Dogg's vest and shirt. "There's something in it that Mordecai wants, but they haven't found its location yet. They're digging through the old archives looking for the traveling journals of someone named *Harper Bellweather*. You find her, and you'll find where the *Book of Days* is."

"What's in it that could be so valuable?" Natascha asked.

"I have no idea," Ren answered. "Gideon said it was written by Baltazaar Gheddi and talks about a lot of Rogue Destiny's origins. Mordecai's getting ready to move on, so I need to get back. Tell Medesto I'll contact you as soon as I know more."

"That's a good start," Natascha replied. "It explains the ransacking of the *Order of the Memento Ex-Libris* archives. Harper Bellweather is one of the field agents. I met her once, years ago. That gives us something to work with."

Ren pulled the pants on and buttoned up the flannel shirt. Natascha checked the street beyond the alley to see if it was clear.

"How many are in there?" she asked.

"Hard to tell from a cat's point of view. So many legs," Ren said. "Twenty or so prisoners from Lazaranth, Mordecai's entourage, and half a dozen cybernetic soldiers."

Natascha gave him a wry grin. "You seem to have picked up right where you left off. Nice to see the old Ren back in action. So Mordecai's really in there, huh? I'm curious what he looked like."

"Tall, scrawny, not really what you would expect in a mysterious crime lord," Ren said. "Except for a cheesy goatee, there's nothing too sinister about him at all." He sat down to pull on Doggs' boots.

"Did you hear any talk of the machine that brought them to this world?" Natascha asked.

"Nothing on any machine," Ren replied. He pulled a handkerchief from his coat pocket and wiped the blood from the unconscious man's nose and face so he could study Doggs' features in the glow of a streetlight. He tilted the face at different angles until satisfied he knew enough to create a convincing likeness of the criminal.

Ren looked up into Natascha's dark brown eyes. They held his attention. The two of them were alike, yet so different. She was self-assured, and a brilliant fighter, like him. But she was kind, honorable, and honest. Ren smiled at her and transformed himself into a perfect replica of the man in long johns lying unconscious at his feet.

Natascha handed him Dogg's studded-leather vest. Ren slipped his arms into it and buckled on the holster. He looked at Natascha, his thoughts suddenly serious.

"There's something else," Natascha said. "What aren't you telling me?"

"After Mordecai goes down," he said, "I'm going to claim my slipstream and going to search for Claymore. Part of me wishes I had never agreed to come back. I should have stayed in *The Crimson Masque*. I was happy there."

"Happy?" Natascha said. "Living as someone else."

"I'm not always comfortable in my own skin," Ren said. "I've hidden behind a thousand faces, so it's hard to know the real me sometimes. I find it easier to be other people."

"Mucluc seems to like the real you," she said. "Medesto said you were watching out for him."

"Mucluc's different," Ren replied. "He doesn't want anything from me. There are no expectations in our friendship. We just are. To Gideon, I'm simply a tool to get what he wants, nothing more."

"Then don't do it for Gideon," Natascha said. "Or Claymore. Or the Raconteurs. Do it because it's the right thing to do. The fate of worlds hang in the balance here. We can't allow Mordecai to use *The Book of Days* to tilt the balance of power in his favor. If Rogue Destiny falls, all of the Mythic Cosmos will be left vulnerable."

Ren picked up Doggs' fallen pistol. He flipped open the cylinder and saw two empty chambers. He checked the cartridge belt around his waist, but there were no bullets. So, Mordecai's underlings were not as well armed as they appeared. He closed the cylinder and holstered the pistol.

"I miss how things used to be," Ren said. "Back when we

were just righting wrongs and chasing down bad guys with Claymore. Why do things have to change?"

Natascha nodded. "Those were good times," she said. "but they're gone now. My father used to say: *The only truism in life is nothing remains the same for long.* What happened to Claymore was a crime. But it pales in comparison to what he's battling now."

"Here, take this in case we need to find each other," Natascha said. She pulled out a small round leather case from her trench coat and handed it to Ren. "I'll have its companion with me as long as we're in-world."

Ren unsnapped the flap and flipped it open. Inside was a companion compass, a common tracking device used by the Raconteurs. It was identical to the one Claymore had given him just hours before when his partner tracked him into Adezhda, the city of assassins. The large needle wobbled back and forth, searching for true north. Under the needle, a smaller red arrow moved with Natascha as she paced back and forth in the alley.

"Thanks." Ren attached the compass to his gun belt. "I'll be in touch." He turned away to hide the anger building at not being able to help Claymore. Natascha caught his arm.

"I'm glad you came back, Ren," she said. "I miss this too. Us working together, I mean. You should consider staying on with the Raconteurs after this is over. You and I can look for Claymore together."

"It's something to think about," Ren said with an unconvincing smile.

"Be careful," Natascha cautioned. "Do not underestimate your enemy. Mordecai may appear nonthreatening in person, but don't forget who he is. He's not to be trifled with. Let's get through this one, then we'll figure out where to go from there." A sadness filled her words that Ren didn't understand. Maybe it was because she knew he would not be coming back after this was over.

Ren winked. "You know me, careful as a church mouse."

Natascha laughed and shook her head. "I'll bind Doggs' hands and legs before he wakes up. We'll take him with us to Rogue Destiny when we leave."

Ren left the alley wearing Doggs Borland's face and dressed in his clothes. He ambled back toward the bookseller's shop. The body he borrowed was bulky and awkward, with too much extra fat. The scent of Doctor Enigma's green mist hung in the foggy air.

Ren was on his own now, and happy the Raconteurs would not be there to stop him from doing what he was about to do. If everything went smoothly, Mordecai would be dead in the next couple of minutes, and he would escape in the ensuing chaos.

Ren reached the bookshop and ambled down the back stairs, imitating Doggs Borland's loping gait step for step. The guard looked up but offered no challenge. "You get rid of the cat?" he asked with a smirk. Ren grunted a reply as he entered the basement entrance.

Now that he was no longer down on all fours, Ren had a much better vantage point to take in the library. The basement under the bookseller's shop was long and wide. The bookshelves were built with a distinct art nouveau style of architecture. Its design was in direct contrast to the architectural style of the rest of this world.

The rows of bookshelves were nearly empty now. Their contents discarded into piles around the room, with Harper Bellweather's journals and notebooks stacked neatly into wooden crates, long canvas bags and backpacks waiting to be hauled away with them when they left.

The criminals traveling with Mordecai were a diverse group from many worlds and genres. The underlings wore a mishmash of clothing they had scavenged during their travels. All but a few appeared to be human. A creature Ren could not identify ambled across the floor on wide flat feet, carrying two giant canvas bags of pilfered writings from the bookshelves.

Its sinewy, malformed body ended in a blunt snout. Cat-like eyes watched everything going on in the room. Bits of bright orange- and black-speckled skin peeked out from under its torn prison uniform. Saggy pants, shredded and dirty around the cuffs from travel, covered its squat legs. Whether it was a fantasy character or a science fiction one, Ren didn't know or care, but in a room full of extraordinary characters, it stood out from everyone else. Only the Grimm Jester and Dark Angus gave off a more formidable presence.

Dark Angus may have been human once, but he was not any longer. He remembered Gideon's words about how he found it interesting Mordecai himself would lead such a motley, unmanageable crew of fugitives instead of relying on his own loyal people. Ren agreed there was something peculiar about that.

The Grimm Jester floated in the darkest part of the wide room, even further away from him. The monster had saved Ren's life the night before from Mordecai's underlings. Their brief conversation took place behind a nightclub called *The Pithy Fool* shortly before the establishment burned to the ground due to a disagreement between Ren and the gangsters of Rogue Destiny.

The mere memory of the ghoul sent a shiver down Ren's back. Now that he was in close proximity to the monster again, he could feel whatever was behind the dark hood stare at him from across the room. He ignored the uneasiness and focused on what he was there to do.

With luck, Ren would end this quickly and get back to *Bad Mojo* before Natascha. Gideon would be furious once he learned Mordecai was dead, but he was not staying around, so that did not concern him. If the Raconteurs failed to see the brilliance of his logic, it was not Ren's problem. Mordecai Davos would no longer be any trouble to anyone, and *The Book of Days* would stay lost. Problem solved.

Mordecai stood where Ren had left him, talking to Tomas. Ren grabbed an unattended crate of notebooks and moved across the floor toward his target. No one in his immediate vicinity paid him any attention. Everyone focused on filling boxes and bags or examining the few books still on the shelves. Mordecai had his back to Ren. The cowboy in black and commander of the soldiers, Silium Cinque Niner, stood to the far side of Mordecai, allowing Ren a clean shot.

The two doors leading in were being closely watched. No one was getting in or out without going through the armed soldiers. That left the narrow street-level windows as the only means of escape. No one would expect an attack from inside the room. Ren hoped the gunshot would cause enough confusion, so he could make his escape through the barred windows where no one could follow him.

Ren set his box down on the far end of the long table, pretending to sort through its contents. Mordecai stood a dozen paces away from him. He took a deep breath and thought of the *Gentlemen of the Open Road*. Mordecai had ordered their deaths simply because they were his friends.

The door at the back of the room swung open. Out of the corner of his eye, Ren saw two men enter. He kept focused on Mordecai, even as they crossed in front of him. He held the gun at his side, hidden from view by the table. The newcomers passed so close to him the leader bumped Ren's shoulder.

"Pardon me," the man said. The sound of the words pulled Ren's attention from Mordecai. Though the trickster could not see his face, he knew the voice instantly. The swagger, the bravado. The same cocksure confidence he displayed from the first day they met all those many years ago. Claymore Ives was standing in front of him.

# Chapter 13
# An Unexpected Turn of Events

Claymore walked past Ren to Mordecai. He carried a rifle over one shoulder, a backpack over the other, and a holstered pistol on each hip. His nicely dressed companion followed. Mordecai looked up as Claymore reached him.

"Mr. Ives," he said, raising an eyebrow. "This is a surprise. I was under the impression you had other business to a tend to." His eyes shifted to the pack Claymore carried. "And what is this?"

"A show of my loyalty," he said. "The night you broke us out of Lazaranth Prison, I heard the cyborg mention he knew a place you could use as a central base. But he said it would require gold."

Claymore swung the backpack from his shoulder onto the table. It jingled in the musical language of loose coins. Every head in the room turned at the sound. "My business in the City is done, and I'm at your disposal. If you'll have me." He untied the flap and tipped the pack over. Gold coins cascaded over the maps and charts.

Ren smiled to himself. Claymore always knew how to make

an entrance. Those were the same coins he and Claymore had stolen from Mordecai's lackeys the night before. His partner was simply returning Mordecai's gold to him. Ren fought the desire to call out his partner's name. His mind reeled with amazement at how Claymore got to Mordecai so quickly. The Raconteurs had just located the criminal themselves.

Mordecai still appeared skeptical. "How were you able to find us?" he asked.

Claymore smiled. "You just have to know your way around the Mythic Cosmos. Besides, the path of destruction you've left behind was an easy trail of breadcrumbs to follow."

Ren realized his opportunity to kill Mordecai was quickly passing him by. He slid the pistol from its holster and lifted it level to his waist. The angle of the hip shot would be difficult, but not impossible. He cocked the hammer back.

A brawny hand grabbed him by the wrist. Ren looked up into the cold eyes of a massive brutish man, bearded with collar length stringy hair.

"What'd think you're doing there, Doggs?" the man spat. The grip on Ren's wrist tightened. The brute slammed his arm against the table, knocking the pistol out of Ren's hand.

He drove a fist into the trickster's stomach. Ren fell to his knees, gasping for air and fighting the urge to retaliate. The brawny man loomed over him, leaving open his midsection, legs, and groin. Defending himself was at the top of a very short list of the moral absolutes Ren held. When someone posed a threat against him, he fought back—not doing so was an anathema to him.

On the other hand, Ren's first rule of shape-shifting was to play out the part he was playing to the end, regardless. Never give away the deception. In a heartbeat, he decided the real Doggs Borland would never win a fight against this hulking man, so neither could he. Every eye in the room was on him as the man gut punched Ren again.

Another swift punch followed. Ren dropped to the floor. The brute had no real fighting skill, just a lumbering street fighting technique, but he was as strong as an ox. He kicked Ren in the side, the back, and in the head. The man's rage grew greater with every blow. All Ren could do was curl up, focusing all his energy on one thing. Not losing the shape he was in.

As the beating continued, Ren felt his hold on Doggs Borland's form slipping. He pulled himself into a tighter ball as each kick brought him closer to the edge of returning to his true shape. He felt nauseous. The effort to hold the shape took all his willpower.

The beating abruptly ceased. Lowering his arms from his face, Ren saw two pairs of boots in front of him. One set he knew was from the brute pounding on him. The other he followed up to the face of Claymore. His partner had the man's arm locked in his grip.

"That's enough, Addison!" Claymore ordered. "He's done."

The bald man snorted. He gave Ren one last kick in the stomach. The trickster rolled onto his back, blood oozing from his nose. The man laughed and stepped back. Ren glared at him through half-open eyes.

Mordecai came over, shadowed by Silium Cinque Niner, and Dark Angus. "Mannford Addison! What is this all about?" he asked.

Addison picked up the fallen pistol and slammed it down on the table in front of Mordecai. "Ask Doggs," the big man growled into his beard. "He was sneaking up on you with his gun drawn. What else could it mean except he meant to shoot you?"

Mordecai Davos glared down at Ren. His gray eyes narrowed, suddenly cruel and vindictive. "Then Mr. Borland will pay for his treachery. Get him up and bind his hands. We will dispose of him on the way."

Addison pulled Ren up from the floor by his shirt. He looked down at four red laser sights pointed on his chest. The brute forced Ren's head to the table, while his hands were bound behind him.

"Claymore," Mordecai said. "Help Addison guard the traitor."

Claymore took a step toward Ren, drawing a knife from his belt.

Ren twisted around to see what Claymore intended to do with the blade. Was he going to stab him right there? He never thought he would have to fight Claymore, but often wondered who would win in such a confrontation. No one was going to kill him without a fight, not even his old mentor and friend. His muscles rippled as he started to shift, but a strong hand grabbed his arm.

"Hold still," Claymore said. He cut off something hanging from Ren's gun belt in a quick slice of the blade and held Natascha's companion compass up for the room to see. "Where'd you get this?" his partner asked.

Ren's mind went blank, and he abandoned his attempt to shift. Lying was as natural to him as breathing, but his head was still spinning from the beating and sudden appearance of Claymore. No answer came to him. "It's only a compass," he stammered, telling himself the stammering was part of the act. "I found it outside in the street when I put the cat out."

"Cat?" Claymore asked. He looked back at Ren.

"You idiot!" Addison backhanded Ren. The trickster's head snapped back. "You want us all to get caught? You don't just pick up anything you find on the street. Your mama ever tell you that?"

Addison raised his hand again, but Claymore grabbed his

arm. He shoved Addison against into a bookshelf, his forearm pressed against the man's throat.

"I said that was enough!" Claymore shouted. His partner stared at Ren for several heartbeats, a questioning look in his eyes. He gave Mordecai a wry grin and held out the compass. "This is a tracking device. I *told* you the night of the prison escape, it was only a matter of time before they showed up." He dropped it to the floor and crushed it under his boot heel. "That's why you need my help. The Raconteurs know where you are. You need to leave this place now."

Mordecai turned to a man standing nearby. "Porter, return to Lady Absynthe and let her know we need to depart immediately." The small man nodded and left through the side door.

Mordecai stared ahead in thought for a moment. "This changes our strategy. There's no need for us to hide in the shadows any longer. We will implement the scorched-earth policy immediately and burn these Raconteurs to ashes, leaving no evidence we were ever here."

Ren could see the words cut through Claymore. His partner stuck a finger in Mordecai's face. "You're not doing that," he said. "Go after the Raconteurs if you want. I have no allegiance to them, but I will not let you harm the *Logos Personae*. If She dies, millions and millions of innocent souls will die with Her, and that will bring the wrath of every Raconteur down on you. Trust me when I say you do not want that. Not if you ever hope to reach your prize."

Dark Angus stepped forward. The sound of his boots broke the tense silence. Claymore glanced over at him, not intimidated by the imposing dark cowboy. Five tiny red dots appeared on Claymore from every side—laser sights from the soldiers' rifles. With his hands still tied behind him, Ren slipped in front of two of the dots, blocking them from reaching his partner. Mordecai sized up Claymore with his eyes, seemingly not bothered by the outburst.

"The last time we spoke," Mordecai said. "You told me you could acquire certain items from a certain library. Can you still do that?"

"Without question," Claymore answered. "Just let me know what you need."

"Excellent. Your service will be of great value to us," Mordecai said. "And to show my gratitude, I will honor your request and spare the life of the *Chosen One*. But we need to leave this world at once."

"Thank you," Claymore replied. He stepped away from the criminal. The soldiers' laser sights stayed on him. "I can get what you need. Although it'll be difficult to get in and out undetected, I've done it before."

Mordecai motioned to the shadows at the back of the room. The crowd separated as the Grimm Jester floated out from the darkness and hung suspended in the air in front of its master.

"Good, the Jester will take you there," he said. "His method of travel rivals Lady Absynthe's machine. No place is beyond his reach, even a hidden library. Once the book is obtained, you will rendezvous back at our camp. But be warned, the road the Jester travels was not meant for mortals. Your journey will not be pleasant."

Claymore nodded, unfazed by the comment. "Good enough, let me talk to my informant and let him know his services are no longer needed."

Mordecai turned to the scholar at his side. "Tomas?" he said. "It's time to leave."

Tomas raised his hands and spoke to the room. "Take what you can carry from the crates that I have marked. We will leave in small groups so as not to attract attention." The scholar gathered the world maps and ley-line charts spread out over a table, returning them to the leather satchel he carried over a shoulder.

Mannford Addison pushed Ren into a corner where two of the soldiers stood over him with guns. "Watch him until we're ready to leave," the big man said.

Both soldiers wore dark military uniforms with a reflective helmet covering the upper half of their faces. Both were females, each with a half-cloak thrown over one shoulder with different ranking insignia on it. Each carried carbine rifles, with a small sidearm on the front of their belts, and an impressively large knife strapped to a leg.

Ren slumped down in the corner. Getting out of the ropes would be no problem. Getting out of there alive, however, was another issue. Across the room, he watched Claymore make his way through the bustling activity to the man he had arrived with earlier. Ren considered trying to get a signal to his partner that he was here, but dismissed the idea out of hand. Not even the two of them together could take the entire room.

Ren watched Claymore talk to the one he had called Chauncey Wainwright. By his dress, the man did not appear to be part of Mordecai's crew. His tweed suit was not dusty or worn from travel. It was in the style the residents of this world would wear, so obviously Wainwright was a local resident. Ren wondered how he fit into all this.

The man in the tweed suit stood in the far corner by himself. He made no effort to help. Claymore spoke in low tones, then handed him a small leather coin purse. The man put the pouch into a coat pocket without counting it. They shook hands, and Chauncey Wainwright slipped out the side door.

Mannford Addison grabbed Ren's bound arm and shoved a gun barrel into his side. "MacGregor, with me," he growled. Another large man grabbed Ren's other arm, and he was marched to the back door. He glanced at Claymore as he went past, waiting for his former partner to say something, to prevent the brutal murder that was about to take place.

Claymore watched impassively as Ren was escorted out the door. His partner's face held no expression, his eyes strangely cold and vacant. Even though Claymore didn't know it was his partner standing there, he was going to do nothing to stop a man from being led off to his death. That bothered Ren more than his own impending death.

# Chapter 14
# Blood Ties

Natascha watched the bookseller's storefront from across the dimly lit street. Ren had just reentered the building in the guise of a fugitive whose face he had borrowed. The trickster had said he'd seen no sign of the portal-creating machine that brought Mordecai and company to this world, but she knew it had to be close.

She pulled the scarf left behind at the monastery in the Russian novel out of her pocket and put it to her nose, smelling the familiar fragrance again. Her mother's favorite, jasmine and lavender. They had not seen each in the years following her father's death.

Victor Pyotr Anatole Zarkov first donned the gas mask and trench coat of Doctor Enigma as a young man in his twenties. He became a founding member of a group of pulp heroes, *The Exceptionals*. Upon his death, Natascha took his place within the group as the new Doctor Enigma. But she could never get past her loss.

Then one dreary winter's day, an odd little man in a black suit named Gideon Dumas visited her flat. He offered her an escape from her past, and a chance to make a difference on a more cosmic scale. She jumped at the opportunity and left her homeworld to join the Raconteurs to continue her father's legacy, and to forget. She never looked back.

Until now.

Idalia Jyotsna Devi was a repressively strict mother, but a brilliant scientist. Loving, in her own way, but intolerant of any shortcomings that she felt kept Natascha from achieving her full potential. The long hours of studying the arts of alchemy and chemistry, along with delving into the darker branches of the physical sciences, made for a horrible childhood. Her sanity was only saved by her father. He would often steal her away for an afternoon to study combat techniques and the proper usage of a multitude of weapons. She cherished the relationship with her father above all else in her life.

The echo of boots on cobblestones brought her focus back to the present as several dark figures emerged from the bookstore. Three of the four people carried large packs, while the fourth followed as their armed escort, unencumbered except for a short rifle. The group headed down the sidewalk, past the darkened shop windows. The hour was late, and the streets were empty. As good an opportunity as any to locate her mother and this mysterious portal machine of hers. Natascha stuffed the scarf back into her coat pocket. She slipped on her gas mask and followed the group along the other side of the rain-slicked street. The filters inside the mask allowed her to penetrate the soupy fog well enough to keep her quarry in sight.

She followed them down the street for several blocks until the buildings changed from brick businesses and apartment tenements to the business district of Old London.

The four crossed a wide-open plaza and disappeared down the stairs, leading to an underground subway system. Natascha followed silently from a distance. The subway platform was dimly lit and empty of commuters at this time of night. She kept the evenly spaced pillars between her and her quarry to avoid being seen.

The air grew colder as she continued deeper into the bowels of the London Underground, past signs saying *Under Construction- Restricted Area- Keep Out.* The group stopped at a boarded-off wall. One man slid a panel of plywood from the wooden barrier, and one by one, they disappeared into the darkness on the other side. Natascha moved quietly to the opening and slipped inside after them. Her night vision adjusted easily to the changes in lighting.

An abandoned subway tunnel stretched left and right in front of her. She followed the flashlight beams of the people ahead of her. The wooden platform creaked softly underfoot as she moved across it. She slowed her pace so as not to give away her position. A scurrying noise caught her attention. The scratch of claws on wood. Just a rat, she hoped, but the scraping indicated something bigger than a rat hid in the blackness. The motion detector in her mask registered movement to her left. Natascha turned, drawing her Peacemaker in one fluid motion. A pair of small eyes gleamed in the darkness, level with her own. She could make out the hunched silhouette of something large crouching in the shadows. The Peacemaker hummed as she clicked it on and raised the weapon.

A snort erupted from the blackness, followed by the thump of hooves scraping the platform surface. Natascha gripped the Peacemaker tight as the massive shape broke from the darkness and lumbered toward her. The wooden landing vibrated under its weight.

Natascha had no time to move out of the way before the creature was upon her. She fired the Peacemaker, hitting it dead center in the chest. The crackle of the lightning-gun broke the silence of the dark subway platform. The kaleidoscope of lights from the electrical arc of the weapon cast distorted shadows all around them.

The monstrosity was seven feet tall, bipedal, with the large, twisted horns of an ox and the hunched back of a razorback boar. Scars zigzagged its mangy fur, and large stitches were visible across its snout and face. The humanoid beast wore only tattered pants and an ill-fitting blanket wrapped around its shoulders.

The creature's hide was a patchwork of thick, coarse hair separated by the grisly scarring that ran the length of its body. Its hands were disfigured and unnaturally split, as if someone had attempted to give the hooved beast opposable thumbs.

The beast's eyes rolled back into its misshapen head as the electrical tendrils snaked over its torso and shoulders. The electricity coursing through it overpowered the creature. The beast slumped to the floor in a heap and lay still. Its breath came in short rapid puffs while its tiny eyes watched Natascha intensely.

Natascha lowered the Peacemaker. "You do not need to fight me," she breathed. "I am not your enemy, but I know where you come from. I know about the hideous experiments you endured that cut and reshaped you to resemble a man. Who would not want to escape from those atrocities?"

The brute gave a snort, grunting words from a throat not intended for human speech. "We have new master now. She protects us. No more cutting. No more pain."

"Your new master is every bit as evil as Moreau ever was," Natascha said, her voice soft and empathetic. She took a step toward the beast, her gloved hands in front of her. "I can help you."

The creature came off the floor with a guttural roar. Its hooved feet dug grooves into the wood as it lunged at her. It caught the Raconteur by surprise. She brought the Peacemaker up but could not get a shot off before the monstrosity was upon her. The massive body slammed into her. Its momentum took them both over the edge of the five-foot platform. Natascha grabbed for anything to stop her from going over the side, but nothing was within reach.

The oxen-boar pitched headlong into the open abyss of the rail lines and Natascha fell with him. The weightlessness in her stomach gave way as gravity took control. She dropped the Peacemaker and crashed on the rail line, entangled with the monster.

The horned monstrosity hit the stone floor headfirst with a loud crunch and lay still. She landed hard on the ground near him, slamming her skull on a thick rail. Only the protective metal sheathings of her gas mask saved her from having her brains splattered all over the rails.

Natascha pushed herself up, dazed and struggling to get her bearings. Her head spun as she stumbled away from the beast, searching for her ray gun. She turned back to the creature. It lay crumpled on the subway tracks, its great horned head twisted to one side at an unnatural angle.

The Raconteur shook away the stars floating in her vision. Her Peacemaker lay on the ground. She walked over and picked it up. The smooth casing of the weapon was cracked, and the round dish-shaped muzzle bent. She sighed, hoping it still fired, and returned the pistol to its holster at her side.

Natascha spun at a noise behind her. A small, hunched shape raced down the tunnel until she lost it in the darkness. She followed the abandoned railroad tracks, until a light appeared far down the subway tunnel. The noise caused by her fight with the beast would have alerted anyone near of her presence. She strode forward, confident of who would be waiting for her.

Further down the abandoned tunnel, she came to the source of the light. An odd-looking craft sat haphazardly on the subway rails in the middle of what looked like a makeshift camp. The glow of lanterns hanging from rafters cast an eerie softness over the strange machine that brought back forgotten memories of a time before Natascha's life was torn apart.

An antiquated printing press, complete with flywheels and cranks, sat atop a flat platform of polished wood and shiny gold metal. A typewriter from a bygone age sat on a low podium in front of a plush leather chair at the center of the craft. Four monitors angled toward the control panel so the driver could see all screens at a glance. Natascha recalled seeing rough blue-prints of such a machine many years ago on a workbench in a secret laboratory that she was not supposed to be in.

Next to the fifteen-foot machine, a raven-haired woman knelt on the running board. She wore a short black jacket with a white frilly blouse and dark slacks tucked into high boots. Mordecai's soldier stood nearby with a gun leveled at Natascha. The other three new arrivals slept on the ground, their heads rested on the packs, oblivious to the Raconteur's presence.

The black haired woman laid her wrench down to clean her hands with a rag. "Natascha, darling, it's been too long," she said without looking over. "How was your encounter with Gyri?"

"Your beast is dead, Mother," Natascha said. "It attacked me, and I could not reason with it."

"Gyri was a hybrid of a wild boar and an ox, dear," her mother replied, standing up. "Never much potential in the way of brain capacity, despite Doctor Moreau's noble attempt to lift him up the evolutionary ladder. You haven't said if you liked the design of my greatest invention."

"It's lovely," Natascha quipped and slowly drew her Peace-maker. "So, you finally solved *Qui Li Jong's Theory of Perpetual Distance*?"

Her mother turned to her and smiled. "I knew you would

appreciate what this machine represented." She sounded actually emotional for a moment.

"Then I have to ask you," Natascha said, "how are you capable of drawing enough energy to jump such distances?"

"It draws its power directly from the ley-line. But, unfortunately, you have to unravel the line before you can redirect it. The cost of that, sadly, is the ley-line itself."

A low growl came from behind Natascha. She spun around and raised her damaged Peacemaker. A shadow crouched in the darkness behind her. A wolf as big as a prehistoric cat stalked out of the blackness. Two more of Doctor Moreau's obscenities of nature flanked the beast.

The first looked like a hyena-pig hybrid, tusks jutting from a doglike face. It waddled forward on two stubby legs, then fell forward on its long front arms. The last creature that appeared was a cross between a lumbering bear and a massive silverback gorilla, whose simple presence exuded a brutal strength.

"Mother, why can't we ever just talk?" Natascha asked. She backed away from them, her Peacemaker held ready. The weapon had enough charge left in it to take down two, maybe all three. She hoped.

"I go by *Lady Absynthe* these days, my dear," her mother answered.

"That's sounds a bit over the top, don't you think?" Natascha sighed. "Who are you running from now?"

"The list is long and distinguished," her mother responded with a laugh.

"And now you're working for Mordecai Davos?" Natascha continued.

"Mordecai does not own me or my beautiful Portalith Machine," Idalia replied. "I am merely a hired gun, always searching for new streams of revenue to fund my next scientific experiment. Mordecai pays very well. Besides, he freed me from Lazaranth Prison. What price can we put on our freedom?"

"Close friends of mine died at the hands of Mordecai's people," Natascha snapped back.

"That is unfortunate," her mother said. "But we are scientists, dear child, and our scientific curiosity overrides everything else. My machine mirrors the ley-lines, drawing power from them to replicate their twisting of time and distance. Those that suffer for the sake of science are of little consequence when compared to discovering a way to move across the Mythic Cosmos unhindered by distance. I thought you, of all people, would be impressed by that. Your father would have been."

"And you're using it to help a madman!"

Her mother smiled. "Oh, sweet one, aren't we all a little mad?" She finished cleaning her hands and tossed the rag into a toolbox.

"Father wasn't," Natascha countered. "He was a good man and would never have let such a dangerous machine fall into the hands of someone like Mordecai Davos."

Her mother laughed. "You did not know him as well as you think you did. Your father was the only man I will ever love, and the only person I ever opened myself up to. But he had his sins too."

Natascha took a small, cautious step toward the Portalith Machine. The motion screen inside her gas mask registered eight individuals around her, five humans and three beasts. Then she picked up another presence that remained in the deep shadows beyond her mother's machine. Something she had yet to see.

Idalia Devi gave a low, menacing chuckled that Natascha knew all too well.

# Chapter 15
# Into the Eye of the Serpent

"What are you doing here, mother?" Natascha asked. She needed to stall for time until she could pinpoint the final unknown entity. If she knew her mother, it would be the most dangerous of her pets.

Idalia let go a laugh. "I was hiding in Lazaranth under an alias. It was quiet, so I could think. Decide what to do next."

"You were hiding inside Lazaranth Prison?" Natascha scoffed. "Who was after you?"

"That's not important, my dear," Idalia replied. "All that mattered was no one would ever find me there. Mordecai Davos somehow learned of my Portalith Machine, and came to me inside Lazaranth with an offer. He would free me from my cell and give me protection from those looking for me in exchange for use of the Portalith."

"And now you're his little lap dog?"

"Hardly," her mother scowled. "I told him no one but myself will ever pilot it and since the machine was hidden where no one would ever find it, he would need me to retrieve it. He didn't like that answer and it's been a bone of contention between us ever since."

"So why is he tearing up old archives?" Natascha said. Her patience grew short. "What is he looking for?"

"Again, not your concern." Her mother smiled in the way she did when she knew her vagueness bothered Natascha. "All I can say is, once Mordecai finds this little goo-gaw he's looking for, he will take Rogue Destiny from those who now control it. Now, please remove that infernal gas mask. Let me see your beautiful face after all this time. I never understood your father's insistence on you wearing it."

"I'm fine, thank you," Natascha said. Her hand slipped into her coat pocket. She had enough somnambulic gas capsules on her to drop everyone in the room. But her enemies were too spread out to guarantee she could get everyone at once.

"That's how it's going to be, then?" Lady Absynthe said. There was a genuine sadness in her voice. "Very well." She raised a hand. The three creatures moved in around Natascha. She was ready for them.

Natascha released the *dissipating mist* that made Doctor Enigma ethereal and ghostlike. The green mist floated up around her as the wolf leaped with a roar. The bared fangs would have caught her in the throat if they had made contact. As it was, the beast passed through the gaseous form of the Raconteur, landing on the ground next to the rails in a tangle of limbs. It whirled back around at Natascha as the massive ape-bear lumbered at her.

Natascha shot the monstrosity with the Peacemaker, hoping the weapon hadn't taken too much damage from her fall. The ray-gun belched an arc of electricity at the creature. It convulsed from the voltage flowing through it. The hyena-pig gave a high-pitched, laughing cry and rushed forward.

Something hit the ground at Natascha's feet. She glanced down to see a silver disk the size of a half dollar. It exploded in a cloud of pink gas and sparkles that intermixed with her own green mist.

"You forget yourself, my darling," Idalia said. "Your father and I worked together on the design of Doctor Enigma's gadgets, so I know your secrets. It was only a matter of time before the Raconteurs showed up and I wanted to be ready to welcome you."

Natascha looked at her mother in disbelief as something solid hit her in the side. She flew across the railroad tracks, entangled with the hyena-pig.

Idalia Devi continued talking in a pleasant tone. "I knew even then that your father and I were never meant to last. We were too different." Natascha strained to hold the snapping jaws away with both hands. The beast chomped at her throat like a rabid dog. Idalia walked over and ripped the gas mask painfully from her face.

"You were the only thing we did together that turned out good," she said wistfully. "The only thing I am still proud of. It saddens me it has come to this."

Natascha rolled onto her back, holding tight to the creature's throat. She pulled her boots up under her and heaved with all the strength in her legs to push the beast away. The creature struck the front of the Portalith machine and howled in pain.

She searched for her Peacemaker. It lay on the tracks ten feet from her. She dove for it, grabbed it, then climbed to her feet. "Call them off!" Natascha ordered. She pointed the weapon at her mother.

"Enough!" Idalia barked loudly. She raised her hand and all three of the creatures stopped where they stood. "Natascha, it does not have to be like this."

Natascha backed away from the three predators. "Yes, mother, it seems it does."

"Very well," Idalia answered. "You are as beautiful and

strong-willed as ever. A lily among the briars. But I cannot let you interfere with my ambitions, not when I am so close to success."

There was movement in the shadows to her right. The wedge-shaped head of an enormous snake rose from the dark and swayed in front of Natascha. The serpentine figure glided smoothly into the light. Its long body stretched over fifteen feet, covered with dark green, mottled scales that seemed to ripple as it slithered toward her. It was a snake in all aspects except for the human-like torso and arms.

The Raconteur raised her Peacemaker, but before she fired, she was caught by the eyes of the snake. Her willpower faltered as the serpentine pupils locked on hers. She fought to pull the trigger, but her muscles went limp under a power that was not her own, that stripped her of her ability to resist. The Peacemaker slipped from her fingers. Natascha stood immobile, drawn deeper and deeper into the emerald eyes of the terrifying creature.

The body of the serpent curled around her, possessive yet not touching its prey. The head swayed hypnotically as the reptile's long tail twitched cat-like behind it. A shiver ran down Natascha's spine. Her muscles refused to respond to her commands. The gaze paralyzed her entire body. It felt like she was falling into a black abyss, although she knew she had not taken a step from where she stood.

Something slid along the side of her boot, curling about her ankle. It took a moment, but Natascha realized it was the serpent's tail. It wound around both her feet. She wanted to scream. She needed to scream, but the commands she sent her body remained unanswered. She could not move an inch.

The snake's head came in close to her face, never breaking eye contact. Natascha remained trapped in her own body, in a dimension of blackness where nothing mattered but the giant serpentine eyes engulfing her. All she could see were the slits of the two pupils that threatened to devour her whole. There was nothing else, only her and those eyes. Everything else was varying shades of gray and black. The only sound was her mother's distant voice, far away and dreamlike.

"I always feared one day I would be forced to move against your father, so I created weapons to counter every one of his fanciful gadgets. You call yourself a scientist, but you still have much to learn. I am truly sorry it came to this, my sweet Natascha. I had hoped you and I would never have to go up against one another."

Beads of sweat rolled down Natascha's forehead, stinging her eyes. Her jaw muscles locked and ached from being unable to relax them. The muscles cramped in her face and neck. The terror of not being able to move, to protect herself, was almost more than she could take. Just like when she was a child.

Natascha had never allowed fear to control her. Her father had taught her that as a young girl. If someone can make you fear, they can influence your actions. Let them kill you before they control you. In the mystical halls of Shangri La, she had trained her mind. She learned that there was always an alternative to giving in to fear, even if it meant running away. Something she had done many times before.

"That's enough, Maquna," Idalia commanded. "I believe she gets my point." The serpent pulled its eyes from Natascha's, and the Raconteur felt the hypnotic control of her body release. She dropped to her knees, dazed and exhausted. She raised her head and saw her Peacemaker resting on her mother's lap. The snake, Maquna, slithered up to the machine next to her.

The people Natascha had followed to the subway tunnels stood behind Idalia. The Moreau beasts spread out around her.

"You are so much like your father, always fighting unwinnable causes."

"You're not the one who found him dead!" Natascha spat.

"How many times must I insist I had nothing to do with his death?"

"Until I believe you," Natascha muttered.

"You and he were always so close," Idalia replied, a touch of venom in her tone. "I never understood why you chose to follow his hollow crusades to thwart evil instead of exploring the darkest secrets of creation with me. You and I would have been magnificent together."

She lifted the Peacemaker and pointed it at Natascha. "I think it's time for you to go, child. Mordecai will be here shortly, and he does not have the affection for you that I do."

Natascha struggled to her feet, her head still spinning from the serpent's mesmerizing gaze. She saw her mother's thumb slide the gauge to its highest setting. The hum from the Peacemaker increased.

"Do not come after me," Idalia said. "Do not try to harm my Portalith or attempt to take it from me. And please give Gideon Dumas a message. Tell him we are coming to take the City, and there is nothing he can do to stop us. Mordecai Davos has a coalition of powerful allies. The Raconteurs have no idea who they are up against. There will not be a second warning for you, my beloved daughter."

"But Mordecai still has to find what he's looking for first," Natascha interjected.

"Yes, he does, and that gives you time to rethink your allegiances, my dear. You do not want to be standing in our way when the reckoning comes."

"I'll stay with the allegiances I have. Thank you."

Idalia gave her a hollow smile. "We both loved you very much, I hope you know that." Natascha thought she saw a tear well up in the corner of her mother's eye. "I will leave you with a final word of caution, my dear. No one involved in this is as they seem. Remember that one truth. It may keep you alive."

A smarmy-looking man appeared in the light. "Mordecai sent me to let you know to prepare to leave, ma'am. The Raconteurs have located us, and we need to depart immediately." He looked at Natascha. "Oh, I apologize. I didn't know you were in the middle of something."

"Mr. Porter, please finish loading my things into the Portalith," Idalia said with a sly smile. "She was just leaving."

"This is not over, mother," Natascha said. She braced herself for what she knew was coming next.

"Now that is something we can both agree on," Idalia said. "I fear this war between us will never be over until one of us has joined your father in death. Goodbye for now, sweet daughter of mine."

Idalia Devi pulled the trigger of the Peacemaker, and a multi-colored beam of electricity struck her daughter. A jolting flash of pain coursed over Natascha. The last thing she remembered was the complete lack of emotion on her mother's face before blackness took her.

# Chapter 16
# Down the Rabbit-hole

Ren walked between Addison and MacGregor with his hands tied behind his back, still in the guise of Doggs Borland. The night air was frigid. Crystalized ice hung in the fog under the gas lamps lining the street. The leader of the soldiers, Silium Cinque Niner, led them out onto the dark boulevard in tight lockstep, ready to respond to any threat that might arise. Behind them, Mordecai followed with Tomas at his side. The Grimm Jester floated at their shoulders. Claymore and Dark Angus brought up the rear. The cowboy's heavy stride echoed off the cobblestones.

Ren's group was the last to leave the bookseller's shop. Smaller groups had left before them, spaced apart at fifteen minutes intervals so as not to draw attention to themselves. An armed soldier escorted each group to prevent any further desertions.

Under normal circumstances, self-preservation was paramount to the trickster. In any other situation, he would morph into anything, large or small, that would get him out of this predicament. But as it stood, he could not shape-shift in front of witnesses without ripping his mission apart at the seams.

The group walked along the empty streets past a wide canal. Ren was careful to stay on his feet, despite the occasional shove from behind.

"This is as good a place as any," Mannford Addison said. "We'll catch up with you in the subway." He and MacGregor grabbed Ren by the arms and led him up the incline to the bridge. Mordecai's group continued on through the dark streets.

Ren watched the rest of the group disappear into the fog. Claymore didn't glance back. Halfway across the stone bridge, Addison peered over the side. He pushed Ren back against the bridge's stone railing and raised a revolver to his face. "This is what happens to traitors," he growled. MacGregor stood behind them, looking up and down the bridge for any possible witnesses to the execution about to take place.

The real Doggs Borland was a great slug of a man, over-weight with sloth-like movements. The person currently impersonating Doggs Borland was not. Ren dislocated his thumbs and let the ropes slip from his wrists. He grabbed the gun with both hands, twisting it away from his face. Addison was a big, muscular individual who didn't expect any resistance from his bound prisoner. Ren disarmed Addison in one fluid movement. He flipped the pistol around and shot Addison in the left boot. The sound echoed into the still night air mixed with Addison's scream.

Ren spun to the surprised MacGregor and pointed Addison's gun at him. The man raised his hands. Ren relieved him of his firearm and tossed it into the river. He motioned for MacGregor to stand next to Addison. Ren smiled savagely before giving Addison a hard kick in the chest. The bodyguard flipped backward over the stone parapet of the bridge and landed with a splash in the water below.

"Remove your coat," Ren instructed. "Along with the shirt, boots, and pants." MacGregor slumped against the stone support and began undressing as Ren studied his facial details. When he finished, Ren hogtied him with his own belt and covered his face with a handkerchief so he wouldn't see what Ren did next.

Ren quickly dressed himself in the criminal's clothing, not taking his eyes from the bound man at his feet. This was not the Pithy Fool. He was in his element, and a dustup with a couple of low-level lackeys was just what he needed to remind himself of the reason he was there. He threw Dogg's clothes over the railing.

Until now, this job had felt like a burden to him. Nothing but an obstacle to keep him from finding Claymore. But now he was with his old partner again. The familiar rush of adrenaline welled up in him. He was back in the hunt, one of the good guys, and he would go through each member of Mordecai's entourage to get to Claymore if he had to.

Ren needed a new disguise, and MacGregor was perfect. Doggs Borland's face had outlasted its usefulness. Now the trickster needed someone higher up the food chain in Mordecai's hierarchy if he was going to help Claymore.

He left MacGregor tied up on the cold stone pavement and ran after the other outlaws. He was glad to shed the extra pounds Doggs Borland carried. MacGregor was younger and more athletic than Doggs, and Ren made good time down the street. Addison mentioned they were headed for a subway line, but he had no idea where that was. He had to catch up with Claymore and the others before they left him behind.

Three blocks ahead, Ren saw Mordecai's group. He found Claymore among the crowd and reached them as they turned off the major thoroughfare onto the steps leading down into an underground railway system.

They walked through the dimly lit corridors of the subway until Mordecai halted at the edge of a construction area. Mannford Addison removed a large panel of plywood from the boarded up wall, revealing another tunnel. Claymore stepped away from the others.

"Well, I guess this is where I leave you," he said to Mordecai.

"Very good," Mordecai replied. He nodded to the Grimm Jester to join Claymore. "Complete your task and return to camp quickly."

Claymore followed the Grimm Jester across the underground station to the deep shadows on the far side. Ren fought the urge to run after him but knew if he revealed himself, it would not help his partner's situation.

Silium Cinque Niner motioned the two soldiers next to him through the opening. Mordecai and Tomas followed, then Ren and one by one the others filed through.

A short walk brought them to the entrance of an abandoned subway tunnel. They climbed down from the elevated platform and continued down several rows of train tracks to the rest of Mordecai's followers. A lady in a black coat and high boots was packing up equipment and loading the items into an odd-looking machine. Ren caught the scent of Doctor Enigma's ethereal mist. Natascha had been there recently. He searched the tunnel but saw no sign of her.

"Are you prepared to leave, Lady Absynthe?" Mordecai asked. "We have been found out and do not have much time."

The lady in black set the toolbox she held down and turned to Mordecai. "I am, but I have warned you we are pushing my machine too hard. I have made temporary repairs, but I desperately need parts to make the machine whole again."

"We are returning to camp," Mordecai answered, not looking at her. "You can make full repairs once we are off this world. But we need to leave. Those chasing us are relentless."

He turned to Tomas, and they began speaking in low tones.

Lady Absynthe stormed across the room into the middle of their conversation until her face was inches from Mordecai's.

"And what if my Portalith Machine gives out halfway through the process of creating a new line?!" she spat, pointing at her precious creation. "The line could collapse out from under us, and we would all fall into the airless void and die. That machine is the greatest achievement in the history of Rogue Destiny, unparalleled in its power and reach," she spat. "It bends time and space to my will. Nothing like it has ever been built before."

Mordecai stared at her with contempt in his eyes. "Did you not assure me that night in Lazaranth prison, when I released you from your cell, that you had access to a machine that could transcend reality? One that would make my search simple and quick. One that could not be tracked?"

"And that is exactly what I have delivered," she countered. "You did not say we would be jumping from one Book after another in a futile search for some little bauble. I have kept us ahead of any pursuers, but even my Portalith has its limits."

"I should say it does," Mordecai said. "Your device has left a trail, and now our enemies are amassing against us as we speak. We were tracked to this world, and now we must take extreme precautions to make sure none follow us further."

"I have moved us across eleven worlds and millions of miles of distance these last few weeks," the woman said. "No one else could have accomplished that. No one! The Portalith was not designed for such intense use, and I will not risk it being damaged further."

"This is not open to discussion," Mordecai said dryly.

"Maquna, to my side!" Lady Absynthe commanded. From the shadows near the machine, a serpent with a human-like torso came into the light. Its eyes were as cold as death, yet somehow mesmerizing. Ren felt drawn to them and forced himself to look away. A forked tongue flickered in and out as the creature stopped next to the woman.

"Yesss, my lady," Maquna hissed, with a slight bow of the head, never removing its gaze from Mordecai. Rogue Destiny's most dangerous criminal averted his gaze and nervously shifted his stance.

Behind Mordecai, the cowboy straightened to his full height and stepped to his leader's shoulder. The room became deathly quiet. All eyes were on Maquna and Dark Angus as they sized each other up in the thick silence. Silium-Cinque-Niner and his five soldiers raised their weapons behind Mordecai.

Ren watched the scene play out with amusement. Everyone was about to kill each other, leaving him alone with this wondrous machine. Unfortunately, he couldn't allow that. He didn't know where their camp was or how to work the machine. He needed Mordecai alive to get back to his hideout, and it appeared only this woman could lead him there.

Lady Absynthe smiled coldly. "Without me, you have no one to operate the Portalith machine."

Mordecai paused for a moment, then nodded. He seemed to realize the position he was in and said nothing more. There was a notable change in the criminal's calm demeanor. Ever since Claymore had revealed the Raconteurs were closing in, there had been an overt anxiousness in Mordecai's body language that had not been present before. He returned to his conversation with Lady Absynthe.

"I apologize," he said. "I will make it a priority to collect the parts necessary to fully repair your portal machine. Now, may I ask if we are able to make one more stop before the return jump to camp?"

"I believe I can make that happen," Lady Absynthe said, sliding a hand down Maquna's scaled neck. "Where are we headed after that?"

Tomas handed her a piece of paper. "It's a horror novel called *Surviving a Bad Romance on the Eve of the Apocalypse*. A story for juveniles, but extremely dangerous, nonetheless. According to separate journal entries, Tomas has deduced Harper Bellweather passed through there several times. Where better to hide something of valuable?"

Lady Absynthe read the details on the paper. "I will get us there," she said coldly. She pulled on long black gloves and placed a pair of goggles on her forehead.

"Thank you, M'Lady," Mordecai replied.

"What about those following us?" Tomas asked.

Mordecai smiled. "I've decided to go through with our scorched-earth contingency plan," Mordecai said. "We will burn this world to dust so no one can follow us further."

# Chapter 17
# Hard Detour

The expression on Tomas' face was one of puzzlement and shock. "But you just assured Claymore we would not do that," he said.

"I will deal with Claymore when the time comes," Mordecai retorted. "He is a useful pawn for now."

Mordecai Davos glanced at the people around him, looking past Ren. "Dark Angus, can I have a moment?" The imposing cowboy followed Mordecai across the tracks, away from everyone.

Dark Angus stood dutifully listening to whatever instructions were given to him, though Ren couldn't hear what was being said over the noise. Ren picked up his heavy pack, causally working his way closer to the cowboy and Mordecai until he was within earshot of their conversation.

"Once She has been taken care of," Mordecai said, "there will no one be left to stop us from completing our quest. Asher Grey will not be expecting you. Eliminate her quickly and make for the nearest rabbit-hole. Take Porter and three others loyal to our cause, along with two soldiers, Cyg-Tens and Cyg-Fiver. Once it is done, meet us at camp."

Dark Angus turned away without a word and motioned the two cybernetic soldiers to follow him. They looked to Silium-Cinque-Niner for instructions. The cyborg nodded his permission, and they fell in behind Dark Angus as he picked several others from the crowd.

Ren recognized one man as Marcellus Barczok, a killer and smuggler that Claymore had put in Lazaranth years ago. The second man was an ambling gorilla of a man called Killian Boyd. Dark Angus pointed to another man. He was short and stout with greasy hair, a couple of missing teeth, and still wore his striped Lazaranth Prison uniform under a heavy coat. His name was Iker Gholson. The final man he didn't recognize, but Mordecai had referred to him as *Porter*. He was a small, mustached man with an air of distrust about him. All four men followed the two soldiers and Dark Angus up the subway tunnel.

Ren wondered what power Mordecai held over the most lethal members of his entourage. He knew nothing about Dark Angus, and even less regarding the Grimm Jester, but both obeyed Mordecai Davos without question.

Lady Absynthe climbed aboard the portal generator and settled into the pilot's chair. The snake, Maquna, crawled in after her and curled into a ball hidden from sight behind the seat. She began typing on an antique typewriter. With each clack of a typewriter key, several directional displays appeared on each of the four monitors around her. Her eyes jumped from screen to screen. She grabbed a lever on her right and pulled it down with a clunk. The engines of the machine hummed to life and a soft wind whipped up in the confined area.

She adjusted her goggles and typed furiously on the keys of the typewriter in front of her. Long gloved fingers danced over the keys like a concert pianist. The antique typewriter's clickety-clack of the keys echoed out over the sounds of the engine. The crowd of onlookers backed away as the swirling air around them grew stronger.

The hum increased as the surrounding ground vibrated. The eight globes rose on the half-sphere at the back of the machine. Each hung in the air over the Portalith, then spun in erratic patterns over the machine. A long, wide swathe of emerald light appeared across the ground, disappearing down the subway tunnel. The line passed directly under Lady Absynthe. Ren had traveled his share of rabbit-holes to know the glow of a ley-line, the life veins of the universe. Ren took an involuntary step backward, mesmerized by the sheer amount of power being harnessed in front of him.

The whine of the portal machine's engine hit a crescendo, and the entire platform rose from the ground. Lady Absynthe pulled a black lever on the console and the flywheel began turning. The green of the ley-line turned blinding white.

Ren put a hand up to block the glare as a small swirling circle appeared beneath the machine. Sparks of color flew off the spinning sphere as it grew and lit up the dark with a prism of colors, like a hundred rainbows after a storm. The colorful effect faded a moment later, leaving only a gaping hole.

The ground under the Portalith cracked, and a large rift opened. Lady Absynthe guided the portal-generating machine down into the hole it had just created.

Mordecai, Silium Cinque Niner, and Tomas were the first to disappear down the rabbit-hole after her. Others followed in single file. Ren waited his turn, ready to enter the next world. He was near the back of the line, with only a woman carrying an oversized pack behind him. Two of the soldiers stood at the opening. Their guns were out, making sure no one slipped away from the group.

Ren shouldered his pack. The edges of the circular opening burned with the smell of burnt paper. He walked down the slope into the soft green light of the ley-line. The portal doorway emerged into an underground passageway of concrete and steel. He adjusted his eyes to the darkness and could see they were standing in the maintenance tunnel of some modern city. Large pipes and heavy wires ran the length of the tunnel.

The portal machine sat a short distance off. Mordecai was talking to Lady Absynthe as the last of their party entered this new world. Something still troubled Ren, but he could not put his finger on it. Mordecai's words to Dark Angus came back to him.

*"Asher Grey will not be expecting you. Eliminate her quickly and make for the nearest rabbit-hole."*

Those words played on the trickster's thoughts. *Asher Grey?* He had heard that name before. Why was it important? Then it came to him.

He stopped in his tracks. The woman walking behind slammed into him. The oversized bag she was carrying came off her shoulder and spilled notebooks and journals on the ground.

"Watch where you're going!" she yelled.

Ren dropped his heavy canvas bag and bent down as if he was going to help her pick up the journals. He unbuttoned his vest and shirt instead.

*Asher Grey.* The *Logos Personae.* The Chosen One of this world.

Dark Angus was on his way to kill the her. If the cowboy succeeded, Natascha and the others would perish along with the rest of this world's millions of inhabitants. There was no time to contact the Raconteurs. He was on his own and had to prevent the murder of the one person who kept this world turning.

Two soldiers stood near the portal opening, staring at their new surroundings. Ren hoisted the heavy pack to his shoulder and pushed past the woman who was collecting the fallen notebooks. He swung his pack into the closest soldier and ran for the doorway back to the world of *The Gaslight Adventures of Asher Grey*.

Ren pulled his shirt off and shifted into a raven, flying across the threshold into the world he had left moments before. Bullets tore up the tunnel behind him. He had expected to reenter the subway tunnel under Old London. What only moments before had been a doorway from one literary world to another was now a dark tunnel that seemed to grow longer the further he flew down it.

The smell of rotting vegetation filled his senses. It took a second before Ren realized what had happened. He was inside the ley-line, seeing it in its true form for the first time. The after-effects of the portal machine had left the mystical line an unraveled, dying husk. The tunnel was circular, like a rabbit-hole, but the walls and floor were rough and uneven. A musty organic odor filled the air. It smelled of decay.

Ren had traveled hundreds rabbit-holes during his time with the Raconteurs. And with every one, it only took a step through the doorway to enter the new world. Some rabbit-holes were nothing more than a round hole in the side of a hill or under a Wayward tree. Others lay at the bottom of a wishing well or behind a waterfall. Sometimes it was even a plain-looking door standing by itself in the middle of a forest.

The trickster did not have time to ponder the physics of what was happening. He flapped his wings harder, traveling swiftly down the passageway, when something occurred to him. How far did this tunnel go? He desperately hoped it was not the thousands and thousands of miles that separated worlds. After what seemed liked far too long, he saw a dim light at the end of the rabbit-hole.

Ren flew through the subway tunnels and out into the deserted streets of Old London. Daylight was slowly spreading over the city. Ren searched the fog-shrouded boulevard for the man they called Dark Angus. The grinding sound of an engine trying to start echoed down the quiet street. He shifted back to his true form, landing lightly on the wet cobblestones, and broke into a run. The vague silhouette of a man walking toward the sound of the engine came into view.

He came up behind Marcellus Barczok and gave a sharp whistle. The man turned, meeting the trickster's eyes with his own and morphed into a mirror image of the Marcellus' scarred face and stocky frame.

The real Marcellus Barczok stared back, open-mouthed at the sight of his own doppelganger. Ren took advantage of his hesitation and punched him in the throat to prevent him from crying out. He got an arm around the man's neck, covering his mouth with a hand and dragging him into the shadows of a nearby doorway. Another punch to the face knocked him unconscious. Ren quickly dressed in the man's outer clothes, coat and bandana, boots and buckled on the gun belt. He left Marcellus where he lay and ran down the street, searching the foggy streets for Dark Angus and the others.

He continued toward the engine sounds until he saw a large pickup truck and the ghostly forms of people standing around it. The hood of the vehicle was up and a man in prison garb sat behind the wheel, trying to get the motor to start. Dark Angus stood back in the shadow of a sky bridge connecting the buildings, unmoving and silent as a monolith. He slowly turned his head as the disguised trickster approached. The two soldiers watched Ren walk up.

The grungy little man named Iker Gholson jumped out of the cab with a wrench in his hand, cursing under his breath. "I hate steam power," he grumbled as he leaned under the hood. "Never made any sense to me."

"You have to charge the solenoid before the motor will turn over," Ren suggested.

Gholson stepped back. "Fine, you do it then!" he spat.

Ren climbed into the high cab and fiddled with the knobs in front of him. He found a silver button under the dash and pushed it in, holding it for thirty seconds before turning the ignition key. The engine coughed, then rumbled to life, belching huge plumes of smoke into the air from the vertical pipes attached to the side of the truck's cab. Ren climbed out. "See? Nothing to it."

"Slide over, I'll drive," the greasy-haired convict snapped, stepping onto the running board to climb into the cab. Dark Angus grabbed the back of his jacket and pulled him down. The small man fell to the ground.

"What was that for, ya big oaf?" Iker yelled and scrambled back to his feet. "I answer only to Mordecai, and I said I was driving."

Without warning, Dark Angus drew his pistol and shot him in one smooth motion. Iker flew back and landed in a heap on the cobblestones. The gunshot echoed off the tall brick buildings around them. Dark Angus holstered the pistol and turned to Ren.

"You will drive," he ordered.

"Well, it looks like he won't be accompanying us any further," Porter said looking at Iker with a smirk.

The shape-shifter stared at the cowboy, then slid in behind the wheel. "Where to?"

Dark Angus got in on the passenger side. He pointed to a group of towers in the distance. "There," he rumbled. "That is where we will find a flying craft."

# Chapter 18
# Back into the Light

Natascha woke to pure darkness. Something covered her face, a sensation of gossamer-thin cobwebs tickling her skin. Her mother's silken scarf. It lay draped gently over her like a burial shroud. A warning to stay out of her affairs. The faint scent of perfume lingered in the air. She gave an involuntary shudder and pulled the scarf off. She hated her mother's macabre sense of humor.

The blackness surrounding her was complete, with no sound except the slow drip of water echoing in the dark beyond her. The cold, damp air told her she was still in the subway system where she had fought her mother's pets and been attacked by the serpent creature, Maquna.

The Raconteur pushed herself off the cold concrete, shivering in the damp air. She was disgusted with herself for allowing her mother to distract her so easily. Her body still tingled from the effects of the Peacemaker. Her own weapon used against her, she mused. Not one of her finer moments. How long had she been unconscious? Were the others looking for her?

Her gloves were missing, along with her trench coat. She

searched the dark for her gas mask and weapons, but found nothing. The coat contained an arsenal of tactical weaponry. Her mother knew that, so of course they had to be taken from her. She sat up, gingerly testing for injuries. Besides a throbbing headache and sharp pain in her shoulder, she felt strong enough to stand.

Her body trembled as she climbed to her feet. Not from the cold, but from the remembered sensation of Maquna slithering around her. She couldn't shake the feeling of the monster's tail coiled around her ankle, the creature's eyes holding her helplessly in its gaze. It was all in her head, but she still shuddered at the memory. It felt like dozens of snakes still squirmed over her naked skin. She had never experienced the loss of all her basic motor skills before. With one last involuntary shiver, she fought to calm her mind. There was still too much work to do.

She couldn't allow herself to give into the imaginary fears her mother always conjured against her, especially when she was a young child. It never failed to throw her off her game. She had always known their worlds would one day collide. When she met Maquna again, she would not be caught so unaware.

Her temples continued to throb as she slipped the false heel from her boot off and pulled out the small round disk hidden inside. She held it in her hand until the warmth from her palm caused its face to glow. The light pushed back the blackness around her and helped to remove the dark shadows shrouding her mind.

She was at the edge of a concrete platform overlooking what seemed to be in a different tunnel of the long-abandoned subway line. After replacing the heel of her boot, she scanned the area with her light, trying to determine which way to go. Both directions looked the same, with no point of reference to indicate where she was. There was a slight breeze from the left tunnel. It smelled less stale than on the right, so she turned that way. Soon, she came across boot prints in the slimy mud and followed them.

The ordeal with Maquna still lingered, but that fear was not the issue. The real problem was the possibility of running into Mordecai's people while she was in hostile territory with no weapons.

The footprints led back to the tunnel where the body of Gyri still lay on the tracks of the underground railway. The blackness crushed in on her. Farther on, the scent of ozone and burnt paper filled the air. It grew stronger as she reached the abandoned section of the subway tracks where she had found her mother. The area was in shambles, with random debris everywhere. The spot where the portal engine had sat was now a huge smoking hole that looked identical to the one that had led her into this world.

Her mother and the criminal madman she worked for were gone, along with the curious machine that could bend time and space. But now there might be a reluctant shape-shifting trickster hidden among their ranks. That meant the Raconteurs could go home, their mission now complete.

Natascha searched through the debris for her coat and gas mask but found neither. Her mother had left her alive out of some twisted sense of affection, but she would never be so stupid as to risk Doctor Enigma following her down the rabbit-hole. Her mother's deepest fear was losing control of her technology to Gideon Dumas and the authorities of Rogue Destiny.

She retraced her steps down the tunnel to the barrier separating the construction from public access and ducked through the hole in the wooden barrier. The sound of railway cars rumbling to a stop reached her as a few early morning commuters waited along the platform to board.

The Raconteur took the stairs that led out of the subway into the early morning light. The fall air held a bite, so she stood there a moment, letting the sunshine warm her bones. Traffic on the streets was minimal, telling her the hour was still early. Overhead, large airships passed above the city, throwing their shadows across the streets and buildings. Natascha watched them, waiting for her body to lose its chill. She needed to find Medesto and the others. No doubt they were searching for her, but Old London was enormous. Logically, they would approach the locals for help.

Once the sun warmed her a bit, she made her way toward the Raconteurs' safe house, contemplating whether to tell Medesto about her mother's involvement in all of this. With the loss of her gear, they would want an explanation about what had happened.

Natascha reached a small grocery store that fronted as the field house an hour later. She entered the grocer's shop and gave the clerk her credentials. A tall elderly woman came out of the backroom, and they shook hands. Medesto had left hours ago, but the young man working the front counter offered Natascha a ride back to *Bad Mojo*. The long walk to the slipstream would have done her good, but she had already made the others wait long enough. At least their mission had been successful. Ren was among the enemy, and she could not return to Rogue Destiny fast enough. She decided during the car ride she would tell no one about the humiliating defeat at the hands of her mother and her pets.

*Bad Mojo* sat where she'd left it, the landing lights on and the engines quietly rumbling. She climbed out of the horse-drawn cab and stomped up the ramp, exhausted, saying nothing to anyone. She hoped they would see her sour disposition and have the courtesy not to ask questions.

Everyone watched her head to a supply cabinet. She pulled down a suitcase containing her back-up equipment. She opened the top to see a gas mask lying on a neatly folded overcoat. Next to it was a shiny Peacemaker holstered in the Raconteur's standard leather belt. She took small consolation in the fact she kept a spare mask and coat onboard any slipstream she might travel on. Closing the suitcase, she looked around, noticing the gnome was not there.

"Where's Medesto?" she asked.

"He's in the cockpit with Sinjin," Charley said. "Something is up, but he wouldn't say what. Are you okay? Where's your coat?"

Natascha gave the young tech a forced smile and nodded. "I'm fine. If you'll excuse me." She picked up the suitcase and slid into the lavatory, locking the door behind her. Setting it down on the counter, she opened it, unfolded the long coat and shook it out.

Once she slid her arms into the sleeves and fit the gas mask on, she felt a weight lift from her. The feelings of vulnerability and inadequacy disappeared. She pulled on the thick elbow-length gloves and checked the functionality of her equipment. The back-up coat was no substitute for the one taken from her, but it would do until she got back home.

The encounter with her mother left her shaken and unsure, like most of her childhood. But now she was no longer Natascha Devi. She was the deadly, unpredictable, mysterious Doctor Enigma. A girl needed to keep up appearances.

There was a knock on the door. "Natascha?" It was Medesto.

Natascha pulled her mask off. "What?" she answered.

"I need to talk to you. We have a problem."

# Chapter 19
# Journey to the Clouds

The inside of the truck's cab was silent as Ren navigated the winding cobblestone streets of Old London toward the towering sky docks. The truck's manual transmission and gear shift were something he was not familiar with. Every time he changed gears, the grinding of metal accompanied it. He glanced over at the passenger side where Dark Angus sat. The wide brim of the cowboy's hat shadowed most of his expressionless face. Menace and rage hung heavy over the dark figure.

The trickster had been around enough death to recognize he was a disciple. He could almost taste it in the air around him and his skin crawled with a sense of impending violence.

The drive to the sky docks seemed to take an eternity. All Ren had to guide him was the visual image of the distant towers. Several wrong turns later, the road finally opened onto a vast parking area. Ren stopped the truck off to the side and everyone climbed out, concealing weapons in duffle bags and under their coats. A dozen towering sky ports disappeared in the gloom above them. The port was heavy with commerce, even at the early hour. Delivery trucks were busy being loaded and unloaded between every tower. Dirigibles of varying sizes hung in the air, waiting for permission to dock.

Dark Angus led the way, his broad frame carving a path through the morning crowd as the people parted before him. Ren and the others followed. The soldiers brought up the rear, carrying their gear as the cowboy headed toward a lift at the base of the closest tower. They crowded onto the freight elevator with several dock workers and their pallet of goods. A young girl, not yet out of her teens, held a toolbox and stood at the back of the lift. She was fresh faced, wearing dirty green work overalls. She smiled sheepishly at Ren from under the cap and goggles on her head. The steel gate closed, and the lift rose.

Dark Angus turned to one worker. "We need to hire a ship to take us east over the sea."

"Where you looking to go?" the man asked.

The cowboy pulled out a wrinkled map and pointed to a spot in the middle of the Atlantica Ocean. "There," he grunted.

"*The Forbidden Island of Antediluvia*?" the clerk said, choking on the words. "Ha, good luck finding someone to take you out there. That place is cursed."

Dark Angus turned away without a word and waited in silence until the lift stopped. When the doors opened, he strode onto an open deck, his boots heavy on the steel-grated floor.

A voice behind Ren spoke. "You looking for a ship to take you to the *Forbidden Island*?" He turned to see the young woman from the elevator. "I know one who'll do it for a reasonable price," she said, pointing out the wide curved windows. "It's docked there across the way. Tower 7. Ask for the *Sky Zephyr*. My father's the pilot and I'm first mate."

Ren was reluctant to get someone so young and innocent looking involved in what he knew was going to end up a bloody mess. He admired her spunk but shook his head. "We'll find someone else. Thank you for the offer, though."

"No one else will go out there," the girl insisted. Ren ignored her and walked after Dark Angus. He looked back to see her scowling at him, but it did not bother him. He had just saved her life.

Dark Angus stopped at the front desk of a company called *Skyways Air Shipping* and thrust the map in front of the clerk at the counter. The man stopped his paperwork and peered over his glasses perched on his nose at the paper in the cowboy's hand.

"I need a ship to take me to this island," Dark Angus rumbled. He was getting more agitated by the second.

"Sorry, we don't haul passengers, only freight and livestock. You'll have to find—"

Dark Angus reached over the counter and caught the smaller man by the throat, lifting him from the floor. "What you haul does not concern me," the cowboy said darkly. "I said I need your ship to take me to this island." The air grew thick, and the shadows deepened around him. His black duster bristled with dark electrical sparks.

Ren glanced at the growing crowd. The bustling crowd started slowing down and staring—Dark Angus was drawing too much unwanted attention to them. The people with Ren were all killers, and none of them would hesitate to open fire on the crowd if they felt threatened. Ren could see this turning into a bloodbath at any moment.

He laid a hand on the arm of the cowboy's coat, expecting the feel of rough denim. Instead, it was like touching cold, oily cloth and not quite solid, like the sleeve and coat were part of the thick arm underneath it. Even odder, the wrinkles in the coat's material did not move in a natural way. It was as if the duster was inseparable from the arm underneath it.

Dark Angus slowly turned to look down at Ren. He could

feel the terrible heat of his wrath shift from the man he held aloft to himself. Ren pulled his hand away.

"Not here," Ren hissed. "If we make a scene, we'll never get you your ship."

"He's right, Angus," the man called Porter said. He touched the cowboy's arm and pulled his hand away immediately. "You start shooting up the place and we'll never reach the *Logos Personae*."

Dark Angus stared down at them. His brooding expression was indiscernible. He set the trembling clerk back down and stepped away from the counter. "Then find me a flying ship," he growled.

Ren scanned the crowd for a way to calm the situation before Dark Angus exploded into deadly violence. He spotted the young woman who had offered her father's ship, the *Sky Zephyr*, still watching them.

"Stay here," he said. The young girl met Ren halfway as he approached. She set her toolbox down at her feet.

"Believe me now?" she asked with a smirk. "Told you no one goes out there except *us*."

"Your ship still for hire?" Ren asked. The girl stared back into his eyes with fierce pride and determination.

"Yes, it is," she said. "The *Zephyr* can get you there, but the price just went up. I'm Lizbeth Larocque. My father is Syd Larocque, captain of the *Sky Zephyr*. I need to be getting back to let my father know we got work. We can leave within the hour. Tower 7, Level 19, Bay 237."

Lizbeth picked up her toolbox and walked away. Ren watched her cross the sky bridge toward Tower 7 until he lost her in the crowd. He knew any ship they chartered would have crew members he would need to protect, but their safety was secondary to stopping Dark Angus from reaching the island. This young girl would now be in the mix, and Ren would have to get them out of the way when the shooting started. Lizbeth reminded him of Charley, full of life and potential. She was not expendable—that would be a problem. It was not her fault she was being pulled into this. He found Dark Angus tormenting another desk clerk about a charter to the *Forbidden Island*.

"I found us a ship," Ren said.

The cowboy glowered down at him. "Show me."

# Chapter 20
# The Sky Zephyr

Bay 237 was one of eight docking stations on Level 19 of Tower 7. The *Sky Zephyr* was held aloft by a massive air bladder and secured to the dock with heavy ropes. The young woman met them at the gate. She had changed clothes from ragged overalls to a practical work shirt with denim jeans and heavy boots. She welcomed them aboard. Dark Angus strode purposefully onto the dirigible, glancing over the wide deck and taking in every detail.

The ramshackle dirigible was fifty feet long and a third of that in width. She was older and more weathered than any of the other ships around her, but seemed sturdy enough. Presently, an older man ambled out of the wheelhouse. He was a lean figure, with a working man's demeanor and shaggy gray hair hastily pushed under a work cap.

The captain of the *Sky Zephyr* held out his hand to Dark Angus, but the cowboy ignored the gesture. Porter stepped forward and shook the outstretched hand. He gave him a greasy smile. "A pleasure, I'm sure," he smirked. "Shall we get this going?"

Syd Larocque gave a broad smile. "Yes, we shall. But first I have contract papers ready to sign in the wheelhouse. All we have to do is settle on the fee."

Dark Angus pulled a pouch from under his coat. "This will be sufficient for your services."

The dirigible captain took the pouch and weighed it in one hand, then untied the top. His eyes widened when he looked inside. He pulled out a gold coin to look at more closely.

"Yes, that is adequate payment," he said—the hand holding the coin trembled. Lizbeth grabbed the money pouch and coin from her father. She dropped the coin back in and pulled the drawstrings tight.

"Shall we catch the wind?" she said. Ten minutes later, the *Sky Zephyr* pulled gracefully out of her dock and into the skies over Old London. Ren remained in the guise of Marcellus Barczok, standing at the door of the wheelhouse as he watched Syd Larocque navigate through the treacherous skyways over the city.

The air around the sky ports was thick with traffic as they headed southwest out away from the city. The hull shook in smooth rhythm with the chug of the airship's engine. A thick trail of black and gray smoke trailed behind the vessel. Lizbeth sat on a stool to one side of her father.

The wheelhouse had its walls crammed with memorabilia from a lifetime of hauling goods. Old photographs pinned all around the front window, along with a child's homemade crafts. A clay figure of a frog and a handmade coffee cup perched on a small table, holding down the corners of the map. A dried rose hung from a string in between the front windows, likely a symbol of love found, or love lost.

Ren leaned against the doorjamb and watched the captain handle the controls of his ship with the precision of experienced hands. He took in everything in front of him and locked it into his memory in case the need ever rose for him to navigate the airship. Ren grabbed the door to steady himself as the ship sharply deviated course to avoid a large garbage scow moving across their path. The weightlessness of the ship's movement played tricks on his legs.

He had flown a couple of dirigibles before, so the ship's navigation was familiar. The left side of the control panel moderated the flow of gas into the giant bladder overhead. The other side controlled the steam engine vibrating under his feet. Then he realized he wasn't the only one watching how the captain navigated.

The man named Porter seemed to be familiarizing himself with how the craft operated, too. Ren didn't know if Porter was his first name or his last, but the smarmy little man had a nervous twitch and a smug mustache. His eyes were in constant motion, taking in everything around him, always with a slight smirk on his lips. He watched the captain's every move as Syd Larocque worked the ship's wheel, flipping switches and pushing buttons that controlled both the air bladder above them and the chugging engine below.

An icy wind blew across the open deck of the dirigible as they hit the open English countryside, eventually gaining an altitude of several thousand feet. Ren took a step inside the pilothouse to escape the harsh chill and assess his situation. The ship's captain and first mate were innocent, but their lives would be forfeit once they reached the island. The trickster would have to be ready to prevent it when that happened.

A gigantic shadow appeared behind him, filling the tiny wheelhouse doorway. The shadow Dark Angus cast was unnatural, engulfing more area than the laws of physics should have allowed. The young girl shrunk back against her father. He put a protective arm around her and held her close.

"How long to the island?" the cowboy asked the captain.

"We're still a hundred from the western coastline. After that, it's another 700 miles over the Atlantica to the Forbidden Island. At top speed and if the winds are with us, we should reach her by mid-morning tomorrow. Can't make the *Zephyr* go any faster than she can go." Dark Angus' expression remained unchanged. He turned and walked away without a word.

Ren saw Syd's hands starting shaking as he steadied the wheel. His brief interaction with the dark cowboy had an effect on him, as it did everyone. Their eyes met, and Ren wanted to reassure him he and his daughter were safe as long as he was there, but Porter was studying the three of them intently. Instead, Ren shrugged and said, "Just get us there as quickly as you can. Dark Angus is not a patient man." He left the wheelhouse and found the hatch leading below deck. If he was going up against this many dangerous outlaws, he needed to get a bearing on what he had to work with.

The cargo hold went nearly the full width of the ship and half its length. At the front, under the stairs, were the sleeping quarters with several tiny cots and a dinette set in the small galley. The actual cargo space echoed the financial woes of the *Sky Zephyr's* crew. The hold was empty except for a workbench and the tools needed to keep the dirigible flying. A series of chains and hooks hung from a winch connected to the beams of the main deck above a wide loading hatch. There was a wooden door at the aft end of the ship's hold. The deep rumble coming from behind it told him it was the engine room.

Opening the door, he found a windowless room with a large steam-powered engine. It seemed to draw its power from a strange, multifaceted crystal sealed in an octagonal compartment with thick inset windows on all sides. Tendrils of electricity stretched from the crystal to the windows and danced in erratic patterns. He closed the door and sighed. There was little down there to help him clear the ship of Dark Angus and his lackeys.

Discouraged, Ren grabbed a rough wool blanket from a cot and returned to the top deck. He found a bench across from the imposing presence of the dark cowboy, who stood motionless, staring out over the sea. Something about the massive figure told Ren he may have been human once, but was no longer. He searched his memory and felt he should know something about who this Dark Angus was, but nothing came to him.

One of the cybernetic soldiers climbed out of the hold, carrying a long duffle bag. Ren remembered her name as Cyg-Fiver. A half-cloak lay over one shoulder, concealing part of her metallic arm. She dropped the bulky bag on the deck, sat down on a bench, and unzipped the duffle. She fitted several segmented pieces together into a nasty-looking short rifle the length of her arm, then pulled out a clear cylinder and clicked it in place under the center of the rifle.

The projectiles inside the cylinder were small circular spheres, each the size of a pebble and filled with a bright fluorescent liquid. Ren guessed there were about thirty shots before the weapon would need to be reloaded. The second soldier joined her a few moments later. Ren knew her as Cyg-Tens.

Ren watched them from across the deck. They were nothing like the criminals who had escaped Lazaranth Prison. Both moved with the compact alertness of a trained soldier, constantly aware of their surroundings with spring-trap reflexes ready to react at the first sign of trouble. Cyg-Fiver glanced over in his direction before he ended his thought. They would be a problem.

The trickster was unintimidated by the distrustful glare he received from the soldier and decided it was time to get things rolling. Finding out what he could about his enemy was a good place to start. He approached Cyg-Fiver with a casual, unassuming gait.

As he reached her, she pulled a small handgun from somewhere on her person. It was no bigger than her palm, but looked lethal, nonetheless. "Step back," she said calmly, pointing the weapon at Ren's face without bothering to look up at him. She remained focused on the ammo clip in her other hand.

Ren raised his hands. "I just thought maybe we should coordinate our attack on *Asher Grey* before we find her tomorrow. I'm Marcellus Barczok."

"Nothing to coordinate," Tens said in a matter-of-fact tone. "We find the ship, kill everyone on board, and burn it out of the sky."

Ren crouched on the deck a few feet from the soldiers. "Is that going to be enough firepower to bring down a dirigible?"

She slipped the pistol back under her body armor and lifted the gun she had been assembling. "This is a plasma impulse rifle. I assure you, it will bring down a wooden airship in a matter of minutes. This will be over quickly, and we can return home to continue fighting in the Great Struggle."

"Where's home?"

Cyg-Fiver finally made eye contact with Ren. "I don't like being here, and I don't like talking to you. I have my orders. I do my job, then we can leave this accursed place."

Cyg-Tens removed the glove on her right hand with her teeth, revealing a metallic skeletal hand and arm that ended at her elbow. With the turn of a metal clasp and a twist, the arm came off. She fit the end of a gun into the empty socket until it clicked. A small red light on top of the weapon lit up. Her arm was now a weapon.

Then she pulled out the largest gun in her bag. It was sleek without being bulky—high tech with a sleek barrel and dangerous look.

"Hey!" she said, tossing the rifle to Cyg-Fiver. The other soldier caught it and checked the settings on the side before pulling off the cartridge beneath the stock to check the ammo.

Once she was done with her duffle bag, Cyg-Tens zipped it up. She picked it up and walked toward the wheelhouse, but stopped halfway and turned back. "Our homeworld is called Gaia 7. It's in the Book *Under a Blood Red Sun*."

Ren knew his charm would eventually break her down, even if he ended up with a bullet in him for his efforts. Most people just needed to feel unthreatened before opening up, apparently even mechanically enhanced soldiers. Cyg-Tens followed her comrade and disappeared from sight around the far side of the wheelhouse.

Something played at the corners of the trickster's mind. A soothing voice teased at the edge of his thoughts. Every literary world had a Muse of some type. A non-sentient force that guided the world's narrative. Some Muses were more aggressive than others, but all would take hold of you if you let them. Ren felt the Muse of this world pressing down on him the same way as the one in *The Crimson Masque* had.

This time, however, it took no effort to shut his mind and push the invisible presence away, like clearing away smoke with the wave of a hand. He wouldn't repeat the same mistake and succumb to Her influence again. His to-do list was growing longer by the minute. He had a world to save, a master criminal to stop and then figure how to bring his wayward partner back to the Raconteurs.

Ren found a spot away from the frigid night winds and huddled under a blanket, trying to ignore the cold. Lizbeth appeared from the hold, carrying two steaming mugs. She sat next to Ren and handed him one.

"This should warm us up a bit," she said cheerfully. "It's hot chocolate. Sorry, we're out of marshmallows."

"This will be fine, thank you," Ren said as he took a sip. The hot liquid warmed his mouth and throat as it went down. "Are we still on schedule?"

"The winds have been favorable. We should reach the island by late morning." The girl huddled around her cup of cocoa like it was a blazing fire. She stared across at Dark Angus, her expression shifting to cold fear. The cowboy in black stood at the railing like a dark monolith, gazing out over the calm sea below them.

"So what's so forbidden about this island?" Ren asked, trying to distract the girl from the menacing presence of the murderous cowboy.

"They call it *The Forbidden Island of Antediluvia* because of what you'll find there," Lizbeth said. "The entire island is covered in fog, with high mountains and deep valleys and inhabited by unspeakable things forgotten by time, primitive monsters and ancient horrors. We've run many expeditions out there over the years because the money's good, and no one else will go near it. Big-game hunters like to go there because you can hunt things you can't find anywhere else in the world."

"Why were you eager to take us there if it's so dangerous?"

"We're desperate for the money," Lizbeth admitted, then took another drink. "Since Mama died last year from the consumption, Papa's not been himself. Mama was everything to him. He's drinking again and disappears into the opium dens for days on end. I've been scraping up what business I can find. I love my father, but the business is about to go under. We're behind on the payments for the *Sky Zephyr*, and if we lose her, we'll be out on the street."

Ren sipped his cocoa. "How long have you been doing this?"

"Since I could walk. Back in the day, we had a fleet of five. Lost two ships to pirates and one in a storm. After Mama passed, we had to sell the other airship and let the crew go because times were so bad. Your party doesn't look like hunters, so you must be looking for the treasure?"

"Why do you ask?" Ren asked.

"We've brought several expeditions out there, hunting for a treasure that's supposed to be buried on the island. They say a cult worshiped a great beast called the *Shaaglamoria* for centuries before completely disappearing. It's rumored they left behind a king's ransom in gold and jewels somewhere among the ruins."

"What's a Shaaglamoria?"

"*The Worm-that-Devours-the-World*," Lizbeth said in low tones. "It's the beast that rules over the island."

Ren finished his cocoa and handed the cup back to her. "Thank you."

"My pleasure," she said with a yawn. "I'm turning in. Dawn will be upon us before we know it. Try to get some sleep."

Ren didn't know if he should tell her the truth or not, but decided the girl needed to know she and her father were in danger. He thought about what Claymore would do in this situation and glanced at Dark Angus and the soldiers to make sure they were not overheard.

"Lizbeth?" he whispered.

She turned around with a quizzical look. "What?"

"When we get to the island tomorrow, things are going to get nasty. These people I'm with are dangerous."

Her eyes went wide. She looked at Dark Angus across the deck, then at the cyber-soldiers. "What do you mean?"

"We aren't here hunting any treasure," Ren said. "They mean to kill someone of great importance to this world. I'm here to stop them. Once the shooting starts, you need to hide with your father somewhere below deck until I take care of things up here."

He wasn't sure why he had warned her or why he cared what happened to two strangers he would never see again once he left this place. He'd have to think about that. This was not the time nor place to develop a conscience. Lizbeth nodded and went into the wheelhouse with her father. Ren heard the click of the latch as the door locked.

Ren kept to himself the rest of the night, never taking his eyes off the pilothouse and the two people he'd said he would protect. He ran a dozen scenarios through his head about how he should stage his attack, but the reality of his situation was sinking in. He was up against five heavily armed criminals and his only course of action would be to take them down one by one without alerting the others. That would not be easy.

The air grew colder as a cloak of blackness settled in over the world. He tried to sleep, knowing he would need all his wits about him once they reached their destination. He dozed off from time to time, wrapped in a thick blanket as the freezing, high-altitude air ripped through him.

# Chapter 21
# The Forbidden Island

Ren woke to a bright morning sun in a clear blue sky. He was cold and sore from sleeping on the bare deck and stood up to stretch the kinks out of muscles, wondering about the possibility of some breakfast. Then reality itself shifted around him.

He caught himself on the railing as a flash of vertigo washed over him. It passed as soon as it appeared, but the trickster knew what it meant. The dirigible had crossed into the narrative bubble of the Story. They were close to the *Logos Personae* now.

Dark Angus stood in the same spot he'd occupied all night, unmoved by the rippling change in the reality around them. He could have been a marble statue. There was a horn blast from the wheelhouse. Ren looked out over the front of the airship, across the blue seas of the Atlantica. In the distance he could see the high mountains of a mist-covered island, just as Lizbeth had described it.

*The Forbidden Island of Antediluvia.*

Ren scanned the deck for the position of everyone on board. Captain Syd and Lizbeth were still in the small wheelhouse with the door shut. Killian Boyd and Porter came up out of the hold, strapping on gun belts and buttoning up shirts. Cyg-Tens and Cyg-Fiver followed them. Each soldier carried their long duffle bag over one shoulder. A half-cloak with military insignia lay over their other shoulders, concealing their metallic limbs. Dark Angus strode to the wheelhouse and Ren rushed after him. He knew this was it. Once things were in motion, there was no going back.

As the giant cowboy approached, the door opened, and a grizzled face appeared. "Just the man I was coming to see," said the captain of the *Sky Zephyr*, a big smile on his unshaven face. "The winds were kind, and we're hours ahead of schedule. That's your island right over there." Dark Angus ignored him, pushing past without a word, and took the rifle off its mounting over the front window. He handed it to Killian.

"It is time," the cowboy rumbled. "Take them below."

"I'll do it," Ren said, stepping in front of Killian. He drew his sidearm and motioned the captain and his daughter out of the wheelhouse. "Come with me."

Syd looked at the pistol being pointed at him. "What is this? I got you to the island," he protested. "Who's going to fly you back?"

"You don't need to worry about that," Ren said. He glanced at Lizbeth, and as if reading his mind, she took her father's arm and led him to the cargo hold. She stopped at the steps and looked Ren in the eye, uncertain and defiant. He dared to give her a quick wink. She held his eyes a moment longer before taking a deep breath and going down the stairs after her father. Once the two reached the bottom, Ren motioned them deeper into the hold. Syd stepped in front of Lizbeth.

"I won't let you hurt my daughter!" he said, his voice trembling. "She is all I've got. Kill me if you want to, but leave her alone! Take my ship. I don't care." There was a desperate pain in his words. Losing his daughter would destroy him.

"I'm not going to hurt either of you," Ren whispered. He stepped back and put a finger to his lips, then fired a shot into the floorboards of the ship. He waited a moment for effect before he fired a second shot.

"Hide yourselves and stay quiet," the trickster ordered. "I'll be back when I can."

"Where are you going?" Lizbeth asked. "Don't leave us down here alone!"

"Up on deck. I'm going to get you your ship back."

The young girl grabbed his arm. "You're going to get yourself killed."

"I'm the hero here," Ren replied with a smile. "I'll be fine." He started up toward the stairs as Killian Boyd appeared at the top. Lizbeth pulled her father in to the shadows under the staircase.

"Is it done?" the big man asked as he stomped down the steps.

"Of course," Ren answered. "I know how to shoot someone." Killian ambled past him, not content with that answer. The trickster let him.

"Good," Killian said. "We need to dump the bodies, so they don't stink up the ship when the day heats up." He glanced around, looking for the two bodies, but stopped when he saw Lizbeth and her father crouching under the stairs.

Ren leaped on Killian from behind and got an arm around his throat. They struggled on the steps. The larger man tried to pull him from his back. Ren fought to maintain his choke hold. Killian slammed him against the wall, but Ren held on tight, kicking the bigger man's leg out from under him. They tumbled onto the cargo hatch.

Killian landed hard on top of Ren, jamming a hard elbow into the shape-shifter's side. All the air in Ren's lungs rushed out, and his grip loosened. They rolled over, Ren trying to keep the upper hand, but Killian punched him in the face.

Lizbeth and her father came out from under the steps. Lizbeth edged around Ren and Killian to a panel of buttons. The combatants separated, and Ren rolled onto his feet. Killian got to his knees and drew his gun. Lizbeth stood behind him. She caught Ren's attention, pointing to a hooked winch hanging above the trickster's head. Ren glanced down to see that he and Killian stood on the closed cargo hatch. He raised his hands in the air.

"I couldn't kill them!" Ren argued. "The old man knows where the treasure is hidden!"

"Treasure?" Killian growled, his pistol leveled at Ren, but his voice was piqued with curiosity.

"You think we came out here just to kill some girl?" Ren asked. "Dark Angus has been holding out on us. He and Porter are in on it together. I heard them talking. They're planning to kill us, so they won't have to split the gold." Ren looked up the stairs with a show of fear and sadness in his eyes. "Fiver and Tens are probably already dead."

Killian gave him a hard look, his common sense wrestling with his avarice. Then he shook his head. "You're lying. There ain't no treasure, Marcellus," he said with a smirk and raised his gun. "That's the problem working with a bunch of criminals. You can't trust any of them."

There was a clank and Ren jumped up as the cargo doors dropped out from under them. He grabbed the hitch hanging above him with both hands. Killian Boyd disappeared out the open hatch. Lizbeth pushed the handle to the hatch down. The cargo doors slowly closed. Ren dropped down with a sigh of relief.

"Do you have anything down here you can defend yourselves with?" Ren asked. Syd rushed to a cabinet and opened it with a set of keys from his belt. He pulled out an antique bolt-action rifle.

"That will have to do," Ren said as he reloaded his pistol. "Shoot anyone who comes down here if it's not me." He started up the stairs.

"Are you sure you don't want some help?" Syd asked as he loaded a single round into the rifle. He dropped more shells into his shirt pocket. "You had trouble with just the one, and Lizbeth will not be up there to help you."

Ren rolled his eyes and ignored the comment. This was exactly why he avoided personal interaction with people. They never understood his methods. He preferred people admire him from afar, as anonymous faces in a crowd who kept their opinions to themselves.

He ran up the stairs of the ship's hold, ready to end this one way or the other, and emerged onto the mist-covered deck of the *Sky Zephyr*. High mountainous crags stretched to the sky on either side of the airship. The temperature outside had risen considerably in the short time he had been below deck.

Dark Angus stood at the door of the wheelhouse, watching Porter pilot the dirigible through the mountains. Both soldiers kneeled at the railing of the ship's bow, their weapons at the ready.

Ren yelled and Dark Angus turned at the sound. He shot the gunslinger in the chest. Dark Angus staggered away from the doorway as Ren emptied the gun into him. The cowboy dropped to his knees, then fell forward onto the deck. There was no blood splatter on the wooden planks, which Ren thought was strange, but his focus turned to the soldiers. He dove to the deck as shots whizzed by him.

The trickster rolled behind a water barrel to reload his

pistol. As he pushed the bullets into the cylinder, he peeked over the rim of the barrel to check the whereabouts of the cybernetic soldiers. They had spread apart from each other, firing at Ren as they ran. Cyg-Tens crouched behind the rigging that held the blue air bladder to the ship. Cyg-Fiver disappeared around the wheelhouse.

Ren returned fire, careful to conserve what ammunition he had left. The soldiers' fire splintered the wooden deck and barrels around him. This was going better than he dared hoped. Two of the enemy down and three to go.

A massive shadow fell over him. He looked up and a steel hand grabbed him by the throat, lifting him from the deck. Ren choked out a cry of surprise and stared into the empty, emotionless eyes of Dark Angus. The trickster fought for oxygen as the cowboy's iron grip slowly crushed his windpipe. The brute grabbed Ren's pistol before he could fire and pulled it from his grasp.

Porter peeked out from the wheelhouse, watching for where the bullets were coming from. "We're coming up to an airship!" he shouted.

The increased pressure on Ren's throat stopped. Dark Angus turned to look toward the front of the ship. Ren twisted his face around to see what the cowboy was looking at. Two hundred yards ahead of them, barely visible through the mist, floated a dirigible held aloft by a giant red air bladder. Ren made a desperate attempt to change his shape, but the lack of oxygen cut his efforts short. The cowboy pulled the trickster close.

"Who are you?" he rumbled. His breath was as putrid as an open grave.

"I'm the hero," Ren choked out. The corner of the cowboy's mouth curled into a cruel, bemused smile. It was the first emotion Dark Angus had displayed, and Ren did not like it. The hand around his throat tightened, and his vision blurred. Ren's head grew light, and darkness overwhelmed him.

"No, you're not." Those were the last words Ren heard before Dark Angus threw him over the railing of the airship.

# Chapter 22
# The Monster Beneath the Lake

Ren opened his eyes to the sound of himself crashing through the jungle canopy, bouncing off one branch to another, before free falling for several heartbeats. He slammed to a sudden stop in something soft and thick.

He pulled his face out of the mud and looked around. He found himself lying at the edge of a misty lake. The flapping of wings and skittering of unseen things filled the shrouded jungle all around him. He fought to get upright, but the claylike muck weighed him down and clung to his clothes. With a great effort, he pushed himself to his knees. He had returned to his true form.

There was a noise above him. A whistle. He looked up as a barrel crashed through the branches and splashed into the lake a hundred yards out from the shore. Moments later, there was a muffled explosion under the water, followed by a gush of water that rose fifty feet into the air.

The lake settled as gentle waves lapped up onto the shore. Beyond the explosion, the water churned and rippled to life. A writhing mass of snake-like appendages broke the surface, then disappeared as something big moved across the dark waters.

The surrounding ground shook. A giant gray foot slammed into the ground next to him. It was round and the width of a tree trunk. Ren backpedaled through the mud to avoid getting crushed as the long neck of a sauropod lowered its head to the water.

Several other dinosaurs joined the first one to drink at the water's edge. Ren struggled to get to his feet and out of the way of the enormous animals. Marcellus Barczok's mud-caked clothing weighed heavy on him as he waded through the thick muck toward the tree line.

He glanced back at the shoreline as the surface of the lake exploded. A huge tentacle whipped out of the churning water, wrapping around a dinosaur's neck. The animal cried out as it tried to free itself, but two more curling appendages reached out and pulled the poor beast into the water. The water turned blood red as the thrashing dinosaur's movements slowed. Moments later, the lifeless carcass was pulled out to the center of the lake by the thick tentacles before it disappeared into the gloomy depths.

Ren stared at the scene playing out before him, trying to comprehend what had just transpired. The doomed sauropod was a hundred feet long and weighed several dozen tons, yet whatever lurked beneath the surface pulled it down into the dark water with little effort.

He decided it was time to leave and peeled off his mud-covered jacket. It landed with a loud smack in the muck. He slipped out of the suspenders and ripped off the button-down shirt. Once his arms were free, he shifted into a black raven and flew free of his clothes.

The black bird was an easy shape to assume. The form fit him like a second skin. With a flap of wings, his body was out of the binding clothing, and he took flight. He ventured a quick look back, only to see another sauropod wrapped in tentacles and being dragged into the water. The desperate honking of the animal filled the jungle. The remaining dinosaurs panicked and stampeded back to the protection of the dense jungle. He turned away from the carnage and focused on getting through the trees to the airships.

He flew up through the giant twisted branches, dodging clusters of huge, exotic-smelling flowers, each with a blossom the size of an automobile. One reached out and snapped at him as he flew past. He corrected his course to avoid it and almost hit a humongous snake sunning itself on a nearby branch.

Following the thin beams of sunlight through the foliage, Ren broke the jungle canopy in time to see the *Sky Zephyr* closing in on the other airship. Dark Angus stood silently on the deck, slowly waving a distress flag. Behind him, a plume of smoke rose from the ship's hold.

A man wearing a pith helmet stood at the railing of the other dirigible. *Wanderlust* was painted on the side in decorative lettering. The *Sky Zephyr* slowed as it approached. Next to the man wearing the pith helmet, a serious-looking, heavyset man stood holding a long gun. A third person, a woman, was priming an explosive charge at an open gate on the railing. The crew of *Wanderlust* appeared friendly but cautious to the newly arrived vessel.

"Ho, *Sky Zephyr*, are you in distress?!" the man shouted in a thick English accent across the gulf between the airships. "We heard gunfire. Is there anything we can do to assist?"

Ren realized the smoke was a ruse to allow the *Sky Zephyr* to get close enough to *Wanderlust* to fire on her. He yelled a warning to the man, but it came out as nothing but the caw of a bird.

The Englishman leaned farther over the wooden railing. "Sir, do you have wounded aboard? We have someone with medical training who can treat them!"

Dark Angus stepped up to the railing. An unnatural shadow spread out over the deck behind him. His deep voice boomed across the gap between the ships.

"Asher Grey!" the cowboy shouted. "Is she aboard your vessel?"

"May I ask your business, good sir?" the man in the pith helmet replied with proper English manners. Ren dove for *Wanderlust* as the *Sky Zephyr* came alongside, hoping to reach it in time. He didn't.

Darkness rose around the cowboy like a gathering storm, and he drew his pistols with lightning speed. The Englishman and the man at his side had no time to react before Dark Angus emptied his guns into them. They fell back onto the deck in a rain of blood. The woman setting the explosive charge rolled behind a barrel and returned fire with her sidearm.

Cyg-Fiver stepped next to Dark Angus. The plasma rifle in her hands gave off a series of 'poof' sounds as small projectiles strafed the side of *Wanderlust*. Each tiny orb burst open upon contact with the wood, splashing a luminous red and orange liquid across the surface that sizzled for a quick second before igniting into open flames. The fire grew quickly, spreading along the wooden vessel as if under its own power.

A man appeared in the doorway of the wheelhouse, and fired several times from a rifle. Bullets struck Dark Angus in the chest. He stumbled back, but raised his pistols and returned fire. The woman at the railing crouched and ran for safety. The man covered her with gunfire until she was inside.

Fiver shielded herself behind Dark Angus as the hulking man took several more hits. He grabbed the railing and sank to his knee. *Wanderlust* burned at a dozen different points. It was only a matter of time before the air bladder failed and the airship plunged to the ground.

Ren watched all of this play out as he dove toward the

airships, considering his best course of action. At the stern of *Wanderlust* sat an object with a large canvas draped over it. He couldn't tell what it was amid the flames and thick haze, but hoped it would be adequate cover from the gunfire. He landed behind it and morphed back into his true form.

Ren lifted a corner of the canvas and smiled. He pulled the cover away to reveal a shiny Gatling gun mounted on the deck. There was a strongbox next to it near the railing. Inside were a dozen neatly stacked two-foot long ammo clips. He grabbed one, fit it into the slot, and pulled back the release. The Gatling gun's base was well oiled and swung around with ease. Ren grabbed the hand crank on the side and turned it on the *Sky Zephyr*. Deafening gunfire thundered across the deck as bullets strafed the airship.

Cyg-Fiver and Cyg-Tens dove for cover, but Dark Angus was not so quick. He had just pulled himself back to his feet when the high-caliber bullets ripped through him. The giant figure staggered back. Ren turned the crank until the barrels of the gun rang empty, hoping the otherworldly gunslinger would finally stay dead. He pulled the empty clip out and tossed it aside. By the time he replaced it, the *Sky Zephyr* had turned away and disappeared into the thick mist.

The deck of the *Wanderlust* fell silent. Ren made a quick shift to one of his stock characters, the ne'er-do-well Axel Prospero. He grabbed a greasy towel from the strongbox and wrapped it around his naked waist.

The woman emerged from the wheelhouse, and the man with the rifle stood behind her. Both held their weapons on Ren as he stepped out from behind the Gatling gun with his hands raised, posing no threat.

"How did you get on board, and why are you wearing only a towel?" the woman demanded. She wore a leather vest fitted with ammo clips and pantaloons tucked into riding boots. The automatic pistol in her hand matched another holstered to her leg. Her western-style cowboy hat was curled tightly on both sides and pulled down to shade her eyes from the blistering sun.

Ren quickly fabricated a story to match the circumstances of his situation. These people were primary players in this world, and if they were on Asher Grey's ship, they would be among the Story's heroes. It was in their nature to help those in need. He could work with that.

"My name is Axel Prospero," Ren choked out. He leaned forward with his hands on his knees, feigning exhaustion. "I was a prisoner of those air pirates. They kept me locked up and naked in their hold, but I managed to get free when they attacked your dirigible. I swung to your vessel on a rope."

"What are air pirates doing out here?" the man demanded. "There's nothing of value on this island."

"They were hired to hunt down and kill someone named Asher Grey," Ren said. At the mention of the *Logos Personae's* name, the man and woman glanced at each other. They knew the name, which meant she was somewhere on board.

Ren realized if he was going to save Asher Grey, he needed these people to trust him. Like every good lie, there had to be just enough truth woven into his story to make it believable. He had just helped drive off the *Sky Zephyr* and prayed they would believe he was who he claimed to be. The last thing he wanted was to have to fight his way to Asher Grey. There was no time for that.

The man hurried across the deck to where their two dead comrades lay. He was tall and dressed in the same high boots and dark pantaloons as his companion. His slicked back hair left his rakish looks on display. Biceps bulged under the rolled-up sleeves of the crisp dress shirt he wore. He held a short-barreled rifle with an ornately carved stock.

"Where's Asher Grey?!" Ren shouted.

"She's below deck," the woman said impatiently. She followed the man and stood over her lost comrades.

"The air pirates could be back at any moment," Ren said. "We need to get her off this island."

"In due time!" the woman snapped. She and the tall man dragged the bodies of their fallen comrades up along the side of the wheelhouse, away from the flames. The woman kneeled and said a prayer over them as the man wrapped each of their dead comrades in a tarp. There was a look of deep pain on their faces when they turned their attention back to the fires raging all around them.

Ren dashed across the burning deck to the main hold. He tried to avoid the scorched areas, but still singed the soles of his naked feet. The wood planks cracked and buckled underfoot, weakened by the intense heat of the spreading fire. He had to locate Asher Grey before the entire ship went up in flames. He ran halfway down the stairs and jumped the last few steps. Timbers above him creaked as if ready to collapse at any moment. The airship's hold filled with smoke and flames, but through the haze he saw a female attempting to free a crewmate pinned under a fallen support beam. It was a young woman. "Asher Grey?!" he shouted.

The girl looked up at him. "Who are you?"

"If you're Asher Grey, you need to come with me!" Ren stated with a smile. "Trust me, I'm here to help."

"No, I'm not Asher," the girl answered, pointing behind Ren. "She is."

Ren turned to see the woman from the upper deck rapidly descending the stairs.

"You're Asher Grey?" he asked, bemused that in the confusion, he missed such an obvious twist of events.

"I am," Asher said flatly. "And I don't need saving, thank you."

"You need to get off this ship," Ren said.

"Not without my crew." Asher looked at the girl. "Tiana, where's Solomon?"

"He went down to check on the crystal," the young girl said. "What happened? We were in the middle of breakfast and there was gunfire. Now the entire ship is on fire!"

"Edmund and Wilson are dead," Asher said in a matter-of-fact tone. "This man drove off the ship that attacked us, but it could return at any moment." Her gaze darted to Ren. "We need to abandon the ship."

"Where's Sethen?" the younger girl asked.

"He's on deck getting the escape balloon ready," Asher replied. "Hurry, we don't have a lot of time."

Ren wove around the burning debris until he reached Tiana. Her eyes narrowed in distrust. But with the ship burning down around her, Ren knew she was in no position to refuse his help.

He slid past Tiana and bent down next to the trapped crewmate. He wedged his feet under the burning timber. With a grunt of effort, he lifted the beam high enough that Tiana could pull the man out from under the smoking support beam. Ren let it fall back and rolled free.

Tiana cradled the man's head in her arms, tears in her eyes. "Phillip, thank God you're alive." Phillip moaned and his eyes opened. Ren helped him to his feet. "Who are you?" the crewman asked.

"Just a helpful stowaway," Ren said.

Phillip looked at Tiana, who shrugged. "Okay, but that doesn't explain your lack of clothing," he said.

"Solomon!" Asher called out. "We're abandoning ship. Get deck-side!"

# Chapter 23
# Firefight in the Mist

Asher Grey led her crew to a winding metal staircase at the back of the hold, away from the flames and debris. Ren helped Phillip up the stairs and onto the smoke-filled deck.

"Wait here for Solomon, then get to the escape balloon," Asher commanded. "I have to get some documents." She disappeared to the wheelhouse. Phillip sat down on the deck, and Tiana tended to his bleeding leg. Ren stretched his aching muscles.

A mallet-sized hand grabbed Ren's shoulder, spinning him around. A crashing blow to his face from a metal fist sent him flying across the fiery deck. He looked up to see a giant of a man looming over him. Ren backed away, then realized the impact of the blow had broken his hold on the disguise. Axel Prospero was gone. He was Ren B'gatti again.

The behemoth stood over him, momentarily aghast at the sudden change in Ren's appearance. He hesitated for a heartbeat before he came at the shape-shifter again, his barrel chest heaving. The man had narrow hips and a powerful handlebar mustache that covered most of his cleft chin. He wore a pinstriped tank top that clung tightly to his hairy chest with skin-tight pants and knee-high black boots laced in white. The gears inside his metallic right leg and right arm whined when he moved.

Asher appeared from the ship's hold, with her leather satchel slung over a shoulder. "Solomon, don't!" she yelled. "He's here to help—" She stopped mid-sentence to gawk, open-mouthed at his current appearance and nakedness.

Ren struggled to get up as the burly man continued to circle around him, shifting his weight on the balls of his feet like a boxer, his hands up in a comedic fisticuffs fashion. "Foul demon, you will harm no one here!" he bellowed. His nostrils flared over his mustache as he threw another right hook at Ren's head.

The shape-shifter dodged the punch and landed three hard blows into his opponent's side. The big man was unfazed and returned the attack with a crushing left-handed uppercut that sent the trickster flying through a wall of flames. He landed hard at the base of the Gatling gun.

Ren had sprung back to his feet by the time Solomon found a way around the flames. The bull of a man came at him through the smoke and ash, his eyes ablaze with bloodlust, determined to finish the intruder. But Ren waited for Solomon to cock his metal arm back, then swung the Gatling gun around with all his strength. The enormous machine gun spun easily on its oiled tripod and caught Solomon in the back of the head, knocking the mustached man to the deck. He shook the blow off and pushed himself up with a roar.

Behind Solomon, the larger airship broke through the mist. The *Sky Zephyr* had returned. Cyg-Fiver and Cyg-Tens stood at the bow with their weapons ready to open fire as soon as they cleared the haze of fog.

"Get down!" Ren yelled. Tracer bullets ripped through the railing and along the deck of the smaller airship.

Cyg- Fiver focused her plasma rifle on the Gatling gun. Pops of glowing fire hit the weapon and the surrounding deck. Each one sizzled on contact, burning through any metal or wood it touched. The burning plasma spread across the surface of the ship at a frightening pace.

Tiana helped Phillip to the doorway of the wheelhouse. Blood trailed behind them. Solomon shielded his head with his metal arm, as bullets ripped up the deck around him. Bullets strafed across his back, and he collapsed on the burning deck. Gunfire erupted from the wheelhouse behind Ren. Asher returned fire on the *Sky Zephyr* while Sethen dropped his rifle to help pull Phillip to safety.

Ren raced to the mounted gun. He grabbed a magazine from the strongbox and slid it into the feeding mechanism on the top of the Gatling gun. The intense heat of the acidic plasma eating through the gun's metal burned his arm. It was more intense than anything he had ever felt, even though no flames were visible. The magazine finally clicked into place, and Ren took hold of the hand crank.

Solomon stumbled through the smoke. His bullet ridden body leaned against the Gatling gun. He shoved Ren away from the crank with a bloody hand. Something in his eyes was different. His rage was directed at the *Sky Zephyr* now and no longer at the trickster.

"Get the others off the ship," he roared. "There's an escape balloon under the front of the air bladder." Solomon turned the crank handle with a massive hand. The Gatling gun spat fire and death back at the other airship. Bullets raked across the airship, splintering the decks and railing around the wheelhouse. Solomon pulled the empty magazine out and pushed in another one.

The moment the Gatling gun stopped firing, both cybernetic soldiers stepped back into view. They rained bullets down on the *Wanderlust*. Solomon answered with another salvo of bullets, following the *Sky Zephyr* across the sky as it began to circle again.

The *Wanderlust* was losing altitude, and Ren knew one more pass from the *Sky Zephyr* would bring her down. Asher and Sethen ran out of the wheelhouse, watching airship in the distance.

"I have to get you off this ship!" Ren yelled to Asher.

"How? The escape balloon is gone," Asher replied. "There's no way to get everyone off safely."

"Not everyone, just you," Ren replied. "Don't ask me to explain, but you're too important to die."

Ren looked out over the top of the jungle canopy. They would have to hide down there until he could figure how to get Asher safely off the island. Nasty things waited among the trees, but they'd have to take their chances. *Wanderlust* was lost and would not be in the air much longer. To stay here meant Asher would die. If that happened, it meant the world itself would die with her.

Out to their right, the *Sky Zephyr* had completed her turn and was coming in for another pass. The airship was about a hundred yards out and closing fast.

"There's no time to argue," Ren said.

Asher gave an angry laugh and pushed him away. "I'm not leaving without my crew."

"You can't stay here!" he yelled. "You'll die!" The *Sky Zephyr* closed the distance between them.

"Then so be it!" she said defiantly. "There are worse things than death!"

In the distance, the sound of a technology not from this world echoed over the jungle. Ren recognized the roar of powerful Coldfire engines and turned toward the direction of the noise. It could mean only one thing.

*Bad Mojo* burst through the mist covering the island and

slammed into the side of the *Sky Zephyr* with the sound of rending metal and breaking timbers. The airship shuddered from the impact and pulled away from *Wanderlust*. Ren saw Medesto and Sinjin in the window of slipstream's cockpit.

"Time to go," Ren said. "Our ride's here. I promise I'll come back for your crew."

Asher pulled herself up to her full height. She was taller than the trickster's five and a half feet. "I told you I'm not going anywhere without them," she repeated, leaning against the railing favoring a bleeding leg.

Ren had to protect Asher Grey at any cost, even if she refused to cooperate. He sighed and shoved Asher over the railing. It wasn't the most heroic move, but Asher Grey was off the burning airship.

He dove off the airship after her.

# Chapter 24
# Of Monsters and Flying Monkeys

The impact of *Bad Mojo* slamming into the airship shook the Slipstream to its engine mountings. Natascha Devi crouched on the steps in full Doctor Enigma regalia. Next to her, Tempest held two long guns, ready to go topside when the order was given from the cockpit. They stood below a hatch leading out to the ship's observation deck.

Medesto's deep voice came over the intercom. "We're clear," he said. "Find the *Logos Personae*. Make sure she stays safe."

Natascha pulled the release handle and pushed the hatch open. She climbed out to the deck, followed closely by Tempest. The glare of clear blue skies, blinded her momentarily. She blinked until she could see the mist shrouded island below them. Mountain peaks broke through the sea of thick fog.

The collision with *Bad Mojo* left the side of the airship crushed in. It separated the two dirigibles and forced the *Sky Zephyr* to retreat. Tempest handed Natascha a rifle. Tempest raised her own and fired as the lofty blue air bladder sank into the hazy white beneath them. Natascha joined her, shooting indiscriminately before the ship disappeared. They were too far away to do any damage but wanted the *Sky Zephyr* to know they were a threat.

To their right, a smaller airship with the name *Wanderlust* written along its bow floated in place, listing to one side and on the verge of falling from the sky. The gas bladder sagged considerably, deflated and losing air in several of its internal chambers. Her decks were engulfed in flames and torn up by gunfire. Natascha spoke into the comm in her hand. "Sinjin, bring us in closer. We need to find a place where we can board."

"Understood. Hang on," Sinjin said. *Bad Mojo* slowly circled the burning craft so they could survey the damage. "Tell me where you want me to put her."

Natascha fervently hoped the trickster had kept the *Logos Personae* safe. She glanced at the sky. It remained a deep blue, giving no indication of any disruption in the flow of the narrative. That meant Asher Grey was still alive. This world's entire existence depended on the survival of that young woman. Her life mattered more than anything else's. That was the cruel truth of the universe. Natascha needed to get on that ship.

Her concerns disappeared moments later when she spotted two figures rise out of the misty shroud beneath them. It was a young woman being held aloft by what appeared to be a winged monkey. The woman struggled in the simian's hands, but his grip held her tight. As they drew closer, Natascha could see she was furious. Tempest raised her rifle.

"Hold on!" Natascha yelled. "I know that flying monkey!"

The airborne monkey flapped his wings in a slow rhythm as they got closer. He dropped his screaming passenger into the hands of Natascha and Tempest. They lowered her to the sky deck as the woman thrashed in their arms.

"Let me go! I need to get back to my ship!" Asher yelled. She tried to stand on her bloodied leg, but the pain forced to lean against the railing for support. She reached for her sidearm, but both her holsters were empty.

"We need to get you to the infirmary," Natascha ordered.

"No, take me back to my crew!" she yelled. "You don't understand! Something is terribly wrong! I don't belong here! I need to be with them!"

The winged monkey landed in a crouch on the deck behind them. He stood up, and the apish features melted away to reveal the exhausted face and naked body of Ren B'gatti. The feathered wings folded in and disappeared into his back, and the coarse fur covering him from head to foot receded into his skin. The shape-shifter's skin tones swirled in wild patterns for a moment, then settled into the color of ashen bones.

"Good work, B'gatti," Natascha said with a grin. The trickster's antics always amused her. "But aren't you supposed to be somewhere else, spying on someone?"

"Something else came up," he explained. "This is Asher Grey, the *Logos Personae* of this world. She's injured, but alive. I disarmed her while we were flying. Didn't need her shooting anyone. There are still survivors on the *Wanderlust,* and I have to get back over there."

Asher calmed herself. The young woman's breathing was heavy, her face pinched as she fought the pain. Natascha bent down to examine her bleeding leg.

"I need to speak to the changeling, please," Asher said softly.

"Ren?" Natascha called. He stepped over. Asher looked him in the eye. Ren stared back for a moment before the *Logos Personae* punched him across the face. He stumbled back while Asher lost her balance and fell to the deck. She pushed herself up, breathing hard.

"You had no right to take me from my ship!" she screamed. "Fly me back there now!" She hobbled after him, wincing whenever she put pressure on her wounded leg. Natascha and Tempest grabbed her arms as she lunged at Ren again. She kicked the empty air, trying to reach the trickster.

"Calm down, we're going back for your crew," Tempest said.

Natascha spoke into a small communicator in her hand. "Medesto, we have Asher Grey. She's safe, but there are others on the *Wanderlust*. We need to rescue them before the ship goes down."

*Bad Mojo* maneuvered alongside the *Wanderlust*. A ghostly figure appeared on the deck through all the gray smoke. A giant of a man stood at the railing, waving his arms and warning them off. The side of his face was red and blistered from the heat. His clothes were scorched and smoking. Blood from several bullet holes ran down his shirt. Natascha could not hear what he was shouting, but he was desperately motioning them away.

Asher leaned against the railing. "Solomon! Why is he... Oh, no." Her face went white.

"Sinjin, pull back!" Natascha shouted into the comm.

The slipstream's engines revved, and *Bad Mojo* tilted away from the burning airship. The dark silhouette of Solomon stood out against the wall of flames and smoke. He leaned on the rail with his head lowered. A second later, *Wanderlust* exploded in a thunderous fireball that engulfed the airship. The concussion of the blast knocked everyone on the observation deck from their feet.

Natascha covered her head as chunks of debris and burning wood rained down on the slipstream from the sky. Shredded bits of the air bladder floated like confetti. The flaming remains of the *Wanderlust* fell into the mist.

Asher's face was pale and frozen, her wide eyes filled with tears. "They're all dead." She sank to the deck, her entire body shaking with grief. Her head came up. She looked up at Ren. "See what you've done?!"

"You'd be dead too if it wasn't for me!" Ren shot back. "And your life is infinitely more important than theirs were!"

"Not to me it's not!" Asher screamed in his face. She swung at the trickster again, but Ren was ready and stepped out of her reach.

"Ren, don't," Natascha ordered. "This is not the time."

There was a cry, distant and barely audible over the engines.

"Quiet!" Natascha snapped. "Somebody's shouting!"

"Help!"

"It's coming from over the side," Tempest said. She was the first across the observation deck and leaned over the railing. "There's someone down there."

"Sinjin, slow down," Natascha said into her radio. "We have someone dangling off the side of the ship." *Bad Mojo*'s engines wound down, and the slipstream slowed to a near stop. Charley remained with the distraught Asher while Natascha and Tempest ran across the top of *Bad Mojo*. Natascha leaned out over the railing of the observation deck. Halfway down the hull, she saw a man clinging to the narrow ribbing on the side of the ship.

Natascha unlatched the top of a supply box attached to the deck. She fastened a safety tether to the railing and buckled the belt around herself. "Pull me back up after I have him!" she yelled to Tempest. She climbed over the railing, sliding down the side of the slipstream until her foot caught on a narrow lip of metal. She inched over within reach of the man and grabbed his free hand. His grip was weak, and he had difficulty getting a foothold, but with great effort she pulled him up to her. Tempest pulled them both up onto the observational deck. The man was bleeding through his shirt and could barely stand. Together, Natascha and Ren helped him sit down.

Asher limped over to him and hugged him close. "Sethen,

you're alive," she said. "I thought I had lost you! Were any of the others able to jump with you?"

Sethen shook his head gravely.

"How did you survive?" Asher asked. She put her hand on his cheek.

Sethen choked back a sob. He collected his thoughts, then raised his eyes and pointed at Ren. "I saw that one push you over the side of the ship. I ran to the railing to see his shape change into some sort of flying creature and stop you from falling. The next thing I knew, the crystal exploded. I leapt from *Wanderlust* without a thought. The concussive blast threw me into the side of this vessel."

Tempest came over to them. "There's no one else out there," she confirmed with a rare show of emotion. She bowed her head and turned her back to everyone.

"I can't believe they're gone," Sethen said. "Solomon, Tiana and Wilson, brilliant hunters. Alison and Edmund, two of my dearest friends." He pressed his forehead to Asher's and pulled her close to himself.

"You must hate me," he whispered to Asher, tears rolling down his face. "I abandoned our friends."

Asher took his head in both hands and kissed him. "Of course not. If you had stayed, you'd only be dead, too."

"I'm sorry for the loss of your companions," Tempest said. "But we need to get below deck before that dirigible comes back. Then we'll get you home."

One by one, they descended the ladder to the interior of *Bad Mojo*. Asher refused to let anyone help her or Sethen. Natascha remained on the observation deck, watching the darkening sky. There was a rumble that shook the air. It was not thunder, but more of a trembling of reality itself.

For a brief moment, all of creation crackled around the ship —the trees, the mountains, the very air itself was alive with an electrical charge. Lightning flashed in the distance, and bursts of red embers floated on the air. The clear blue sky rippled in the disturbance's wake. Then, letters and words appeared across the surface of the sky, like they were from a book.

"It's starting," Natascha said out loud to no one.

# Chapter 25
# Turning the Tide

Medesto stomped out of the cockpit of *Bad Mojo* and down the steps to the main hold. Even as events were spiraling out of control around them, he formulated possible remedies to this fresh problem. Nothing came to him. He walked up to Tempest sitting in a leather flight chair, applying a bandage to Asher's injured leg.

"I thought we were leaving," Charley said. "The *Logos Personae* is safe, and Mordecai is getting further away from us by the minute."

Asher Grey sat quietly, staring off into space and absent-mindedly fingering the pistol in her lap. Medesto didn't have time to worry about where she had found a firearm. She was safe for the moment. Sethen sat back in the chair next to her, his eyes closed.

"Not quite yet, Charley, but soon," Medesto said. "Where's Natascha?"

"Still on the observation deck," Tempest said.

"I need to talk to her," he replied.

"I'm goin' with ya," Raffles said. Medesto led the way up the steps, out onto the windy deck atop *Bad Mojo*. Natascha stood at the rail, staring at the sky.

"How far along is it?" Medesto asked as he walked up.

"Still in the early stages," Natascha answered. "Have you told the others?"

"Not yet. I wanted to talk to you first," the gnome answered with a glance skyward. He searched the gathering clouds for the coming firestorm. Ash had begun to fall like snow on the deck. Lightning flashed overhead and a slow rumble of thunder sounded in the distance. The wind was growing warmer and more volatile by the minute.

Raffles shaded his eyes against the lightning flashes. "A *Never-Never Event*, da *Big Goodbye*, da *Crucible Effect*. I seen too many o' dese befor'. We nearing da end of da story cycle, but da continuity broken, so da narrative not sure where to go next. Dat storm you see building up out dere is da world breakin' down in front o' our eyes. If we don' do sumthing 'fore we run out of words, it be da end o' everyting."

"Okay, let me think," Medesto said and rubbed his eyes. "We've been in worse scrapes."

"Have we?" Natascha replied quietly. The electrically charged storm moved in rippling waves across the sky and the number of red fire-bursts increased. "We have no idea how close to the end of the narrative we are, so we could reach critical mass at any moment."

The gnome glared at her, but before he said anything, the hatch opened. Ren's head appeared. "What's the holdup?" he asked, climbing onto the deck to join them under the darkening sky. "I saved the *Logos Personae*. Why're we still on this unforsaken island?"

"Asher Grey is out of harm's way for now," Medesto said. "But we have a bigger problem. The Narrative is stalled, and we can't leave until we figure out how to get it going again. If the Story doesn't find an ending, it will eventually implode in upon itself and burn up."

"So another *Crucible Event*?" Ren replied. "Just like in the *Angels of Avalon*?"

Medesto shook his head solemnly. "I'm guessing *Wanderlust* was vital to reaching that ending. Without it, the Story has lost its way." The gnome scratched his beard and stared at Ren for several heartbeats. "When you were in *The Crimson Masque,* you blended in with the Narrative. The Muse accepted you as a part of the Story without question. You didn't challenge the events in the Book but ran with them."

Ren gave Medesto a quizzical, uncertain look. "You want me to be Talbot Mundi again?"

The gnome shook his head. "No, but I am talking about playing kabuki theater. We take the place of the *Wanderlust* crew and give the Story an ending."

"Will that work?" Natascha asked.

"I have no idea," Medesto said. "But there's no time to try anything else. We need to find out what Asher Grey and her crew were doing out here."

"Den let's do dat," Raffles said.

Medesto led them into the hold of the slipstream. Tempest and the others looked up as they reached the main deck. Medesto went straight to Sethen and Asher. "How many were in your original party?" he asked.

"There were seven of us," Sethen said. He was shirtless and had bandages tightly wrapped around his chest. Small blotches of red stained the white linen. "I led the expedition. Asher was the tracker and guide. There were two hired rifles, the captain, and a crew of two. Why is that important?"

Medesto made a mental count of the Raconteurs. With

Asher and Sethen, they had seven. That was enough to replace the crew of the *Wanderlust*. Raffles was the outlier, but he was non-human, so he'd have to play mascot. He felt Asher's eyes boring into him.

"Who are you people?" Asher asked.

"That is a good question," Sethen said. "Where are you from? Flying around in such a strange ship. Are you French? You look French!"

"Yeah, we're from France," Natascha said, throwing a look at Medesto. "Can I ask what brought you out here? This place is called the *Forbidden Island* for a reason. Maybe we can help."

Sethen rolled his eyes. "Ha, I knew it!" he said with a laugh. "What you need to do is mind your own business and stop piggybacking on our expeditions. Find your own beast to hunt."

"So, you were hunting something?" Medesto asked.

"We came here to kill a monster," Sethen said.

"Like what I saw in the lake this morning?" Ren said.

"You saw the Shaaglamoria?" Sethen exclaimed, his eyes full of surprise and excitement. He stood up quick, flinching in pain. Asher grabbed his arm to help support his weight.

"If it's the big tentacled thing that has a taste for dinosaurs," Ren admitted. "Yeah, I saw it."

"Sethen, you should be in the infirmary?" Tempest asked. "With your injuries, these chairs cannot be comfortable."

"I'm fine, thank you," Sethen said. He winced as he laid back in his seat. Asher sat up in her seat next to him, pistol on her knee.

"You're not separating us," Asher said softly. "Sethen stays with me."

Sethen stared at the floor, lost in thought. "That's the monster we were searching for," he said with a grim smile. "We took the contract offered by the English government to search this island and destroy the *Shaaglamoria* after the first expedition disappeared without a trace. Over the past year, the beast has been terrorizing parts of England, destroying entire villages along the eastern coast. It's only a matter of time before it reaches one of the major cities, like Old London. Hundreds have died, and thousands more will follow if we don't stop it." His voice wavered as he stopped to catch his breath.

Asher exhaled deeply and put a hand on his knee. "The monster resides in the deep lakes of the island," she said. "Hibernating until it has to eat again. We found fresh a dinosaur carcass yesterday, so we knew we were getting close. We were trying to drive the creature from the lake with depth charges when the other airship attacked us."

"The Shaaglamoria is an ancient creature," Sethen continued. "It was worshipped by the inhabitants of this island until they disappeared hundreds of years ago. That is, if you believe the legends."

"So, can you still kill this thing?" Medesto asked.

"I honestly don't know now," Sethen said. "With *Wanderlust* gone, we have no weapons, no nets, no harpoons."

"Then let us help you finish what you came here to do," Natascha said. "You can have any glory or riches that come with killing this Shaaglamoria. We just want to see it killed."

Sinjin's deep voice came over the speaker on the wall. "Medesto, we have something coming up underneath us. Something big."

Medesto followed Ren to the window. The gnome pressed his face to the glass and tried to see what was under the ship, but the angle wasn't right.

"What is it?" Asher asked.

"I think we dropped a burning airship on top of your monster," Medesto said. He pressed the com button. "Sinjin, keep us out of its reach until we figure out our course of action."

"Roger that," Sinjin replied. *Bad Mojo's* engines rumbled, and the route thrusters kicked in. The slipstream leaned to the side in an evasive maneuver. Medesto grabbed the back of a seat to keep from sliding across the ship's hold. He leaned toward the window and looked into the mist. A deafening roar erupted from the jungle below them that shook the ship.

Medesto watched *Bad Mojo's* shadow move over the fog—then an enormous shadow appeared beneath it. Giant tentacles as thick as the gnome's body broke through the surface of the mist, followed by a behemoth-sized monster from the depths of the darkest of nightmares. The Shaaglamoria's blunt head had a dozen eyes. Long tentacles came off the crown of its head, trailing along its eel-shaped body. Electrical currents coursed over the oily hide. Fishlike fins, large and small, navigated the body as it flowed through the air like a serpent through water. It came out of the fog straight at them.

"*That* would be what I saw," Ren stated matter-of-factly.

*Bad Mojo* leveled off. The ship's speed increased, and with it Medesto felt a sense of momentary relief. The slipstream could easily outpace the creature, and he breathed the first easy breath since the *Wanderlust* had been blown out of the sky.

Suddenly, he spotted the *Sky Zephyr* in the distance, heading toward them. Several small orbs of sizzling fire streaked past the Bad Mojo, leaving contrails of red in their wake. Another hit the side of the slipstream close to his window.

"Come on, Ren!" Medesto said. "*Operation Kabuki Theater* is underway."

Ren reluctantly tore himself from the window. "Where are we going?"

"To build this world a new ending," Medesto answered. "First thing we need is an airship, and there's only one left on the island. I need you to get us to the *Sky Zephyr* before that monster destroys it."

Medesto hurried to the back of the cargo hold and pushed a button on the control panel. With a loud clank, the rear loading ramp slowly opened. A blast of hot air blew in, along with white ash and debris from a world slowly disintegrating around them.

"Why do we need an airship when we have *Bad Mojo*?" Charley asked as she followed him to the ramp.

Medesto motioned Charley over to him. "We can't use *Bad Mojo* because she's not of this world," he whispered. "The Narrative won't accept her as a substitute for the *Wanderlust*."

"Of course," Charley whispered back. "Field work is more complicated than I ever imagined it would be."

"We have to mimic the original storyline of the Novel as closely as possible, so we need to use as many things as we can that are connected to Asher Grey's world."

"The Raconteurs aren't from this world," Charley argued, sounding even more confused. "How's that going to work?"

"We're sentient beings," Medesto answered. "The Story is fine with that for some reason. Think of it like this. The Narrative is a great river. If there are any major disruptions to the flow of its continuity that obstruct the flow of the narrative, terrible things can happen. We have to keep things flowing by creating a fresh path for the Narrative to follow and fooling it into thinking we are the *Logos Personae's* dead comrades. We act like nothing is out of place and hope we can ride it out until we bring the Story to its new conclusion. But there is something I need you to do while I'm gone."

Medesto glanced over at Asher and Sethen. They were both staring in his direction. "Pull up the last couple of chapters of *Asher Grey and the Forbidden Island* on your machine. Find out as much as you can about the ending and how they killed this Shaaglamoria. Specifically, where Asher is when that happens. And look for any details that might be important."

"I'm not following," Charley said.

Medesto leaned in closer to her. "This is Asher Grey's story. That means she'll play a major part in its climax. If we are going to save her world, we need to keep her as close to the original storyline as possible. The rest of us just have to be here as place-holders. Also, if you have time, learn what you can about Asher and her continued adventures throughout the entire book series. Trust me, it's important we know everything we can."

Charley nodded and started tapping commands into her scanner. The turn of events and sudden danger they faced visibly shook her. "I'm not getting a solid signal from the WayFinder," she said. "The storm outside must be disrupting the ley-line signals. It's fading in and out."

Medesto placed a hand on her shoulder. "Just keep trying and stay calm. I know all of this is overwhelming, but we'll get through it if we keep our heads. Any second thoughts about working in the field?"

Charley nodded slightly and sighed. "I never should have left my lab. The most dangerous thing I had to worry about there was running out of snacks."

Medesto looked around for Raffles. He was looking out a window at the beast following the slipstream. "Rabbit, you coming?" Medesto asked. "Time to finish paying off that debt to Gideon. This isn't radioactive zombies or psychotic leprechauns, but it should be fun."

"'Bout time," the rabbit huffed, jumping down from his seat. "All dis talkin' and stratagizin' was beginin' ta bore me."

"Won't this be too dangerous for him?" Ren asked as they walked out to the end of the open ramp. "I thought he was just our guide."

Medesto let go a laugh. "Raffles? Trust me, he'll pull his weight. So how many are we up against here?"

"We started out with seven, but I whittled down the numbers

as best I could. Some guy named Porter and a couple of dangerous science-fictional soldiers with cybernetic weaponry. Then there's their leader. They call him Dark Angus. I killed him twice already, but he won't stay dead."

"I know that name," Medesto mused. "He's from the *Weird West* genre. Dark Angus, the Grave Dancer. Doctor Enigma brought him in, if I remember correctly. Went to Lazaranth Prison for shooting up a shop in Rogue Destiny. Rumor is he's some kind of embodiment of vengeance. His family was killed by bandits, and he was left for dead hanging from a tree. But the rope broke at the moment he died. Now he straddles that silver cord between life and death, looking for the men who killed his wife and children. He wandered his world, showing no mercy to the guilty. How he ended up in Rogue Destiny is anyone's guess, and why he'd agree to work for Mordecai is even more puzzling."

"There are two crew members on board, hiding below deck," Ren said. "The ship's captain and his daughter. I promised them I'd be back. So, how we doing this?"

"We circle around through the mist and come in from behind," Medesto explained. "Hit them hard and fast, and with any luck, bring back the *Sky Zephyr* in one piece."

"And the giant wyrm?" Ren asked.

"We avoid it if we can," Medesto said with a shrug. He turned to the others. "Ren's going to carry Raffles and me to the dirigible. Natascha, tell Sinjin to keep *Bad Mojo* within sight of the *Sky Zephyr*. We'll need you and Tempest to draw their fire, keep them focused on the slipstream until we get on board. You'll find any kind of long gun you could need in the traveling bag under my seat."

"And if you're killed by this gunslinger who refuses to die?" Tempest asked.

Medesto shrugged his thick shoulders. "Then you're on your own to figure something else out. This is the best I got."

Ren backed away from everyone as he shifted. Muscle, bone, and sinew morphed until great feathered wings sprouted off his back. He grew in stature to well over six feet tall, broad and muscular, with an angelic face.

"Let's do this," he said.

# Chapter 26
# The Down and Dirty of Things

Medesto and Ren looked out over the misty jungle of the Forbidden Island. Raffles waddled up behind them, hoisting his backpack over a shoulder. The air was thick and stifling, but the view of the island below them was mystic and strangely beautiful.

"Are we ready for this?" Medesto asked. Raffles scrambled up a pant leg to his back, his tiny claws digging into his corduroy jacket and the skin beneath it. Ren came up behind Medesto and gripped him under the arms.

"Hold on," Ren said. He stepped off the ramp into the nothingness, taking the gnome and jackrabbit with him. Broad wings spread as they caught the wind and became airborne. Medesto knew he was heavier than he looked, but the winged angelic shape-shifter held him tight as they made a wide arc to come in behind *Sky Zephyr*. Ren flew them in below the line of mist to avoid detection from the airship's crew. The thunder and lightning continued to rage high above them. The falling ash swirled in the air around them.

"Remember, we need the airship in one piece," Medesto said to his companions. "And don't kill anyone unless you have to.

We just need to take control of the vessel." He made the mistake of looking down at his feet. Through the thinning fog, he could see tops of jungle trees a hundred feet below. There were two things he was not fond of. Extreme heights and open water. He closed his eyes tight. Gunfire erupted in the distance.

"Over dere!" Raffles yelled into Medesto's ear. The rabbit's breath smelled like the compost of rotting vegetables. "I bet da beast found da *Zephyr*. We need to get to dem before it tears her apart."

Ren cleared the hazy mist, and they spotted the hideous Shaaglamoria entangled in the rigging of the *Sky Zephyr*. Long tentacles swarmed over the decks of the ship. The gigantic monster's stunted head peeked over the railing. Its long body disappeared down into the mist.

At the bow of the airship, two soldiers fired into the tangle of tentacles writhing across the scorched deck. Eruptions of fierce blue fire burst off the mottled skin of the beast. The smell of sulfur and plasma and burning flesh filled the air. The massive head of the monster came up onto the deck and crashing through the railing. Its flailing arms reached out for the soldiers.

Ren flew across the front of the craft. The high-pitched sound of engines rumbled below deck. Whoever was flying the ship was pushing the engines to their limits, forcing the airship forward, and trying to *break itself* free. Despite straining the ship's capabilities, the Sky Zephyr remained locked in the grip of the Shaaglamoria.

"They're going to burn out the engines, and she'll be dead in the air!" Medesto yelled, pointing to the wheelhouse. "Ren, get control of the ship and turn the engines off!"

Ren nodded his agreement. He swooped down under the giant air bladder that held the airship aloft. A tentacle lifted off the deck toward them. Medesto felt Ren let go of him and Raffles as the appendage slammed into the trickster. Ren sailed backward in a tangle of feathery wings and flailing limbs before disappearing over the side. Medesto didn't have time to worry about that. He flew in the air, slamming his dragon skin boots into the towering figure of Dark Angus. He was as solid as iron and hit the cowboy with the full momentum of his body.

"You take down da black hat!" Raffles yelled, still clinging to the gnome's shoulder. "I goin' have a talk wit da squidgy 'bout lettin' go of da boat."

The rabbit leapt from his shoulder and landed on a mottled tentacle slithering across the deck. There was a flash of a silvery wire and the end of the appendage separated from the trunk and splatted behind Medesto as the gnome landed hard on the deck. Raffles rode the severed limb up, spinning the wire in the air above him, and disappeared into the writhing mass of coils.

Dark Angus crashed in a heap. Medesto reached for his sidearm, but the holster was empty. He searched for his missing revolver amid the chaos, but his pistol was nowhere to be seen. In desperation, he ran at Angus, hoping to get to the cowboy before he recovered. Dark Angus had climbed to his feet by the time the gnome reached him.

Medesto met him with a solid punch to his midsection that caused Angus to stagger back. He followed it with blow after blow until his fists ached. The Grave Dancer stood well over six-feet in height. The gnome barely broke the four-foot mark. He threw all his considerable strength behind each punch. It was like hitting a stone wall. The gunslinger showed no visible pain, but slowly, Angus was forced back.

Medesto had the gunslinger against the railing when the Grave Dancer suddenly caught his fist with one meaty hand and smashed him in the face with the other. The impact rattled the Raconteur to his core and sent him flying back into the slithering tentacles. He scrambled to get out of the reach of the flailing appendages. On the other side of the deck, the two soldiers continued their assault on the Shaaglamoria, but their efforts seemed to have little effect on the giant wyrm.

Dark Agnus strode forward and drew both of his long-barreled pistols—but as they came down, Medesto rushed back and caught both wrists. A battle of willpower and physical strength began. Dark Angus gained leverage over his shorter opponent and forced him back one step, then two. Medesto struggled to gain traction on the slimy surface of the deck, but only slid further back. The revolvers came down closer to the gnome's face.

Medesto gritted his teeth and pushed back against the cowboy with everything in him. The Raconteur had a jaw of iron and the punch of a battering ram. The blood of Nordic giants flowed through his veins. Volsaang's Bane was the lineage of his family's bloodline, handed down from parent to child for generations. It was his family's most treasured possession. It was his gift and his curse. One family member carried it each generation, and this was Medesto's time. He had inherited it from his father on the day of his birth. His father got it from Medesto's grandmother on the day he was born. Volsaang's Bane made him nearly invulnerable. No one was stronger than him.

Without thought, Medesto pulled Dark Angus forward, using his momentum to flip the gunslinger over him. Both revolvers went off next to Medesto's head, sending splinters into his face. The blast left his ears ringing.

The cowboy flew into the same tangle of tendrils. They wrapped around his neck and torso, holding him tight. He forced his way to his feet and pulled against the tentacles holding him. He began shooting into the mass of flesh. Chunks of yellow meat and dark blood showered the deck until the ones entangling his arms released him. When his guns clicked empty, he threw them aside and pulled out a massive Bowie knife from somewhere under his coat.

He slashed at the tentacle coiled around his neck until the blade sliced halfway through it. He grabbed the dangling appendage and ripped it from its trunk. With a roar, the Shaaglamoria pulled the stub away. Medesto spotted his revolver in the slimy ichor underneath it.

Dark Angus unwound the detached tendril from his neck and threw it aside. He turned back to Medesto. His shadow engulfed the deck as he strode toward the Raconteur with a deadly purpose.

Medesto shook his head. Tiny lights floated in front of his eyes as he staggered back. He shook his head to stop the ringing in his ears. The sound of gunfire around him was muffled and distant. He didn't have time for this. A prehistoric monster was destroying the airship he needed to save this world, and an undead cowboy in a black duster was standing in his way.

The Bowie knife came down. Medesto dodged to the side, but the blade caught the arm of his coat and left a long cut. The wound burned like fire. The cowboy slashed at him again, but the gnome escaped the blade a second time. He kicked one of the cowboy's legs with all the strength he had left. The leg buckled, and the big man fell back. Medesto ignored the burning pain in his arm and ran for the revolver. He dove headfirst, sliding through the slimy gelatinous innards of the Shaaglamoria to reach it. Once he had it, he rolled onto his back. Dark Angus was already bearing down on him. Medesto fired.

The cowboy's head jerked back from the impact. The gunshot left a gaping black hole in the right side of his temple. There was no blood from the wound, only a black liquid that gave off a horrible stench that oozed down the gunslinger's face. The Grave Dancer slumped forward and crashed onto the deck beside the gnome.

Medesto holstered his gun and grabbed the front of the cowboy's duster. He dragged the body to the side railing. The head wound was already closing. If he could get the cowboy off the airship before he returned from the afterlife, he'd consider that a victory. He lifted the massive corpse and heaved it off the ship, but his boots slipped in the yellow ochre underfoot and the body crashed into the railing instead. A lifeless hand twitched and Dark Angus caught himself before he fell through. He pulled himself back up to the deck. Medesto rushed forward, but he was met with a black boot to the face that knocked him back.

Medesto struggled to his feet, covered in slime and monster blood. "Oi, will you die already?" he growled, searching frantically for anything he could throw. A large water barrel was within reach. The gnome tipped it on its edge, then hoisted it over his head with both hands and lofted it at Dark Angus with all his strength. The projectile crashed into the cowboy, knocking him through the railing and off the ship. Medesto bent over, hands on his knees, sucking in much needed air.

"By Dante's beard," he murmured to himself, "I'm going to be sore tomorrow." He spat a glob of blood on the deck. He ran his tongue over his bruised and cut lips. Although he considered himself near-invincible, that punch still hurt. After a quick peek over the side of the airship to make sure the Grave Dancer was gone, he looked around to see where he might help next.

A huge tentacle trailing green and yellow gore crashed onto the deck in front of him. It was as thick as a tree trunk, tapering to a curled tip. The end of it squirmed about, then uncurled. From inside its coils, a furry head appeared. Raffles squirmed free of the dying tendril, pushing it open with his foot. "Sorry 'bout dat, boss," he said. "Squidgies slice up easy enuf, but dey leave behin' a nasty mess."

In his small paw he held a curved, bone-handle grip with a shiny, silver ten-foot wire that glinted even in the dull light. With the push of a button on the handle's side, it retracted into the handle with a zipping sound. "S'cuse me," the rabbit clucked, his fur matted down by yellow-green slime and a look of grim determination on his face. "I see da squidgy's still got some arms left. I be right back."

Raffles spun the silver wire over his head as he approached the monster. "You not see enough of my vorpal string yet, squidgy? Well, I'm just gettin' started." A thick tentacle unwound from the rigging and dropped to block his way. With a whip of his short arm and a flash of silver, the cord sliced through the appendage with ease. The rabbit side-stepped the severed limb as it splatted on the deck next to him. He continued his march toward the head of the Shaaglamoria.

"Get outta here!" the rabbit shouted at the beast. He waved his paw like he was shooing off a stray dog that had wandered onto his property. "Go on! Back to where ya came from!"

A multitude of eyes, full of wrath and destruction, stared at the rabbit for a long, tense moment. A bellow of rage and pain that shook the airship followed it. The Shaaglamoria untangled its remaining appendages from the ship's rigging and its enormous body slid off into the mist. With the massive weight of the wyrm gone, the *Sky Zephyr* righted itself, rocking from side to side.

Medesto was thrown from his feet as the deck shifted under him. Raffles clung to the rigging above him. The air had grown thick and unbearably hot. The gnome wiped his brow and got up, heading to the wheelhouse. Overhead, the intensity of the storm continued to grow. He looked over to see two cybernetically enhanced soldiers, their weapons trained on him.

The engines had slowed, which meant Ren had taken control of the airship. Raffles was somewhere behind him. Hopefully, one of them would notice Medesto's current predicament and come to his aid. Behind the soldiers, huge tentacles rose out of the mist, followed by the blunt head of the hideous beast.

"Watch out!" Medesto yelled, pointing behind them. The warning came too late.

The Shaaglamoria hadn't been driven away. It only changed its strategy, coming up under the airship to the other side. A tendril wrapped itself around one soldier and pulled her from the deck. The other ran to her partner's aid, firing at the appendage from close range. The arm of the monster quivered from the gunfire but wouldn't release its grip on the hapless soldier. Instead, another giant tentacle swept out. It struck the shooter, catapulting her off the ship. The soldier continued firing until she was lost from sight.

Medesto emptied his revolver into the massive tentacle holding the remaining soldier. He knew it would have little effect, but it was better than doing nothing. There was a hoarse cry above him. He looked up to see a small, furry shape drop onto the mottled-colored tentacle and the vorpal wire sliced effortlessly through the thick appendage holding the soldier. The severed end fell with a splat to the deck. Raffles dropped to the deck beside it.

The Shaaglamoria roared in pain and pulled away from the Sky Zephyr, disappearing into the thick mists again. The soldier pulled herself free of the dismembered appendage. She raised her gun-arm, pointing it at Medesto. Raffles stopped in his tracks, looking up into the eyes hidden behind the reflective face guard.

"After I just save ya from a nasty death?" The rabbit clucked, shaking his head in disgust. "Dat how ya wan' ta play dis, huh?"

Raffles' short arm barely twitched, but the lethal wire whipped up. It cut through the soldier's weapon in an instant. She gave a blood-curdling scream and collapsed to the deck, grabbing the severed limb. Raffles kicked the gun away with his foot.

Despite the injury, the soldier reached for a side arm with her remaining hand, but Medesto rushed up and grabbed her body armor with both hands. He flung her over the railing into the open air.

Raffles picked up the front piece of the rifle from the deck. Blood dripped out of the severed end, and he noticed there were still parts of the soldier's flesh and bone fused to the weapon. He handed it to Medesto.

The rabbit grimaced at the grisly sight. "I didn' want to do dat, but she gave me no choice." He whipped the wire into the bone handle and tucked it back in his vest pocket.

"Don't worry about it," Medesto growled. "The cyborg was going to kill us, despite you saving her life. When it comes down to either them or us, there's no choice. We do what we have to." He tossed the severed weapon over the side. "Let's go see what shape the ship's in."

Medesto hurried to the wheelhouse. Ren stood at the helm, guiding the ship out over the jungle. A man in a tweed suit lay unconscious at his feet. Raffles waddled in behind him.

"Any sign of the Shaaglamoria?" he asked.

"Nothing out there but mist," Ren replied. "You both smell awful, but that was an impressive show you put on, rabbit."

Raffles snorted. "A vorpal string is dangerous ting in da hands of someone who know how ta use it."

"Raffles is Mythic," Medesto said. "That's why Gideon sent him with us."

"Like Bijou Antilles?" Ren asked.

"Ya, Bijou is da daughter of the Caribbean," Raffles quipped. "Picaroon Joe live in da wild west. Giant John Tremblay rules the Great White North, an' I am da king of da Bijou."

"So the tall tales you tell are true?"

Medesto nodded. "I saw him go toe to toe with a dragon once."

"She was only a little one," the rabbit said. His dark brown-colored fur lay matted with a greenish and yellow slime, but his face shone with a wide grin. "Just a few hundr'd years old."

"Medesto, take the controls," Ren said. "Lizbeth and her father are hiding below deck. I need to check on them." He darted out the door.

Medesto studied the controls in the front of him. He had flown everything from single prop biplanes to interplanetary starships, so an antiquated airship was no challenge.

Raffles plopped himself down on the floor and leaned against the wall. He propped his feet up on the unconscious man and gave a long exhale. "By da Horned Rabbit, do I enjoy a good dust up!"

Medesto laughed. "I swear, rabbit, at the End of Everything, after the oceans have dried up and the winds stop blowing, and we're left wondering what it all meant, you'll still be standing."

Raffles chortled. "An' don't ya ferget dat." He rummaged through his rucksack. "Ya want part of a choc'late bar?"

"Yes, I do," Medesto said. He chuckled and turned the wheel of the airship toward *Bad Mojo*.

# Chapter 27
# Into the Crucible Fires

Natascha stood atop the deck of *Bad Mojo*, watching the last moments of the battle aboard the *Sky Zephyr* play out. Between the firefight and the flailing tentacles, it was quite a spectacle. She watched the hellish cephalopod slide from the deck of the damaged airship and drop into the thick mists below them. Tempest stood next to her, scanning the area for any sign of the beast through her binoculars.

"They seem to have taken the airship," Tempest said. "But from the looks of that battle, there may not be enough of it left to carry out our plan."

"It's too late for other options. We have to make this work," Natascha replied. She didn't have time for Tempest's fatalistic outlook, but in her heart, Natascha knew she might be right. Improvisation was standard operating procedure for the Raconteurs, especially when the fate of worlds hung in the balance. The *Sky Zephyr* listed slightly to the side as it approached.

The giant air bladder that held the airship afloat was soft and deflated in several places, with barely enough buoyancy left to keep it aloft. The railing was missing along a good portion of the deck, facing *Bad Mojo*.

The port side of the ship was splintered and broken. The end of a severed tentacle dangled off the deck. A broken navigational sail swung precariously in its mounting. Green ichor covered the deck and rigging. Raffles stood beside Ren with a triumphant smile on his fuzzy face and waved as they pulled alongside. Natascha waved back before pulling off her gas mask to find a hideous smell coming off the damaged *Sky Zephyr*.

The craft came to a slow stop beside *Bad Mojo*. Medesto, a young girl and an old man emerged from the wheelhouse. Natascha assumed they were the crew Ren had spoken of. The old man shook his head, his face an expression of utter despair as he surveyed the damage done to his ship. He ran his fingers through thinning hair and put his cap back on. The girl beside him wrapped her arm around him.

The storm overhead had continued to increase in fury. The snow-white ash that had fallen earlier had turned into burning specks of orange embers. Fortunately, the embers burned out before coming in contact with the airship. Natascha's long coat flapped about her in the hot winds. She knew the worst was not even upon them, and they still hadn't figured out how to kill the beast. Every passing minute brought them closer to the climax of the Book and the destruction of this world.

Medesto came to the bow of the *Sky Zephyr* and gave her a thumbs up. Natascha smiled back and waved. She put on an outside façade of confidence, but inside she was deeply worried about the flying condition of the airship. She spoke into her comm. "Sinjin, move us around to the front of the *Zephyr*. We need to tie her on."

"Hang on," came the deep-throated reply from *Bad Mojo*'s pilot.

The slipstream's engine revved, and the ship inched forward. *Bad Mojo* spun slowly into position at the front. Tempest threw a tow cable to Medesto. The gnome tied it to the giant O-ring on the airship. Natascha tossed a second line to Ren. He did the same, connecting the two ships. Natascha waved them over.

Medesto spoke to the captain and his daughter, then turned to Ren. The trickster retook the shape of an angel and carried Medesto and Raffles over the chasm between the ships.

"Sinjin, the *Sky Zephyr* is secured," Natascha said. She scanned the sea of mist around them but saw no sign of the Shaaglamoria. "Keep us moving and let me know if you pick up any movement out there." The increasing winds buffeted the floundering airship. It rocked and creaked in the air.

"On it," Sinjin said. *Bad Mojo* edged forward slowly until the cables pulled taut and the slipstream started towing the airship behind her.

"Well, we did it," Medesto remarked with a deep sigh. His clothes were dripping with a nasty-smelling green mucus. Natascha took a step back from him. "I know the *Zephyr's* not in the best of conditions, but it's a miracle we could save her at all. It'll have to be enough. Where's Asher?"

"Downstairs with Sethen." Natascha led the way to the main hold into the infirmary, where Charley and Sethen waited.

Medesto looked at Sethen. He lay on a bed in the infirmary with his eyes closed. His bandaged chest rose in a steady rhythm.

"I gave him something for the pain," Tempest said. "He'll be out for a while. Asher is getting more blankets from storage."

"Good, that'll give us a moment to talk," Medesto said. "Asher's expedition was here to hunt and kill the Shaaglamoria, so we need to reestablish an ending to the Story. It's up to us to finish what they started."

"How do we do that without *Wanderlust*?" Tempest asked with a scowl on her face. "We have no weapons to bring the monster down."

Medesto ignored her. "Natascha, you have anything big enough to blow that thing out of the sky?"

"Not on me, I'm afraid," Natascha said. She dug through the secret pockets of her overcoat with both hands and set several items on the table. There were four small bottles, each with a different colored stopper and three shiny metal orbs. From a strip hidden inside the lining of her coat, she pulled out seven small somnambulic gas capsules. Each could put a room of people to sleep, but against a beast the size of the Shaaglamoria, all seven together would have little effect on it.

"This is all I have," she said. "The good stuff was in my other coat."

"The one your mother took from you?" Ren quipped.

"That would be the one," Natascha replied. She glared at Ren for pointing that out in front of the others, but knew they were all wondering where she was during the time she was missing. "I followed Mordecai's people. And I ran into my mother and her portal machine in the subway tunnels under Old London. We fought. She won."

"You saw your mother?!" Medesto exclaimed.

Natascha shrugged. "Guess who works for Mordecai Davos and built the portal machine that's transporting him across creation?"

"Your mother is Idalia Jyotsna Devi, isn't it?" Tempest said. Her smirked tinged with a touch of moral superiority.

"So?" Natascha retorted. "You don't choose your family."

"No, you can't," Tempest replied. "But families tend to follow the same path. My mother was a Fleet Admiral who commanded a thousand starships. Yours is a wanted fugitive with crimes that go back many years."

"What are you implying, Tempest?" Natascha growled. After today's events, she was ready to go head to head with the Raconteurs' Chief Security Officer, if only to release the pent up rage inside her.. But there were more pressing problems at that moment.

Charley picked up a vial. "What are these?"

"That one's a florescent tracking compound," Natascha answered. She glanced at Charley and winked, glad for the shift in conversation before things got out of hand. "Those two are liquid light. The last one is a highly concentrated acidic formula for locks and other things that need opening." She picked up one of the silvery orbs with a gloved hand. "These are flash bombs. Great for distraction, but there's not much kick to them."

"I have sumthing in ma pack that might help," Raffles said. He waddled out of the room and returned a minute later, holding two sticks of dynamite.

Natascha examined the ends of the explosives. "They have fuses, but I can modify that. The flash bombs will work like blasting caps. I'll rig wires to a handheld detonator. Even then, it won't be enough to inflict any actual damage to the beast. We need something that can generate an explosion sufficient to mortally wound the Shaaglamoria."

A voice behind them spoke. "An Amaranthine Crystal would do that." Natascha looked over to see the young girl from the *Sky Zephyr* standing at the doorway.

"How'd you get over here?" Tempest spat accusingly.

"I've been around airships my whole life," the girl replied. "Climbing between them is a basic job requirement."

"You can't be here, girl," Tempest said, and took a step toward her.

Natascha slipped in between them with her hand up against Tempest. "The girl is from this place," she said. "Her knowledge could be helpful."

"She's a local and should not be involved!" Tempest replied, trying to keep her voice low but failing. "What if she figures out too much?"

"Then we'll recruit her." Natascha put a hand out. "I'm Natascha Devi."

The young woman shook it. "Lizbeth Larocque, first mate on the *Sky Zephyr*. How can I be of service?" She looked at Ren and smiled.

"What was this you were saying about a crystal?" Medesto asked.

"Remember how the *Wanderlust* was blown to kindling?" Lizbeth said, getting right down to business. "Her onboard engines could never have caused that kind of explosion. That could only mean her Amaranthine Crystal was compromised. It's the aeronaut's greatest fear."

"And every ship is powered by this type of crystal?" Medesto asked, his expression hopeful.

"Of course." Lizbeth moved in closer to them, watching Tempest out of the corner of her eye, but unfazed by the taller woman's irritating disposition. "The Amaranthine Crystal floats in a high-density containment chamber to protect it from exposure to air."

"The plasma weapons the soldiers were using burned through anything they touched," Medesto said. "They must have penetrated the outer layers of the chambers."

"Yup. *Boom*." Lizbeth said, splaying her fingers out for effect.

Natascha couldn't hold back a smile. "That is something I can work with," she said. "But I'll need to see this chamber first. With Lizbeth's help, we might be able to jerry-rig *Sky Zephyr's* crystal into a bomb."

"That's one problem solved," Medesto said. "What did you find out about the ending to Asher's book?"

Tempest glanced at Lizbeth. "Is this something we should be talking about in front of her?"

Natascha sighed. "We've already crossed that line and we're running out of time here. Go ahead, Charley."

"I finally got enough of a signal to load the last chapter," Charley said. "You were right about Asher, Medesto. She is the one who actually fires the shot that kills the Shaaglamoria. In the original ending, the crew entangles the monster in nets rigged with explosives and a harpoon sticking in one of the beast's twelve eyes. Then Asher opens up the chain gun and shreds it to pieces. But we have none of those things."

"So, we improvise," Medesto said. "Natascha, how long will it take you and Lizbeth to have our makeshift bomb ready?"

"I have to look at what I'm dealing with," Natascha answered. "But I'm guessing not more than twenty minutes."

Charley looked up from her scanner. "There's more." She handed the device to Medesto and pointed to a paragraph on the screen. "How do we fix that?" she asked.

Medesto's bushy eyebrow rose as he read the section. "That will be a problem," he said with a glance at the sleeping Sethen. "But we'll worry about that when the time comes."

Medesto gathered everyone in close. His voice dropped to a whisper. "Before Asher gets back, there's an important point to remember. Asher Grey has to be shooting when the bomb goes off. It has to look like she kills the monster. The story can tolerate minor changes to its structure, but the climatic ending must stay as close as possible to what was originally written. Asher has to make the fatal shot. Whatever happens from here on out will be imprinted on the Narrative, creating a new ending for the Book."

"If Asher's out there shooting the monster with us," Tempest asked, "how are we going to prevent her from getting killed?"

"I don't have any answers here," Medesto growled. "So I'm counting on everyone to prevent that from happening,"

"We have a shape-shifter?" Tempest said. "Why can't he pretend to be Asher Grey? He can kill the beast when we blow the crystal, and that'll keep Asher out of harm's way."

Medesto looked exhausted. "That won't fool the narrative. Asher Grey is connected to this world in ways we don't understand. There's a mystical bond between the *Logos Personae* and their Story. She is the Chosen One if you prefer that term, and we need to play this as close to the original Storyline as we can get. Asher must never know how she fits into all of it."

Lizbeth had stood silent, listening intently to everything the Raconteurs discussed. "I didn't understand a thing you just said?" she said, a puzzled frown on her face. "Narrative? Storyline? You're talking like we're acting out a play here? What's a *Logos Personae*?"

"That's difficult to answer at the moment," Medesto said. "If we survive the next few minutes, I'll happily answer all your questions."

"Are you certain you want to know?" Charley asked.

"After what I've been through in the last twenty-four hours," Lizbeth said, "I'm ready for anything."

"Keep that thought and come with me," Natascha said with a somber smile. She led the young woman to the port window and pointed up to the sky. "Anything about this storm seem strange to you? Came out of nowhere, didn't it? And it's getting worse by the minute. Seems to be centered on the *Sky Zephyr* and *Bad Mojo*, doesn't it? Something not quite natural about it, is there?"

"What am I looking for?" Lizbeth asked.

"Just wait," Natascha replied.

Lightning flashed again. Lizbeth's eyes widened, and she stood speechless. On the sky behind the flash of lightning, words appeared.

# Chapter 28
# An Unexpected Ally

*Asher Grey sprinted to catch the 5:10 train to Canterbury Square. She was already late and could not miss her meeting with the Society of Cryptozoology. It was important to get there before Edwin Farnsworth. A contract of this size did not come along every day, and her company desperately needed the infusion of cash to remain afloat. To lose out on another bid to that pompous walrus of a man was more than she could endure. She ran faster.*

The paragraph continued, but Lizbeth turned away. "They look like words from a book," she murmured.

"They *are* words from a book," Natascha said. "Written upon the sky to bring this world into existence. Everyone you know and everything you have experienced in your life has happened inside a series of books called *The Gaslamp Adventures of Asher Grey*. We're currently at the end of the first book, *Asher Grey and the Forbidden Island*."

"You're telling me I'm just a character in a storybook?" Lizbeth asked, her voice faltering. "That I'm nothing more than words on a page? No, that's not possible! I am real. I remember growing up in Old London. My parents are Syd and Bebe

Larocque. I lost my mother last year. I live. I breathe. I feel." She pulled a small knife from inside her sleeve. Natascha stepped back, prepared to defend herself if necessary. Instead, Lizbeth pressed the point into her palm until blood trailed down her hand.

"I bleed!" she said, looking up as if she wanted Natascha to tell her she had not gone crazy.

"You are much more than just words in a book," Natascha reassured her. "You are real, just like the rest of us standing here. But your reality is not everything you believe it to be. I will explain it all in time, but right now, your world is on the brink of destruction. We need your help to save it."

The harsh reality of that statement hit Lizbeth hard. She lowered her head for a moment, then collected herself and swallowed. "What do you need me to do?" she replied.

Asher appeared from down the hallway. Her arms filled with blankets, and she eyed the Raconteurs with suspicion. "Why aren't we headed back to England?" she asked as she set the blankets down.

"We've decided to help you kill the Shaaglamoria," Natascha said.

"I don't care about that anymore!" Asher said. "My obsession with that monster has cost me my crew, my ship and almost my fiancé. I just want to go home to be with Sethen."

"Still, I think it's best if we help you finish the job," Medesto said. "If not, it will keep on destroying cities, and many more people will die."

"How can we possibly kill a creature of that size?" Asher argued. "The Wanderlust is gone. We lost the chain gun, our nets, our explosives. Does your ship carry any armaments?"

"*Bad Mojo* has no guns," Natascha said. "She is more of an exploratory vessel."

"Then we have nothing to fight with."

"The beast's been wounded," Medesto said. "Now is your opportunity to end its reign of terror once and for all." He opened the top of his worn leather traveling bag and dug through it, pulling out a long rifle. He tossed it to Asher. "We improvise. Are you still able to shoot?"

Asher caught the gun, favoring her injured leg, and stared at them. "Why would you help us?"

"Because you need help," Natascha said. "It's as simple as that."

Asher shook her head, hesitant at first, and then with more conviction. "Alright, I'll do what I can, but I want Sethen to stay down here. I won't risk losing him again."

Medesto furrowed his brow. Without Sethen, they would be one person short in pretending to be the *Wanderlust* crew. That might be a problem, but what choice did they have?

"We can do that," the gnome said, glancing at Charley. "Lizbeth, do you have extra clothing on board the *Sky Zephyr*? Anything'll work. Coats, overalls, even hats."

"There's a box in the galley full of stuff left behind by passengers. Not much of a selection. What do you need it for?"

Medesto looked at Lizbeth. "To fool the Muse into thinking we're part of the Story."

# Chapter 29
# Kabuki Theater

The lower decks of the airship buzzed with activity. The crew of the Sky Zephyr worked to prep everything as quickly as possible. Natascha watched the other Raconteurs dig through footlockers and storage cabinets for clothing that would aid in their desperate plan. She had chosen a pair of well-worn jeans, along with a button-up work shirt and a long scarf. She still wore her own trench coat with her gas mask hooked to the inside lining. Medesto walked up to her wearing an olive-colored plastic rain slicker, cut down to fit his short stature. Tempest was behind him, wearing grease-stained overalls and a workman's cap.

"Honestly, how is this nonsense going to accomplish anything?" Tempest asked.

"Wearing an article or two of clothing will lend authenticity to our charade," Medesto replied. "And ground us to the world. Like actors going on stage and bluffing their way through the performance. If we can position Asher to shoot the monster at the moment the dynamite is blown, the Story will have its ending. That's the key to everything."

"Fine, I'll get Asher in position," Tempest replied.

Natascha watched Tempest walk off. "So tell me," she said to Medesto, "is there any chance of this working?" she asked.

"I don't know," the gnome replied. "The Narrative isn't going to just accept us because we're not part of the Story, so blending into the environment will be our best shot. It worked for Ren inside *The Crimson Masque*. Now we just need to recreate the events as close to the original narrative as possible. When Sethen gets here, we'll match the number of crew members on the *Wanderlust*."

"Sethen's on board?" Natascha asked, pulling her gas mask on. She clicked on the internal screens inside the mask. Why were they involving Sethen?

"He will be shortly," Medesto said. "Sethen Rooke was the leader of the expedition, and he has a role in killing of the Shaaglamoria. And we needed a seventh member of the crew. I sent Ren to bring him over through the cargo hatch and hide him below deck. Sethen needs to be here for the Story to play out as it should. But now, we have to move. The end of the book could be upon us at any moment."

"We could use Claymore in this one," Natascha said with a sigh.

"Don't I know it?" Medesto agreed. "Unfortunately, he isn't here, and we only have one shot to get this right, so we need to make it count."

Natascha watched the stout gnome amble away. Medesto knew as much about the inner workings of a story's narrative as any educated scholar in Rogue Destiny. He knew exactly how far they could bend the narrative without breaking it. He had seen more end-of-the-world scenarios than Natascha, so she would have to trust him on this. But she didn't understand Sethen's role in this. She turned back to Lizbeth. "Let's go look at that crystal."

The Amaranthine Crystal was housed at the rear of the airship, beyond the main engine room and below the crew's quarters. Lizbeth led the way down a rickety set of stairs to a humid, dimly lit room behind a thick wooden door. The crystal itself sat entombed in an octagonal box atop a five-foot-tall chamber of wires and pipes connected to the surrounding walls. The shape of the box was the same as the gas streetlights that lined every street in Old London.

The crystal encased behind the thick glass was a foot in diameter. It looked like a massive uncut diamond, floating serenely at the center of the containment chamber. Tendrils of electrical arcs sparked from the purple-red gem, striking the sides of the glass and dancing along its surface. Heavy rivets and metal brackets ran along every seam and corner to hold the windows in place. A tangle of wires and piping came out of the base of the chamber into the floor and walls around it. The base was fastened to the wooden floor with heavy metal bolts.

Natascha removed her gloves and ran a hand across the smooth glass surface that encased the crystal. There was a slight vibration under her fingertips. She sensed the inside was extremely hot, but somehow the sturdy glass insulated the heat inside the box. "Anything I need to be careful with as I dismantle this?"

Lizbeth set her toolbox at the Raconteur's feet and stepped back. "I don't know much about the technology, except that the Amaranthine Crystal is housed in a vacuum-sealed containment field, like an incandescent lightbulb. Once the crystal is activated, the airtight chamber is the only thing that keeps it from exploding."

The young girl pointed to a box attached to the containment chamber. "That's the energy damper," she said. "It controls the amount of power flowing through the ship's engines. Without it regulating the crystal's output, the entire system would overload in an instant. It can only be turned off from the wheelhouse."

"I am not familiar with this material," Natascha said, touching the dense metal bolts that held the chamber house to the floor.

"It's Caerulean Iron," Lizbeth said proudly. "Strongest metal in existence."

Natascha smiled to herself. She could name a dozen metals she had encountered in her travels that were no doubt stronger. Science fiction worlds with unbelievably dense metals used to drill into the core of a star. Fantasy realms with sword blades sharp enough to slice dragon scales. She didn't mention that to Lizbeth, though. Everything was relative to one's life experience, and there was no need to dampen the girl's pride.

The motes of energy generated by the crystal swirled within the box in a hazy glow. They drifted down like snowflakes inside a snow globe to the bottom of the octagonal box.

Medesto's voice came through the speaking tube hanging on the wall. "Natascha, how's it going down there? The clock's ticking."

"Rerouting the power cable back into the containment chamber now." Natascha opened the toolbox. "Give me a couple minutes to get this thing wired." She rummaged through the toolbox.

"Do you have anything big enough to pry the base loose?" she asked Lizbeth.

"No, we don't," Lizbeth said. "The factory installed the crystal when we bought the ship. The chamber was never to be moved under any condition."

"Fortunately for us, we have someone on board who can help with that," Natascha said. She spoke into the communication tube. "Medesto, I need your muscle down here to move the containment box into position."

"On my way."

Natascha pulled Raffles' dynamite out of her coat pocket and replaced both fuses with flash bombs as a point of detonation. She wrapped the two sticks of dynamite together and used strong adhesive tape from the toolbox to fasten them against the glass of the chamber.

The technology of this world was familiar, something the Raconteur could easily work with. She moved with a desperate purpose, her fingers trembling, knowing the end could occur at any moment, or even worse, their gambit would end in failure. She kept the makeshift detonator in the pocket of her coat. The point was to concentrate the explosion in one spot to crack the glass, allowing air to reach the crystal and go boom. That was the hope.

"Is your team always up against the clock like this?"

"Too many times to count." Natascha cut several more wires. She tied them together and bent them out of her way. She wouldn't wire the detonator until they were ready to lower the crystal chamber.

"Well, it looks to be an interesting kind of life," Lizbeth commented.

"It's never boring," Natascha said. "And definitely more satisfying when we're not all about to die." She unclamped the main cable from the chamber's housing. The young girl had a fire in her belly and a certain curiosity about her that was admirable. Lizbeth helped them without question, even under pressure that most would collapse under. Natascha liked her more every minute. If they survived the night, the Raconteurs would have to make this up to Lizbeth and her father.

# Chapter 30
# In Medias Res

Ren lowered Sethen Rooke gently onto one of the sleeping cots in the hold of the *Sky Zephyr*. He had brought the unconscious man up through the cargo hatch under the airship. He was still unsure how a wounded man would be of any help with what they were about to attempt, but did as Medesto requested without question.

With a thought, he released his hold on the form of the angelic being. His body shrank back to its usual five-foot-seven height. The large wings folded in on themselves and disappeared into his back. The linen pants he wore hung loose on his lean frame. His skin tone slowly shifted from a mosaic of flowing reds, earthy greens, and blues to its natural bone-colored hue with splashes of indigo and burnt umber across his chest and arms.

"How is he?" a voice behind him said. Ren turned to find Charley standing in the doorway. She stared at the dark tendrils of concentrated skin pigment creeping over his arms and exposed torso. He ignored her. It was nothing new for people to gawk at the idiosyncrasies of his shape-shifting gifts.

Charley caught herself and looked up at him. Ren didn't

want her to know how desperate the situation was for them. He'd witnessed this scenario play out many times before in his time with the Raconteurs. Sometimes they saved the world, other times, like in *The Angels of Avalon*, they could not.

"He's still asleep from the pain medication," Ren replied. "Medesto insisted he had to be onboard with us. Something about his presence is necessary if we're going to fix the ending properly. This stuff is beyond my understanding." Charley motioned him away from the bed.

"He's not supposed to be alive," she whispered. She peeked around to make sure they were alone.

"Say again?" Ren asked, not sure he heard her correctly.

"I read the last chapter to *Asher Grey and the Forbidden Island* and the first couple chapters of the second book in the series. In the original ending of the first book, Sethen dies during the expedition's battle with the Shaaglamoria. The irony is, he's the only one of the Wanderlust crew to die. Everyone else survived their encounter with the monster."

"Does anyone else know this?" Ren asked.

"Only Medesto," Charley said. "Don't know if he's told anyone else."

"Let's go see," Ren said. He didn't know what the gnome had planned, but he was going to find out. They left Sethen asleep and ran up the stairs to the main deck. Medesto approached them as they appeared from the hold.

"You brought Sethen over?" the gnome asked him.

"Yeah, he's onboard," Ren answered. "Charley told me…"

Medesto cut him off. "He's here. That's all we need to worry about for now. Natascha needs me in the engine room." He disappeared down the steps before Ren could say anything else.

"That was strange," Charley said as she reached the deck. Ren could see all of this insanity was getting to the young girl.

"How you holding up?" he asked.

"Too much talk about the end of the world," the dirty blond-haired tech said. "But at least the monster's gone."

"Oh, de squidgy still out dere," Raffles said. He sat on a bench near them, chewing on a cherub root. "He out there. Lickin' his wounds. Just watchin' and decidin' how to come at us."

"So it'll come back?" Charley asked.

Raffles spit out a piece of root. "Oh, dey always come back. His pride's wounded, and squidgies never let sumthing like dat lie. He jus' waitin' for de right moment."

"How long will he wait?" Charley said, her eyes anxious.

"Depend on its mood." The rabbit spit into a bucket next to him. "Don' worry tho, he'll get over his shyness soon 'nough."

"You've seen those things before?" Charley asked.

"It's one of da Yaga'eldritch," Raffles said. His whiskers twitched as he spoke. "Da Ancient Ones. But dis one just a pup by da look of him. They get lot bigger." He gave a nervous chuckle.

"We just need to be ready for when it does return," Ren said. "Come on, rabbit. Let's go see where we can help out." Raffles dropped off the bench to the floor. He and Charley followed Ren down the stairs.

Ren stopped at the doorway of the engine room. Medesto crouched down to examine the bolts that held the chamber to the ship's floor. He grabbed one with his hand and with gritted teeth, tried to unscrew it. It didn't budge. "I'm not going to break the seal on the crystal if I manhandle this, am I?" he asked.

"No," Natascha said. "It's encased in the strongest metal this world has to offer." Ren saw Lizbeth smile at the comment and Natascha wink at her. "I disconnected the chamber from the ship, so it's ready to be moved."

"Okay then, stand back." Medesto braced himself and pushed against the containment chamber with both hands. The flooring beneath the octagonal chamber cracked and splintered under the force.

He gritted his teeth and, with a burst of strength that did not come close to reaching the gnome's limits, he pulled it back toward him. The crystal chamber tore free from its wooden moorings. With a grunt, he hoisted it off the floor. "Where am I going with this?"

"Bring it out here where I can finish wiring the dynamite," Natascha told him, and left the engine room.

Medesto manhandled the chamber through the narrow doorway. He set it down with a decisive thud that shook the cargo hold. "Any ideas how to get the creature close enough to kill it without blowing ourselves up?"

"We get above the Shaaglamoria and drop the bomb on it," Charley said. "Boom, no more monster."

"Too risky," Medesto said. "Asher has to have a clear shot at the beast the moment the bomb blows. There are too many variables for something to go wrong, and we won't get a second chance. But we need to decide on something quick. We have to be getting close to the final chapter, if we're not there already. We could use Claymore's input right about now. He was always a better strategist than me."

Raffles pointed to the hook hanging over the cargo hatch. "We could go fishin'." He waddled over, stretched up to a switch, and opened the cargo doors. Hot winds and ash blew through the wide opening.

"We lower yer bomb down, den coax da beastie in close with sumthing tasty," Raffles yelled over the wind. "It should be famished after da spanking I gave it. Ya set off da dynamite, crack open the crystal, blow up ya squidgy. What kind of food we got on board?"

"There's a bin of vegetables in the pantry and back bacon in the freezer," Lizbeth said.

"Good," Raffles said, his eyes wide with excitement. "Someone need to go fry up da bacon."

"I can do it," Charley volunteered.

"Charley?" Natascha pulled her Peacemaker out and handed it to the young tech. "Use this to help thaw the back bacon as it cooks. It'll save us precious time."

"Da smell will bring da beast around," Raffles said. "But he still prefer his supper da old fashion way, alive and on da hoof." He looked at Ren.

"What are you suggesting, rabbit?" Ren asked.

"You a skin changer, ain't ya?" Raffles clucked. "You could ride da crystal down and help draw the beastie in."

"You want to use me as bait?" Ren asked indignantly.

Raffles gave a chuckle. "If ya wanna get technical 'bout it. We just need a plump, juicy-lookin' pig to draw da squidgy in close enough to have a shot at blowin' him up." Ren looked at everyone else.

"All right, why not?" Ren said. "Just give me a signal before you detonate the bomb, so I can fly out of there before it blows."

Medesto carried the bulky chamber over to the open cargo doors. He tilted it so Ren and Tempest could wrap the hoist chain around the base and every side. Once they had the containment chamber secured, the gnome hit the button. The chain went taut and lifted the box off the floor.

"Hold it!" Natascha said. "I need to finish the wiring." She handed the detonator to Lizbeth and carefully connected the wires to the flash bombs on the end of the explosives. Satisfied the connection was good, she stepped back.

Medesto put a hand on Ren's shoulder. "You sure you want to do this?" he asked. "Nobody will think less of you if you don't do it. The smell of the meat should be enough to bring the monster to us."

Ren shook his head. "But if it doesn't, I'll be there to lure the creature in. Besides, I'm the only one who can get out of the way fast enough when the crystal blows."

"There's hope for you yet, B'gatti," Medesto remarked with a smile.

"The squidgy's outer shell is like armor," Raffles said. "So blowin' da crystal next to it don't guarantee a kill. We need da chamber near da beast's mouth and head 'fore we blow da dynamite."

"Be careful, Ren." Natascha said. "*In Medias Res.*"

Ren smiled at the words. *In Medias Res*, the official motto of the Raconteurs. *Into the Middle of Things*. That summed up their philosophy perfectly.

Tempest nodded. "Good luck, B'gatti. You're either very brave, or very stupid." Despite the smirk on her face, she seemed impressed by what Ren was about to do.

"I'm sure it's a little of both," Ren replied with a grin.

The aroma of cooked bacon filled the room as Charley came in from the kitchen holding a greasy canvas bag. The trickster took it and jumped onto the suspended chamber.

"So now we just drag the chamber through the mist until the monster shows up?" Tempest asked. "Is that going to work?"

"It should. I hurt da beast pretty good," Raffles said. "It'll be famished."

"We'll find out soon enough," Medesto said. "Ready?" Ren nodded and crouched on top of the containment chamber. He swung the box out over the open cargo hatch.

"The chain looks long enough," Natascha said. "So the ship should be clear of the explosion."

The crystal chamber swayed in the winds whipping through the hatch. The air was hot and dry as the storm intensified. Ren felt a shiver of apprehension as the thought struck him that this might not be as good of an idea as it sounded a minute before.

Medesto yanked on the pull cord of the auxiliary generator

used to power the hitch. It chugged to life. He hit a button to lower the chamber, then Ren and the crystal slowly descended beneath the airship. The last thing he saw of his friends was the detonator in Natascha's hands and Lizbeth feeding out the wire to the bomb he stood on.

As the chamber descended, the reality of being bait to catch a massive predatory monster while straddling a potent explosive sank in. Ren told himself he needed to stop agreeing to volunteer for every dangerous job that came along. He found himself trying to impress the Raconteurs. For some reason, their opinion of him mattered more than he wanted it to, especially Natascha's. But he knew his ego was going to get him killed one day.

Ren held tight to the chain to keep himself from being blown off. For all his vaunted shape-shifting powers, there was no shape he could take that would protect him from a blast of that magnitude. But he could always run. He was good at that.

Claymore's final request was for Ren to watch over the Raconteurs and see that they continue in his absence. If this was the end for him, at least he would have died keeping that promise.

A hundred feet below the airship, the chamber jerked to a stop. Ren and the chamber hung above the rolling mists that covered the island. His desire to not be there grew stronger. He looked out into the thick fog, but saw no sign of the beast. The air felt strangely calm despite the howling winds swirling around him.

Ren took a piece of back bacon out of the canvas bag and nibbled on it. The air grew hotter and dryer by the minute. The skies were dark and shook from the rumbling thunder. Lightning lit the sky from time to time and he could read the giant words etched on the sky over the Sky Zephyr. Sweat dripped down his face, stinging his eyes, which only added to his ragged nerves as he waited for the inevitable return of the monstrous Shaaglamoria. It was time to get into costume. He crouched, focused his mind, and morphed into the largest, juiciest-looking razorback pig he could manage.

The surface of the crystal chamber proved to be a tight fit for the razorback's considerable girth. The winds rocked the octagonal box back and forth, making it difficult for Ren to keep his footing. The smooth metal crown of the round crystal was as slick as ice under his cloven hooves. He plopped his enormous rump down and let out a grunt, leaning against the winch chain to keep from sliding off the side of the box. The hog's coarse hair irritated his nether regions as it rubbed against the metal. At least Claymore wasn't there to mock him for his choice of disguises. His partner would have never let this one go.

He wondered where Mordecai had sent Claymore. What task could possibly require the help of the Grimm Jester? His partner had been free to go anywhere he wanted after he and Claymore parted ways the day before, and yet he'd chosen to chase down Mordecai. He nosed his snout into the bag, deep in thought, and chewed on another piece of bacon. The irony of a pig eating pork was not lost on him.

A deep guttural sound came up from below him. It was somewhere between a throaty growl and a croak. He peeked over the edge. The fog was thick and unforgiving, but he thought he could see movement roiling beneath its surface. A massive shape passed below him. The long serpentine body glided through the mist like a predator on the hunt. Raffles was right. The beast had returned. It was bound to the Story as much as Asher Grey.

The great shadow circled gracefully under the crystal chamber but remained at a cautious distance. Ren exhaled in frustration and sat back down. He needed to grab its attention.

According to Raffles, the beast favored fresh meat, so Ren grunted out several loud piggish snorts.

A throaty snuffling sound grew closer. A tentacle as thick as Ren's waist crept into view, feeling around for the source of the noise.

The silent air around him was unsettling. Even the raging storm winds had slackened since the Shaaglamoria reappeared. Ren knew it had something to do with the monster's role in the overall narrative, but he was too preoccupied to think further on the subject.

Ren peered into the fog again. Twenty-feet below him, part of the creature's massive head was visible. The Shaaglamoria was even larger up close than he imagined it would be. It floated effortlessly in space, its long eel-like body tapering into the mists below it.

A dozen eyes stared up at his piggish form with an unsettling amount of intelligence. The largest one blinked, followed in sequence by the others. Tentacles swarmed off its head like a grotesque lion's mane, reaching out and caressing the chamber with increasing boldness. Raffles' vorpal wire had left many of them nothing more than blunt stubs, but many had already begun to grow back.

The appendages suddenly pulled away. Ren realized a fraction too late what that meant. The beast gave a throaty roar and struck the crystal chamber with the largest tentacle. The trickster flew into the air. Despite his disorientation, he morphed into a raven a moment later. Flapping his wings wildly to get away, he dodged the swinging chamber, but not the enormous maw full of serrated, foot-long teeth. The Shaaglamoria struck with blinding speed and snapped its massive jaws around him.

The sides of the monster's throat contracted, pulling Ren away from the teeth and down whatever the Shaaglamoria used as a digestive system. The crushing pressure caused his body to return to its natural shape. His arms grabbed for anything to hold on to before the beast swallowed him completely.

Ren shifted into a massive saber-toothed cat and sank his claws into the soft tissue of the monster's gullet. He tried to pull himself out of his slimy prison, but the throat muscles constricted around him, forcing the air from his lungs. Unable to breathe, he lost his hold on the prehistoric cat and slid further down its throat. The daylight from the monster's open mouth disappeared and the innards of the monster closed in around him. Panic overwhelmed his senses as the darkness engulfed him.

His last thought as he slid into the bowels of the Shaaglamoria was how his quest of infiltrating Mordecai Davos and his band of outlaws had drastically changed in such a short time. *In Medias Res.*

*Into the middle* of things indeed.

# Chapter 31
# As It is Written, so Shall It Be

Natascha stood in the hold of the *Sky Zephyr*, watching through the cargo hatch as the great mythical Shaaglamoria of the Forbidden Island emerged from the mists under the ship. Tempest was on her left side, Asher Grey was on her right, rifle in hand. Her chest was tight and the breath inside her gas mask forced. They were at the moment of truth. They could hear the distant grunt of a pig as Ren tried to draw the monster out. Their plan was working so far, but now the timing had to be precise.

The misshapen beast swam through the air beneath the mist, circling Ren and the crystal chamber. Its stubby head trailed down to a long eel-like body and tail. Natascha estimated it to be over a hundred meters long. A score of tentacles trailed from the crest of its blunt head. Several were only stumps after its encounter with Raffles, but appeared to be regenerating on their own.

The grotesque creature snaked its way through the mist toward the chamber. It stopped in midair, hovering in place, defying every known law of physics as it searched for the source of aroma coming from the containment chamber. Charges of electricity flashed from its body at irregular intervals. A dozen or more diamond-shaped fins ran down the length of its body, fluttering in the wind like a tropical fish floating in its tank. Its tail tapered out to several long, graceful fins that quivered in unison with the ones on its side. Heavy scales covered the monster's entire body. The lower jaw jutted out from under its stunted nose. Its writhing tentacles drifted like dreadlocks off its misshapen head, encircling both Ren and the box.

The monster sniffed around the chamber, pressing its great snout up against the glass. Then, without warning, the beast slammed the chamber with a tentacle, flinging the wild boar off the top into the air. Ren turned to a raven in a heartbeat, but the creature was faster. With a snap of its jaws, the tiny black bird disappeared into its mouth.

The Shaaglamoria stared up at the airship a moment longer, then with a great roar and twist of its head, dove back into the mist. Its long, finned body arched for several seconds before completely disappearing from view.

"What do we do now?!" Charley yelled in a panic.

"Get up on deck!" Medesto barked. "See if we can track where the monster went."

"What about Ren?" Tempest asked.

The gnome glanced at Natascha, but he didn't answer the question. He stomped up the stairs to the main deck. Half way up, something struck the stern of the airship with the force of a battering ram. The cargo hold tilted violently to one side, throwing everyone off their feet. Asher teetered forward, almost falling through the open cargo hatch. She managed kept her feet under her and fell back into Tempest. Medesto was not so agile. He crashed through the wooden railing of the stairs toward the open hatch.

Natascha landed hard on her back, sliding away from the opening. The detonator jerked out of her hands and disappeared through the hatch. Charley threw an arm around Raffles. She and Lizbeth both grabbed onto the piping running down the wall. Tempest and Asher were in a heap on the other side of her. She watched helplessly as Medesto fell headfirst out the cargo hatch.

Natascha rolled to her feet and fought her way up the slanted floor as the *Sky Zephyr* continued to tilt under them. She dropped to her knees, peering carefully over the side. Medesto hung by one hand from the chain about twenty feet below her, his boots dangling out over nothing. He looked up at her with shock and fear in his eyes.

Medesto grunted and hauled himself up hand over hand, back to the hatch. The angle of the ship allowed his short legs to get a boot on the edge of the opening. He reached out a hand and Natascha grabbed hold, but it took both her and Lizbeth to pull the gnome back onto the tilting floor.

"Tempest, get Asher topside!" Medesto shouted. "Find out what just happened."

"You got the crystal?" Natascha yelled to him.

"Already on it," Medesto answered. He began pulling the chain holding the chamber back up. "I'll be right behind you."

Natascha raced to the galley, Lizbeth, Charley, and Raffles close at her heels. She passed the crew quarters, but a voice stopped her. "Wait, I'm coming with you!"

She turned to see Sethen sitting up in his bed, holding his head in his hands. Natascha looked around for Asher, but she was already on deck with Tempest.

"I had the most terrible dream," Sethen said. "I was floating outside my body and could hear voices talking, but couldn't see who it was. I looked at my own hands and they were burning. The flames moved up my arms, engulfing me. Asher was suddenly there with me, her clothes covered in flames, too. She ran toward me. We held each other as everything around us burned to ash before our eyes. Then I woke up."

Sethen stood up and struggled to button his shirt. He looked directly at Charley. "I heard you said I wasn't supposed to be here. I didn't understand what that meant at first, but now I think I do." Charley returned his gaze, but remained silent.

"Lizbeth," Natascha said, "go to the wheelhouse and check on your father. Make sure he stays safe. The rest of you, come with me."

Together, they climbed from the hold into a nightmarish scene. The Shaaglamoria had crashed onto the back of the *Sky Zephyr*. Its massive body squirmed and crawled its way up the damaged ship, tentacles writhing wildly, intertwining with the rigging and supports of the airship like some great kraken from myth. The air was stifling. Even through her protective gas mask, Natascha's lungs burned from the heat. Every breath felt like she was in a furnace.

Winds whipped over the deck, stronger than ever. The atmospheric pressure had increased in the last few minutes. Now it was thick and stale. Her movements felt sluggish and labored. She looked for the others. Raffles was across the deck, dodging a tentacle. He ducked under one appendage, then jumped out of the way as a second one slammed into the deck. He moved in slow motion. Time was being warped by the fracturing of the Narrative and impending collapse of the Story.

Lizbeth sprinted for the wheelhouse, but she moved unnaturally slow. Tempest and Asher remained near Natascha. No one seemed sure what to do. Asher raised her rifle, then paused. Tempest dug through Medesto's traveling bag, pulling out more firearms. She placed each long gun on the deck next to its corresponding box of ammunition, then started loading them.

Enormous waves of gray smoke swirled across the sky and blotted out the sun. Intermittent fire bursts exploded in the clouds. An inky black rain started falling, covering everything in a dark, oily liquid. Natascha's breath caught in her throat. They were in the final phases of the *Crucible Event*. The end of the world was upon them. Asher Grey's book was coming apart at the seams, unraveling before her eyes and there was nothing she could do to stop it.

# Chapter 32
# That One Moment of Truth

Medesto emerged from the hold, balancing the crystal chamber awkwardly on one shoulder. Natascha shouted at him over the winds, but the words were not in sync with her mouth. "Throw it!" she shouted. "Into its mouth!" There was a pause before he heard her words and looked over. Again, it was several heartbeats before the gnome reacted to what she said.

The Shaaglamoria was halfway up the broken deck under the air bladder when a small furry shape jumped from the ship's rigging in front of it and stood defiantly in its path. The monster's twelve eyes focused on the long silver strand of vorpal lying next to the rabbit and hesitated.

"Dat right, squidgy, you remember me, don't ya?" Raffles yelled. His words did not quite match the movement of his mouth. "C'mon on, you and I ain't done yet." The wyrm was infinitely larger than its tiny foe, but the sting of the rabbit's wire seemed to be fresh in its mind. Raffles waddled toward his foe, whipping the silver wire over his head.

"Rabbit, get its mouth open!" Medesto yelled.

Raffles reacted to the words moments later and swung the wire, slashing through the closest tentacle intertwined with the rigging. The stump of the tentacle pulled back, and the beast's roar of pain and rage shook the ship. Medesto heaved the heavy crystal chamber at its gaping mouth with both hands. It hit the Shaaglamoria with considerable force and wedged inside its massive jaw, locked down by rows of long, sharp teeth.

Natascha shouted. "The dynamite, Asher! Shoot the dynamite!" Her words hung in the air around her. A moment later, Asher reacted. The *Logos Personae* leveled her rifle and started firing. The bullets hit the crystal's box but failed to find the dynamite. She fired several more times before her weapon clicked empty.

"I'm out!" Asher yelled. Strangely, her words were in perfect sync with her mouth, but Natascha had no time to ponder that.

Tempest took the empty Winchester from Asher and handed her another rifle from a different time and era. Asher slowed her shooting with the new gun, taking more careful shots as the Shaaglamoria continued to thrash about in front of her. Sethen stood at her side with another rifle ready. Tempest reloaded the Winchester behind them.

Asher lifted the rifle and waited until the crystal chamber was visible inside the creature's thrashing mouth. She slowly squeezed off a round. There was a spark, and the dynamite exploded—followed by the second a heartbeat later. The monster's head jerked back, and an enormous chunk of jawbone exploded from the side of its head. Green sludge poured from the wound.

The creature's hold on the Sky Zephyr weakened, and it slid back down the deck. Its massive serpentine body thrashed about as its tentacles flailed about, trying to stop itself from falling off the airship. The enormous head slammed into the air bladder above it.

The smoke cleared inside the monster's mouth and Natascha could see the chamber. It was still intact. The dynamite had wounded the Shaaglamoria but had not damaged the crystal at all. The beast roared again, shaking the very reality around it. Its fury rose by the second.

Even wounded, the Shaaglamoria fought to climb farther onto the airship, but every time it wrapped a tentacle around the rigging or rail, Raffles was there to slice through the appendage. The monster lost its grip and slipped back to the stern, but caught itself before it fell completely from the ship.

Asher stopped shooting and lowered her rifle. "That didn't work. Now what?!"

Sethen ran up to Natascha, pulling her aside. His mouth moved, but the words came to her several seconds later. "The vial of acid you spoke of earlier," he yelled. "Give it to me and I can blow the crystal open."

Natascha looked at Medesto. He nodded, and she handed Sethen the tiny jar with the red-stopper. "You weren't supposed to be awake to hear any of that."

"No, I think I was supposed to hear it," Sethen said with a somber smile. He slipped the vial into his vest pocket. "I understand now this is how it has to be. It will put things right, and Asher will be safe. That is all that matters in the end, isn't it? I can't claim to know what is going on, or who you people are, but I do know what I must do."

Asher turned and saw him for the first time. "Sethen, what are you doing here?" Confused, she pressed a hand to his chest. The surprise on her face melted into profound sorrow.

Sethen gave her a stoic smile, but his eyes remained sad. "This expedition was my responsibility from the start, and I have to see it through to the end." He tapped his vest pocket. "This vial is our last chance to pierce the chamber's glass."

"Darling, no!" Asher pleaded. The words echoed on the

wind, louder than anyone else's. They were not broken or slowed by the shifting reality around them. Natascha saw the desperation in her eyes and felt the anguish behind her words.

"It will be alright, my beloved," he replied with a pained smile. "You know this is how it has to be."

"Don't go!" Asher begged. "You'll die if you do this! I'll go!"

"Then you make sure I get back," Sethen replied, putting his hand on hers. "Cover me with your rifle. You've always been a better shot than me."

"This is insane!" Asher cried. "You'll never get close enough!"

Sethen saluted her. "Ma'am, I am a retired lieutenant in Her Majesty's Royal Air Navy. No force in this world can stop me from doing my appointed duty. Trust me, my love, this will all make sense when it's over."

Asher held on to him. "I won't let you walk out there to your death."

"Then I'll go," Lizbeth offered. "I'll blow the crystal and kill the thing."

"No, Lizbeth," Medesto said. "Sethen should be the one to do this." The girl opened her mouth to argue, but the scowl on the gnome's face made her reconsider.

Sethen pulled Asher into him and kissed her. "I will always be with you." He brushed a strand of hair from her face, then looked at the Raconteurs. "Keep her safe, my friends. Everything depends on her. I realize that now."

He ran to the rigging, ignoring his injuries, and started climbing like he was born to it. Once he got into position above the thrashing Shaaglamoria, he yelled to Raffles. "Rabbit, draw the creature's attention so I can reach the chamber." His voiced echoed, out of sync with his movement of his lips.

"You heard him!" Tempest yelled. "There's still a chance to make this work. Asher, keep firing! We need to distract the monster!"

Everyone picked up the guns and opened fire, trying to take the beast's focus from Sethen. Raffles ducked his head and jumped to the railing, scrambling up the ship's rigging out of the line of fire.

Next to Natascha, Lizbeth scowled at Medesto as she fired her rifle. She shouted something at him. The words came out a moment later. "Why'd you make Sethen go?! He's injured! I could have easily gotten to the crystal quicker!"

"I didn't *make* him do anything," Medesto replied. "He went out of his own free will. You heard him—*this is how it has to be.*"

Sethen swung from the rigging to drop in front of the beast. He dodged a thrashing tentacle and dashed forward, pulling the small vial from his vest pocket. He went to throw it, but another tentacle reached around him and pulled him off the deck. The red-capped vial slipped from his fingers. Natascha watched the bottle roll down the broken deck to the edge of the airship.

She looked into the bright orange sky with dismay, a pang of regret in the pit of her stomach. The skies above the airship burned a bright red and orange from the firestorm. The narrative had stalled like a river obstructed by a dam. It could flow no further, and the pressure built to a boiling point. They were out of time, and the Shaaglamoria was still alive. This was it. The final moment before cinder and flame consumed Asher Grey's world.

She caught movement out of the corner of her eye. A black raven flew over the railing into the fray. It had to be Ren.

Natascha waved her arms and yelled to get his attention, but the bird didn't hear her over the howling winds whipping across the deck. Asher stood beside her, firing at the monster's tentacle holding Sethen. Natascha grabbed her arm.

"Asher, tell that bird to grab the vial before we lose it!" she shouted, pointing at Ren. Her voice was suddenly clear and unaffected by the world collapsing in around her.

"Bird?!" Asher shouted back. She gave Natascha a confused look, then her eyes lit up. "The doppelganger!"

Asher handed her rifle to Natascha and cupped her hands around her mouth. "The vial!" she yelled, pointing at the small glass container about to roll off the ship. "Get it to Sethen." Her voice rang out over the deck, loud and clear against the storm raging overhead.

The raven heard her. He circled back as the small vial disappeared over the side of the airship. Ren dove after it.

Long seconds later, the raven appeared, clutching the red-capped vial in its talons. Ren swooped past the monster's thrashing limbs and dropped it into Sethen's outstretched hand.

Despite the tentacle wrapped around him, Sethen twisted enough to cast the small glass vial against the window of the crystal chamber. The vial shattered on impact. Curls of smoke rose from the reflective surface. Sethen fought to get free of the creature's grip. Asher continued firing, but the Shaaglamoria's grip on her fiancé remained unchanged. From out of nowhere, Raffles jumped down from the rigging and, with a swipe of his vorpal wire, cut the snaking tendril in half.

The tentacle's hold on Sethen slackened, and he slipped free. He grabbed a stray rope hanging near him and began climbing up, trying to get beyond the monster's reach. Natascha thought he was going to make it until another curling tentacle reached for him. It grabbed his leg, stopping his ascent.

"Sethen!" Asher screamed. She lifted her rifle and fired again. The shot hit the tentacle below where it held Sethen's leg. She fired again and again. The Shaaglamoria flinched at the impact of the bullets but refused to release him.

Natascha watched as a second tendril wrapped around his waist. Sethen's grip failed, and the tentacle pulled from the rope. The British officer fought with everything in him. He kicked at the beast's head to stop from being forced into the gaping maw.

Raffles leapt onto the ropes and swung the lethal wire. It sliced through the last tentacle anchoring the monster to the *Sky Zephyr*. The Shaaglamoria slid down the deck, taking Sethen with it. Asher continued to fire her rifle, tears running down her face.

Gray smoke rose off the glass of the containment chamber. A second later, a shrill whistle split the air as the corrosive acid ate through.

"Get down!" Natascha yelled to those around her.

The chamber exploded as the Shaaglamoria and Sethen slid off the end of the airship. A massive fireball of spectral colors and smoke spiraled up into the dark sky, engulfing both.

The Shaaglamoria's head erupted in a splatter of thick black and yellow fluids. The earth-shattering explosion rocked the *Sky Zephyr*. Whatever served as the monster's brain matter splattered on the deck and chunks of the black innards rained down around them.

The core of the explosion was so bright the light filters in Natascha's goggles failed to protect her eyes from the flash. The concussive force of the exploding crystal knocked everyone from their feet. She landed on the deck near Asher and Tempest.

"Did we do it?" Charley asked, still momentarily blinded by the explosion.

Natascha climbed to her feet and squinted skyward. "We're still here, so that's a good sign."

The skies above them remained stormy for what seemed an eternity. Then, the falling black rain slowed and the lightning and thunder subsided. The bold words written across the sky faded until they disappeared completely. The ashfall stopped.

The stormy skies overhead cleared as the clouds separated and a bright sun shone down. The tumultuous winds turned to a strong breeze, then dissipated completely. Charley starting laughing as the inky rainfall ceased. Even Tempest looked at Natascha and smiled.

Raffles dropped down next to them. "It a miracle how you Rac'oteers manage ta stay on dis side of da grave," he said, shaking his head.

"Looks like we have ourselves an ending," Medesto said, with a look of relief on his face. "As crazy as it was, the narrative accepted our changes in the events leading up to the monster's death."

"What does that mean?" Asher asked.

Natascha lay back on the deck where she fell. A light, refreshing rain fell from the remaining clouds. "It means it's over. Your world is whole again."

The raven flew down. It landed near Natascha. With a shake of his head, the bird morphed into the naked shape of Ren B'gatti. Waves of colors rippled across his body before settling into an alabaster hue. He looked at Natascha with a tired smile. One eye was midnight black, the other the color of mustard yellow.

"Good job, B'gatti," Natascha said. "I thought we lost you when the Shaaglamoria snatched you out of the air."

"But how'd you get out of the beast's gullet?" Raffles asked.

"Not important," Ren replied.

"We didn' see ya exit out da mouth." Raffles scratched his head in thought. "If ya didn' come out da front door, dat leaves only one other way out." He made a disgusted face and took a step back from Ren. "Dat's a long, dark, nasty road ta travel."

"*Shut up*, rabbit! I said it's not important," Ren ordered. "All that matters is I got here in time to save the day."

Natascha chuckled. "Just go get cleaned up, B'gatti." She looked around for Asher Grey.

The *Logos Personae* stood away from everyone, gazing out at the last of the falling ash. She saw Natascha watching her and walked back to them, a rifle on her shoulder. She leveled the weapon at Medesto and racked in a round.

"I want answers," she ordered through gritted teeth. "And I want them now. Starting with, who the hell are you people?"

# Chapter 33
# Denouement

Ren stood beside Medesto, ready to react if needed. The gnome remained calm, even amused by the unexpected outburst from Asher Grey. "You've heard the saying, *All the world's a stage, and all the men and women merely players*?" Medesto inquired.

"*They have their exits and their entrances*," Asher continued. "Sir Francis Bacon wrote that. So?"

Medesto smiled. "We call ourselves the Raconteurs. We are the ones who work backstage, behind the scenes, to make sure the show goes on as intended. The last line of defense when things go wrong."

Asher's hand gripped the rifle tighter. "I lost my entire crew because of you people. You expect me to believe anything you say? I told you I would help kill the monster, but only if you left Sethen out of it. Now he's dead too."

Medesto raised his hands in front of him, but he did not step toward her. "Let me ask you one question. You've been feeling this growing sense of dread, haven't you? It began when *Wanderlust* blew up, but it was more than grieving the loss of your crew. It was this inescapable feeling that something terrible was about to happen, but you didn't know what it was, or how to stop it. But the moment the Shaaglamoria died, the feeling stopped, didn't it?"

Asher lowered her rifle. "How could you know that?" she asked, tears welling in her eyes. "The despair in the pit of my stomach. It was like nothing I'd ever felt before."

Medesto's shoulders relaxed. "It happened because the natural circadian rhythm of this world was out of sync and events were not playing out as they should. We tinkered with things to put things back in their proper place. It goes by many names, but most commonly as a *Crucible Event*. Trust me when I say Sethen did what he did under his own volition. He knew this was how it had to be, and somewhere deep inside, you know that too, don't you?"

Asher stared at the gnome for a moment. Her hands trembled. She dropped the rifle to the deck and walked away. "I need to be alone."

Ren watched the *Logos Personae* disappear below deck. He turned to see everyone staring at him.

"What?" he said. "I thought you had already left for Rogue Destiny, so I had to take matters into my own hands. How'd you know what was going on?"

Medesto gave him a quizzical look. "Chauncey Wainwright. The local guy you sent to warn us the *Logos Personae* was in danger. He showed up at the field house just as I was about to take off."

"Of course he did," Ren said, remembering the man Claymore gave the leather coin purse to at the booksellers' shop. "I knew he'd come through for me."

Ren smiled at Natascha, but the skepticism on her face told him she wasn't fooled. He was not even sure why he had lied to them, and even felt a little bad about it. He was a hero today and there was nothing to hide.

Still, he found he did not want anyone to know Claymore was involved. He and his partner were going to bring down Mordecai together and that would show the Raconteurs Claymore Ives still walked on the side of the angels.

---

Medesto lifted the support beam and held it up while Lizbeth hammered it into place. He dusted off his hands and scanned the damage to the airship. "That should hold long enough to keep her in the air until we get back to Old London," he said.

*Bad Mojo* towed the *Sky Zephyr* through the sky over a deep blue ocean stretching out beneath them. The salt air was refreshingly cool, washing away the taint of the Forbidden Island and its horrors from Medesto's thoughts. The gnome had fought terrifying things during his travels, but this monster was among the most nightmarish. He would not soon forget it, or this world. They had won the battle, but there was always a period of decompressing afterwards. With the *Logos Personae* headed home to begin the events of her second book, the Raconteurs could continue on after Mordecai.

"How's your father doing?" he asked Lizbeth. "He was pretty upset with us destroying the *Sky Zephyr* to kill the Shaaglamoria."

Lizbeth shrugged. "He'll be fine. I love him, but he can be a bit of a princess sometimes."

"We could not have done this without you," Medesto said. "I admire your resilience. You seem like a very capable individual."

Lizbeth glanced over at him. "You flirting with me?"

Medesto chuckled. "Oh no, nothing like that. You kept your head through everything that happened. Not many could have done what you did."

Lizbeth smirked. "Did I have any choice? With my father the

way he is, it's up to me to keep our business afloat. If I let the world burn to dust, that'd be bad for business. Hard to find passengers when they're all dead."

Medesto laughed. "That's the attitude I'm talking about," he said. "How would you like to come work for us?"

Lizbeth lifted her face in surprise. "You're offering me a job?"

"You saw what happened here today. We need people willing to watch over their worlds. You want to be one of those people?"

"I thought you were leaving after we got to Old London," Lizbeth said.

"We are. And that means we won't be here to keep an eye on *The Gaslamp Adventures of Asher Grey*. But you will be. What I'm offering you is a chance to protect yourself and your world, so something like this doesn't happen again. What do you say?"

"What would I have to do?"

"You play a larger part in this story than you did just a couple of days ago," Medesto said. "You would serve as a liaison between your world and Rogue Destiny. The Raconteurs are always looking for caretakers to watch over things in our absence. Individuals who contact us if our services are needed. You would be the perfect candidate for that. We have a field house in Old London, part of a network we're building throughout the Mythic Cosmos, with the locals in any worlds that we get involved with."

"Still hard to wrap my head around," Lizbeth said. "That everything around me is only words inside a book."

"Don't think about it too much," Medesto warned. "You'll only drive yourself crazy. There's someone there I want you to talk to. His name is Chauncey Wainwright. He runs the field house. He's a good man and could use the help."

"So there are more worlds like mine out there, huh?"

"Tens of thousands more, and every one of them is its own self-contained reality. That's why we need your help. It's too big a job for us to handle alone. The city of Rogue Destiny is the exception. She sits at the center of everything and is the only place in all of creation that is not bound to any book."

"Is that where you and the Raconteurs are headed to next?" Lizbeth asked.

"Yeah, that's where we're from," Medesto said. "When we get to Old London, we'll pick up Mordecai's trail again. Ren knows where this artificial rabbit-hole is located. But first we need to put the *Sky Zephyr* back together as best we can and get Asher Grey to her second book, *Three Deadly Nights in Zanzibar*."

"Take me with you," Lizbeth pleaded, her eyes eager. "I want to see what's out there, all those other worlds. I want to see Rogue Destiny."

Medesto looked up at the comment. "You'd make a great Raconteur," he said. "But your father needs you here and your world deserves a caretaker like you. However, I have an idea you might like."

"What's that?" she asked, a glimmer of hope on her face.

"Whether or not you decide to work for us, we'll pay for a new Amaranthine Crystal and any other repairs the *Sky Zephyr* needs. In return, you help monitor Asher Grey and her stories. She may be the key to your world's continuation, but Asher's going to need someone to watch her back. Someone who's decisive and quick on her feet, like you. We stopped this threat, but there will be others."

"Before you go any further, something's been bothering me," Lizbeth interrupted. There was a rare moment of hesitation in her voice. "Would you answer a question for me?"

"Of course."

"You knew Sethen Rooke was going to die, didn't you?" she asked.

"Yes," Medesto answered. He set his hammer down and got comfortable on the beam he was sitting on.

Lizbeth's eyes narrowed. "And you let it happen, anyway?"

The gnome thought for a moment before answering. "No, we didn't *let* it happen," he replied. "What we did was allow the Story play out as it should. Sethen Rooke wasn't supposed to live past the first book. His death was necessary, so *The Adventures of Asher Grey* could go on as they were written. If he had survived, it would have altered everything in Asher's life that came after. When the *Wanderlust* blew up, the Narrative changed, and we had to act quickly to save the world." His voice petered out.

He took a deep breath and continued. "Think of the Story's Narrative as a raging river, powerful and difficult to interfere with. There are thousands of events happening at the same time to create the Story. The Narrative's strong enough to adjust to minor disruptions in its flow, small ripples that are easily absorbed, but there are pressure points that can throw the Narrative off course. Major changes, like harming the *Logos Personae*, or the death of a key character that alters the course of the Story."

"Or a character surviving that was supposed to die," Lizbeth muttered to herself.

"Exactly," Medesto said with a nod. "We didn't write the Book, but it's our job to keep the Narrative moving forward as it was meant to."

"So, do the Raconteurs always save the day?" Lizbeth asked.

"Unfortunately, no," Medesto admitted. "We got lucky today, and *The Gaslight Adventures of Asher Grey* will go on. But right doesn't always win, and good doesn't always triumph over evil. In the original ending, Sethen sacrificed himself to save the expedition. This broke Asher's heart, but it started her on the path that would take her through the next twelve books in the series. I think Sethen intuitively knew what had to happen and did what he did to fulfill both their destinies."

"What about the rest of the crew?" Lizbeth asked. "Aren't they important too?"

Medesto gave her a sad smile. "That's the greatest irony in all of this. In the original story, everyone on the *Wanderlust* crew, except Sethen, survived the battle with the Shaaglamoria. But like you and me, they were secondary characters to the Story, expendable as far as the Narrative goes. Sethen was intrinsic to Asher's future. If he had lived, he and Asher would probably have settled down, raised a family, and no doubt ended up working at the university like her parents. It's his death that compels her to leave Old London and explore the world, saving it from evil doers over and over in the later books. As cliché as it sounds, everything happens for a reason."

"Then why don't we just tell her that? She seems so sad right now."

"Asher knows this was how it had to be," the gnome replied solemnly. "She may not understand how she knows, and it doesn't make the loss any easier, but she'll always remember Sethen died saving her."

"Wouldn't it be easier if she knew the truth?" Lizbeth asked.

"No, it's best if she doesn't know who she is or her true role in this world," Medesto said. "Imagine knowing that you are the linchpin to the safety of an entire world, and that every soul lived or died based on the decisions you made. She would spend every moment second guessing her actions. That would drive you to madness. She would never have let Sethen face the Shaaglamoria if she knew he wasn't coming back."

He cleared his voice and continued. "Asher Grey is the fulcrum to everything that keeps this world turning, but she is not the only one important to its survival. There may be the *Logos Personae*, but the rest of us are all predestined for something. Sometimes, that destiny is not about riches or glory. Sometimes a person's purpose is to make sure that others are safe, that they continue on. To sacrifice themselves for the greater good. Sethen died a soldier's death to save his comrades in battle. Don't worry about Asher. She'll be fine once she gets to the next book. There are great things waiting for her in future stories. I hope you consider our offer."

Lizbeth nodded, thoughtful. "I'll think about it."

Medesto and Lizbeth climbed down the rigging to the airship's deck. He dropped his hammer into the wooden toolbox.

"So, you're fine knowing that you are nothing more than a character in a book?" Lizbeth asked.

Medesto took out his pipe and lit it. He blew the smoke into the air, where it danced on the wind and dissipated into nothing. "Not much you can do about it, is there?" he mused. "But we are much more than just ink on paper. Aren't we the ones who are truly free? Asher Grey's locked into her narrative, destined to play out the same stories over and over again. You and I are not. We may be secondary characters, but at least we make our own choices."

"And that's enough for you?" Lizbeth replied, pondering his words.

"What can you do about it?" Medesto took in a deep breath of fresh ocean air. "I live, I breathe, I am content with my life. No one could ask for more than that. I've known people who've gone mad thinking too much about such things."

"So, if we are in a book," Lizbeth said, "then someone, somewhere, had to have written that book."

Medesto looked across the blue waters at the English coastline and smiled. "I don't worry too much about the nature of our existence," he admitted. "We obviously came from somewhere, but I'll leave it to the philosophers and scholars of Rogue Destiny to debate the greatest mystery of all. That's enough for me. Let's go get some supper."

Ren B'gatti took a long hot shower to get the stench of the Shaaglamoria off of him. He toweled off and dug through the storage room for something to wear, deciding on a pair of pants that had a tie-string at the waist. The fabric was soft and hung comfortably off his lean frame. He pulled on a loose shirt and left the shower area.

He had volunteered to watch the prisoners locked in the storage hold of *Bad Mojo*, figuring that was better than cleaning Shaaglamoria entrails off the deck of the *Sky Zephyr*. He had already experienced enough of the monster's insides to last him a lifetime.

He leaned back in a chair with his head down, trying to catch up on some sleep, knowing they would soon be back to chasing Mordecai. Doggs Borland snored loudly in a cell next to the one that held the man called Porter. The prisoner sat in the shadows at the back of his containment cell.

"Hey, doppelganger?" Porter said. "I need to speak to whoever's in charge."

"Be quiet," Ren said without opening his eyes. "You'll be back in Lazaranth soon enough."

"No one's taking me back to that hellhole!" Porter spat. "*Not* with what I know."

Ren opened an eye. "And what is it you think you know?"

"I ain't saying any more until I get some guarantees," Porter replied. "The first being a pardon for my part in all this."

Ren sat up. It was obvious the man would not let him sleep. "Just tell me," he said. "Or I'll demonstrate what happens when all the joints in the human body are manhandled by a gorilla."

"No need for violence," Porter said, the confidence in his words wavering. "You Raconteurs think you got this all figured out, don't you? You have no idea what went down that night in the darkness of Lazaranth Prison."

"How'd you see anything if it was so dark?" Ren asked.

"In my old life, I was a vampire's thrall and still carry the blood of the master in my veins. So I see very well in the dark, and there was no mistake as to what I saw."

Porter got off his bunk. His pupils shone with a strange blue light as he walked out of the shadows and pressed his face up to the bars of the cell. "There's a lot more to tell once I get my freedom. Information you Raconteurs will want to know!"

"So tell me," Ren ordered. "What do you know that we don't?"

"There's an old joke that *Rogue Destiny is the most magical place without magic*?" Porter whispered. A sinister smile appeared on his face.

"I've heard that."

"Well, Mordecai's aiming to change that." Porter's smile shifted from sinister to satisfaction. "That's all I'm saying until I talk to whoever's in charge."

Ren laid back in his chair and stretched. "How do you know I'm not in charge?"

"Cause you're sitting in the hold watching the prisoners. I'm guessing your boss is the dwarf or the tall lady with the scowl."

"He's not a dwarf, he's a gnome." Ren could feel *Bad Mojo* slowing down beneath him and stood up to investigate. The conversation was starting to bore him, and their prisoners were not going anywhere. He started for the door.

"The man you are chasing isn't who you think he is!" Porter hollered, a wicked grin on his face. "I was there. I saw everything that went down."

"Goodbye, Porter."

"So, you're going to tell them I got information to barter with?" Porter pleaded.

"Sure," Ren said as he left the room. "Somebody will be down in a moment to take your statement."

Ren didn't know if he believed the criminal or not, but he was not about to tell anyone about their conversation. By the time *Bad Mojo* reached Rogue Destiny, he and Claymore would be back together, taking Mordecai down, so it didn't matter what Porter knew. He climbed the stairs to the main hold.

Natascha collapsed into a leather seat in the galley of *Bad Mojo*. She was sore and exhausted, and her adrenaline levels had not quite returned to normal. She needed a minute to herself and thought hiding in here would give her time to catch her breath.

Everyone but Ren was still on the *Sky Zephyr,* repairing the damage done to keep the airship flying until they reached England. She lay back and closed her eyes, but heard someone enter a moment later. Ren stood in front of an open cupboard, rummaging through the foodstuffs and canned goods stored there.

"Aren't you supposed to be watching our prisoners?" she asked.

"They're not going anywhere," Ren said. "Why are we slowing down?"

"We're approaching Old London and *Bad Mojo* might attract too much attention, so we decided to wait for the sun to go down, then we can bring the *Sky Zephyr* in under the cover of darkness."

"Where's everyone at?" Ren asked.

"Medesto and the others are still working on repairs to the *Zephyr*," Natascha said. "Asher's kept herself locked in a cabin below deck and has refused any offers of food and water."

Ren nodded but didn't reply. He opened a box of crackers

from the cupboard and seemed distracted as he nibbled on his snack.

"You prevented the death of a world today," Natascha announced. "And saved countless innocent lives. That should make you proud."

Something was not right. Ren had been uncharacteristically quiet since the battle with the Shaaglamoria. He had never hesitated to brag about his heroic exploits before. Usually, they couldn't shut him up. Maybe if she changed the subject to something more to the Ren's liking.

"And then there's Claymore," Natascha added, waiting to gage his response. At the mention of his partner's name, Ren looked over and met her gaze.

"What about him?" he asked.

"After this is over," Natascha replied, "how about you and I go search for him? You in your shiny new slipstream and me in *Nevermore*. We could cover twice as much territory that way. It worked well enough when Medesto and I searched for you."

Ren shrugged at the suggestion. "I haven't decided what I'm going to do after we stop Mordecai. I may just fly away and disappear like he did."

Now she knew the trickster was lying to her. Most of the time, Ren B'gatti cared for little beyond himself. He was reckless, reactionary, and pig-headed, with a temperament that reacted to things first and thought about the ramifications after the fact. But he would never abandon a friend who needed his help, most of all Claymore.

"I'm tired," Ren said. "I'm going to get some sleep before we take a run at Mordecai again." He took his box of crackers and left.

Natascha watched him leave. She knew there was more going on than what he was saying and wondered what Ren could possibly be hiding. How did Ren know Chauncey Wainwright? The trickster had never been to this world before, so why would he trust a complete stranger to deliver such an important message to the Raconteur's safehouse?

Claymore, on the other hand, maintained contacts throughout the Mythic Cosmos, so it made sense he might know someone in this book. As she thought about that, the pieces fell into place. There was only one reason Ren would hide the truth from her.

Claymore was somehow involved in this, and Ren had been in contact with him.

She took a deep breath. One problem at a time.

# Epilogue

R en B'gatti stared into the darkness of a large, slanting hole in the floor of an abandoned subway line under the city of Old London.

"Well?" he asked. "Is it safe, rabbit?"

Raffles ambled out of the yawning tunnel. He sniffed the air and snapped off a rotted, curling root stem that poked through the loose dirt. He crouched down, silently touching the floor where the ley-line had ripped the ground open. With an exasperated breath, he stood up and adjusted the small pack on his back with its two fishing knives strapped to it. His long ears poked through the holes of a wide-brimmed straw hat.

"Never seen nuthin' like it," Raffles said, his thick Cajun drawl filled with a cautious excitement. The rabbit brushed the dirt off his tiny paws and scratched his cheek. "Da portal machine we chasin' punched a hole through da floor directly into da ley-line passin' under us. Wat has dat kind of power?"

"And we're sure Mordecai Davos went this way?" Tempest asked.

"That's the passageway Mordecai and his entourage walked through when I left them to chase down Dark Angus," Ren said.

Raffles nodded in agreement. "Judgin' by da tracks, dey have least a day's jump on us, so we better decide what we doing."

"But the tunnel's safe, right?" Charley asked, her voice a little unsteady. "Natascha said the last artificial ley-line she entered collapsed out from under her."

"If we stay spread out, we should be fine," Raffles answered with a nod. "Just tread careful. She's dryin' out around da edges."

"None of you are under any obligation to go further," Medesto told them. "Ren and I can go it alone from here."

"Mordecai has shown himself to be a genocidal threat, willing to destroy an entire world to protect himself," Natascha shrugged. "You might need help."

"Good to hear," Medesto said. "Tempest?"

"I always see things to the end," Tempest answered bluntly.

"We've come this far," Charley added. "I'm curious where Mordecai's headed next."

"Raffles?" Medesto asked.

"Count me in. Most fun I had as long as I can remember."

Lizbeth stood back from the group. "So this is goodbye?" she asked. There was more than a touch of sadness in her words.

"For now," Medesto answered. "And thank you for your help, Lizbeth. We couldn't have saved the day without you. Someone from our field house will contact you in the next couple of days about replacing the Amaranthine Crystal on the *Sky Zephyr*. That will give you some time to consider our offer."

"We need to go," Tempest said. "Mordecai will not wait for us to catch up to him." The tall woman picked up her gear, turned on a flashlight and strode into the tunnel.

Lizbeth shook hands with Natascha and Medesto. Raffles nodded at her. Charley smiled and waved before following Tempest into the passageway. That left only Ren standing there. Lizabeth stepped in and hugged him tightly.

"Thank you," she murmured into his ear.

Ren hesitated for a moment, not used to sudden displays of affection, but then gave in and returned the hug. "You did all the work," he whispered back. "Don't forget to seal up the rabbit-hole once we're gone. You don't know what might come crawling out if you leave it open."

Lizbeth opened her satchel to reveal several sticks of dynamite. "Never traveling without these again. And I meant it when I said *thank you*. If you hadn't been there, my father and I would be dead."

"Just think about our offer?" Ren told her. "You're a real hellion under fire, and that's what the Raconteurs are always looking for."

Lizbeth pulled away. Ren saw her misty blue eyes glisten in the illumination of her flashlight. "Only if it's the first step to becoming a full-fledged Raconteur," she said. "Saving a world is pretty exciting."

The young woman left him there, making her way down the dark subway tunnel. Ren watched the bobbing glow of her light until she was out of sight.

"Ren? Let's go!" Medesto yelled from the tunnel.

The trickster smiled one last time at all that had occurred in the world of Asher Grey. Then he turned his thoughts to what lie ahead as he disappeared down the rabbit-hole.


The End


GLOSSARY OF MAJOR PLAYERS

The Good Guys

Ren B'gatti – Shape-shifting trickster of dubious morals
    and mysterious past.
    Claymore Ives – Founder of the Raconteurs and Ren's
partner.
    Natascha Devi – aka – Doctor Enigma – Senior field
agent for
    the Raconteurs.
    Medesto Bodenhammer – Senior field agent for the
Raconteurs.
    Tempest Vondersteen – Security Officer for the Raconteurs.
Oversees general operations.
    Charley Lovejoy – Tech specialist for the Raconteurs.
    Gideon Dumas – Director of the Raconteurs.

The Bad Guys

Mordecai Davos – The shadowy overlord of Rogue Destiny's
criminal underworld who has kept his true identity hidden,
even from his innermost circle.
    *The Society of the Black Rose* – A secret society controlled by
    Mordecai Davos whose influence extends throughout the
Mythic Cosmos.
    The Grimm Jester – Mysterious wraith under the control of
Mordecai Davos.
    Piqwic York – The overseer of Mordecai's vast fortunes. He
uses his financial expertise to increase the Black Rose's wealth

and help them maintain their dominance over Mordecai's criminal underworld empire.

Odd Bod – Mordecai's Grand Enforcer.

Audette Shoales – Hired killer from the Adezhda, the City of Assassins.

Serralto Cardus – Member of Rogue Destiny's Common Council of Eternal Vigilance and Public Sympathy.

# GLOSSARY OF MAJOR PLAYERS

**The Good Guys**

Ren B'gatti — Shape-shifting trickster of dubious morals and mysterious past.

Claymore Ives — Founder of the Raconteurs and Ren's partner.

Natascha Devi – aka – Doctor Enigma — Senior field agent for the Raconteurs.

Medesto Bodenhammer — Senior field agent for the Raconteurs.

Tempest Vondersteen — Security Officer for the Raconteurs. Oversees general operations.

Charley Lovejoy — Tech specialist for the Raconteurs.

Gideon Dumas — Director of the Raconteurs.

# GLOSSARY OF MAJOR PLAYERS

## The Bad Guys

Mordecai Davos — The shadowy overlord of Rogue Destiny's criminal underworld who has kept his true identity hidden, even from his innermost circle.

*The Society of the Black Rose* — A secret society controlled by Mordecai Davos whose influence extends throughout the Mythic Cosmos.

The Grimm Jester — Mysterious wraith under the control of Mordecai Davos.

Piqwic York — The overseer of Mordecai's vast fortunes. He uses his financial expertise to increase the Black Rose's wealth and help them maintain their dominance over Mordecai's criminal underworld empire.

Odd Bod — Mordecai's Grand Enforcer.

Audette Shoales — Hired killer from the Adezhda, the City of Assassins.

Serralto Cardus — Member of Rogue Destiny's Common Council of Eternal Vigilance and Public Sympathy.

# GLOSSARY OF PLACES AND TERMINOLOGIES

Rogue Destiny — The infamous city that stands at the cross-roads of the Mythic Cosmo.

The Mythic Cosmos — a universe filled with the mythos of every fable, myth, legend and fairy-tale.

The Raconteurs — A self-appointed band of world-hopping troubleshooters who protect the Mythic Cosmos from the corruptive influence of Rogue Destiny's criminal element.

Ley-lines — The mystical pathways that grow from the roots of the Wayward Trees and connect all the written worlds of the Mythic Cosmos.

Rabbit-hole — A doorway between worlds created by the ley-lines.

The Word Canopy — The mystical veil of words that surrounds every world.

The Narrative — The continual progression of a world's Story that must remain uninterrupted and free of outside corruption. If that narrative flow is broken, the consequences will be catastrophic.

The Logos Personae — The main character of a world's Story. The individual who is intertwined with the Narrative and the linchpin to the world's survival.

The Crucible Event — A catastrophic event that burns a world to ash. Occurs at the death the Story's main character, the *Logos Personae*, or when the flow of the Narrative is altered beyond what can be repaired or restored.

# About the Author

Paul Tallman lives in the wet and wonderful Pacific Northwest with his long suffering wife, Tina.

After having worked for far too many years in the insurance industry, he finally broke away from the security of a steady paycheck to pursue writing.

A geek by birthright, he has spent his life in the social awkwardness of his calling, ever since reading *The Lord of the Rings* for the first time in middle school.

Paul can be found holed up away from the society, working on his next book.

He still mourns the cancellation of the TV show *Firefly*.

To find out more about the Rogue Destiny universe visit: paultallmanauthor.com

# Also by Paul Tallman

**A Rogue Destiny**

Rogue Destiny: Beginnings

Ley Lines and Rabbit Holes

9 781648 396502